WHEN YOU WERE MINE

Calamity Falls

ERIKA KELLY

Mistletoe and Silver Foxes
ALL I WANT FOR CHRISTMAS IS YOU
WHEN YOU WERE MINE

The Wild Wolff Village Serials
KISS ME SLOWLY
ANYWHERE WITH YOU
BABY I'M YOURS

Have you read the Rock Star Romance series? Come meet the sexy rockers of Blue Fire:

YOU REALLY GOT ME
I WANT YOU TO WANT ME
TAKE ME HOME TONIGHT
MORE THAN A FEELING

Subscribe to my newsletter to get updates on the next Calamity Falls series coming October 2025. You're going to love Can't Get Over You of #secondchance #nannyforyourex #runawaybride

Get PLANES, TRAINS, AND HEAD OVER HEELS for FREE! I hope you'll come hang out with me on Facebook, TikTok, Twitter, Instagram, Goodreads, and Pinterest or in my private reader group.

This book is dedicated to Olivia Kalb.
Thank you for sharing this journey with me.
It means everything to me.

Acknowledgments

- To Superman: you're number one on my gratitude list for so many reasons, but since we're talking about books: thank you for dropping everything to work on plots and dialogue with me even when you want nothing more than to read the paper and drink your espresso in peace! I see you!
- Thank you, Sharon Pochron, for always being there. You're the best kind of friend.
- Erica Alexander, I don't know what I'd do without you. Thank you for your friendship, your patience, and your wisdom.
- Melissa Martin, you're just AWESOME! I am so grateful for all you do for me.
- Thank you to Melissa Panio-Peterson for standing by my side all these years.
- Thank you to Olivia Kalb for making my books sparkle.
- To Karen, the last set of eyes on my books. Thank you for all you do!
- Thank you, Kenna Rey, for giving me the edit I've been looking for.
- And thank you to the readers, bloggers,

reviewers, and all my author friends who make this job so richly rewarding and worthwhile.

Prologue

Is this real?

Am I actually marrying the love of my life?

Jessica Elsworth wanted to remember every single detail of this moment. The cozy white chapel and the plaster cherubs lifting bouquets of roses on either side of the altar. The officiant in a white rayon suit and a turquoise bolo tie, and his wife's bright yellow sundress and white terry cloth flip-flops, her long fingernails painted a brilliant red.

Jess would imprint this setting, these colors, and the fragrant scent of roses on her mind forever. Not only because she was eloping, but because it was so them. They were wild, reckless, free.

They were outlaws.

They were twenty years old, on their way home after a spectacular failure, but they were fiercely, fully together.

Forever.

As she faced her soon-to-be-husband in the Las Vegas chapel, she grinned at the crazy situation. She might not have grown up dreaming about weddings, but she'd always known she'd love Trevor Montgomery with all her heart for the rest of her life.

Her gorgeous, funny, smart, big-hearted groom began his vows. "I never told you this, but my first memory of us goes back even before kindergarten. My dad backed his truck up to the loading dock at the feedstore. I was kicking my mom's seat just to piss her off, and I looked out the window and saw this little girl doing a monster dance."

Overflowing with happiness and so full of love for this man, Jess cracked up. "Monster dance?" She had no recollection.

"Yep." He took a step back to show her. Lowering his head, he stomped his feet and lifted his arms like he was working a pulley. When he bent over and shook his ass, even the officiant broke out laughing.

"Eh." She waved a hand to dismiss the memory. "No proof it was me. Could've been anybody." Of course, she was teasing, and the glint in Trevor's eyes told her he knew it. Her dad owned the store, and that was exactly the kind of weird thing she'd have done while hanging around.

"You know that expression *dance like no one's watching?*" Fire glinted in her groom's eyes.

She nodded. He was such a passionate man. She loved that about him.

"Well, that's you. You dance like no one's watching, sing like no one's listening, and love like you've never been hurt. Elzy, I admire the hell out of you. You're strong and smart, you love hard, and you're the best person I know." Color flooded his cheeks, and his voice broke. "You caught my attention when I was four, and you continue to dazzle me to this day."

Jess blinked back tears. Two days ago, their world had come crashing down. The bad news had them quitting their server jobs, giving their landlord notice, and packing up the truck to head back home.

But he'd turned it all around by driving them straight to this Vegas chapel.

They might've given up one dream, but he'd fulfilled another, more important one: sealing their future as a couple.

"I love you." His voice was thick with emotion. "That first day of kindergarten when I saw you, I swear to God, the world cracked open. It was the first time I'd ever been away from home, and I didn't know what to make of it, but the moment I laid eyes on you, all the confusion in my mind went quiet. I knew back then, and I know now, you're my best friend, my lover, my peace, my motivation, my inspiration, my North Star, and the love of my life."

"Trevor." His name came out on a gust of breath. She needed to be alone with him, skin to skin. She needed her hands in his hair, her mouth on his. The endless quest to get closer, to merge, to breach the physical separation never, ever went away. If they got lost on a deserted island, she wouldn't care. He was all she needed. Now and forever.

He reached for her hands. "Elzy, you were my reason when I was four, and you're my reason for the rest of my life." He slipped the plastic band on her finger. "With this ring, I pledge my life to yours. I know wherever life takes me, with you is where I'm meant to be."

Now, it was her turn, but she was so full of love and affection, she couldn't think straight. He wasn't just movie-star handsome and built to haul bales of hay. He was the kindest, most generous man she'd ever known. "You've had more time to think about it—"

"Elz, I've been thinking about marrying you my whole life."

Well, when he put it that way, so had she. "I love you." She said it plainly, simply. "You're my best friend, my playmate, my confidante, and my greatest challenge." She blew out a shaky breath. "Not a day goes by when I don't think how grateful I am to have you in my life. I mean, we were eight when my mom died. I don't know how you knew what I needed, but you did. You sat with me, and we didn't say a word. You let me be quiet. You've always known exactly what I need. You see me. You always have."

She slipped the ring on his finger. "Trevor, I vow to love you, take care of you, and walk this life by your side through every storm and battle. And you know what? Forget pledging anything because it's my absolute privilege to spend my life with you. Thank you for loving me. I don't *vow* to love and cherish you—I *get* to."

He hauled her to his chest and kissed her, and with the volatile cocktail of excitement and passion, she knew their connection could light up a night sky.

"Uh, well." The officiant laughed. "Guess I don't need to say it, but you may kiss the bride."

Trevor clutched her bottom and drew her tightly to him. His warmth seeped into her. As they clung to each other, she got lost in the soft, wet, heat of his mouth, the clean, masculine scent of him and the urgent dig of his fingers.

"Okay, then." The officiant cleared his throat. "I now pronounce you husband and wife."

Clasping hands, they practically ran out of the chapel.

Jess floated on a wave of bliss. They burst out the doors into bright sunlight.

"I can't believe it." She tipped her head back and shouted, "We're *married.*"

"We've been married since we were twelve and I built us that treehouse." He wrapped an arm around her waist. "Today, we made it legal." He kissed her. "I love you."

"I love you so much."

"So, what do you think?" Grabbing her hand, he headed to the truck. "Spend the night in the motel or hit the road? Your call."

And this was why she adored him. Two days earlier, they'd found out her teenage sister was pregnant. Instead of staying in Los Angeles to pursue his goals, he'd quit his job and packed his suitcase right alongside her. They'd only been there two years—not nearly long enough to get traction in Hollywood.

They were truly in this together. "We're not going anywhere until we consummate this marriage, mister."

He broke into that sexy grin that made her blood go hot. "I like the way you think."

She grinned, giddy with love for him. "Let's plan on leaving in the morning." She bit her bottom lip. "Consummating is going to take all night."

"Yeah, I don't know about consummating, but there's going to be a lot of fucking."

When they reached his ancient Ford 150, he bent his knees and lifted her into his arms.

She laughed. "What're you doing?"

"This truck's the closest thing we have to a marital home, so I'm carrying you over the threshold." Hitching her higher, he unlocked the door. "Open it." Once she did, he plopped her onto the seat. Then, instead of hurrying to the driver's side, he cupped her cheeks and gazed into her eyes. "You're mine now, Mrs. Trevor Montgomery."

"I always was, Mr. Jessica Elsworth."

When he laughed, his eyes sparkled, and she couldn't believe Hollywood hadn't snapped this man up. He would've been box office gold.

"Take me home, Wild Bill."

"Anything for you." His big strong hands cupped her cheeks, and his tongue licked into her mouth. Every time he kissed her, it felt like he'd just come home from a deployment. His hands caressed and his tongue explored with such *hunger*.

A car drove past, and a woman shouted, "Get a room."

"On it," he shouted back. Smiling against Jess's mouth, he said, "I can never get enough of my Calamity Jane." He shut the door and made his way around to the driver's side.

They'd never fit in their small town. He had no interest in farming, and she wanted so much more than the jobs available in Riverton, Wyoming. Even though they loved their families, they'd just never really connected with kids their age. They only liked hanging out with each other.

Growing up, they'd loved to pretend they were outlaws. They'd ride horses or ATVs, tearing across the land. Using sticks as guns, they'd break into sheds and holler for the "tellers" to hand over the money.

All their lives, they'd dreamed of owning a ranch in Calamity Falls—a town about three hours west. They'd call it Robbers Roost after Butch Cassidy and the Wild Bunch gang's hideout.

The engine rumbled to life, and she brought the bouquet to her nose, breathing in the sweet, delicious scent. "We should grow roses."

"I'll plant you a whole garden." He pulled away from the curb. "A forever reminder of this day."

He was so romantic. She smoothed her hand on the ripped fabric of the bench seat. He'd found this truck abandoned by a farmhand who'd run off in the middle of the night. Trevor worked on it for months to get it going. Why? Because she'd wanted to take an advanced dance class only offered in Caspar. Her dad didn't have the time to drive her, so Trevor did it.

Junior year, someone at school had drawn a heart with Trevor and Jess's initials in the dust on the hood. A few nights later, when he'd picked her up for prom, she'd noticed Trevor had painted it red.

I love this man.

The moment they entered their motel room, Trevor pulled up his T-shirt, exposing his washboard abs, tan skin, and the arrow leading to the thick outline of his cock.

Once he'd tossed the shirt aside, he gave her a lazy-eyed smirk and undid the first button on his jeans. "What's it gonna take to get you naked, Mrs. Montgomery?"

"Honestly? Not much."

Laughing, he gave her an impatient flick of his hand. *Strip.*

But just as she started to unzip the back of her skirt, the phone rang. He sauntered over, leaving the flap of his jeans open. Her mouth watered, and her hands itched to touch his warm skin. She couldn't get undressed fast enough.

"Hello?" Trevor sat on the bed, watching her peel off

her clothes. "Oh, hey. Okay. Yeah, I'll give her a call. Thank you." As soon as he hung up, he stalked over to her. She stood naked before him, and he slid his fingers through her hair, lifting it off her shoulders. "You're fucking gorgeous."

"I hope you still think so after I pop out our ninth baby."

"Sweetheart, I could find chicken bones in the folds of your belly, and I'd still be hot for you."

She laughed. "That was vivid. Who was on the phone?"

"It was the front desk. My agent called."

Her chest tightened. "Oh. Wow." How crazy would it be if he finally got a part now that they'd left LA? She felt a little sick to her stomach. It'd be such bad timing. "How did she even know we're here?"

"She called home."

Her dad had insisted on booking a motel to break up the fourteen-hour drive. Which meant both families knew the itinerary.

"But she can wait." He pushed her breasts together. His hot, wet mouth closed over a nipple, and his tongue flicked back and forth. "Because right now, I'm making love to my wife."

Lust spread in a rush, making her tingle. "Say it again."

As he gazed into her eyes, his thumbs caressed her sensitive peaks. "First, you were that fascinating girl doing a monster dance. Then, you were my best friend and outlaw." He kissed her again. "And now, you're my *wife*."

"My husband." She let out a dreamy sigh. "But let's find out what she wants, or I won't be able to think about anything else."

"Okay." He kissed her on the mouth and then returned to the bed to make the call.

But she already knew. Why else would his agent track him down, other than to tell him he'd gotten a part?

This is good, right?

Yes.

Maybe.

I don't know.

While he punched in the calling card's code, she grabbed her clothes and headed into the bathroom.

Because she was freaking out and didn't want to impact his decision.

This job could change the direction of their lives. What if it was a TV pilot? He'd need to live in Los Angeles. But she couldn't go with him. She had to be with her sister.

What will happen to us?

They'd grown up in the same town. They'd moved to LA together. They'd never been apart.

Okay, calm down. We don't know anything right now.

No, we do know something.

Trevor and I are solid. We love each other. We might have to spend some time apart, but in the end, we'll have the money to help our families and buy Robbers Roost.

So, it's good.

We'll be fine.

As she dressed, she noticed the quiet. She peeked out of the bathroom and saw him in the same position, the cord tethering him to the bed, one arm belted across his chest, his chin tilted down.

With the phone pressed to his ear, he looked concerned. Finally, he spoke. "What if we told them I'd walk?" He twisted his neck from one side to the other as if working out the kinks.

Something was wrong. Quickly, she zipped up her skirt and came out of the bathroom.

"I understand. Okay." His shoulders squared. He drew in a breath. "Yes, I'm sure."

He didn't sound like a man who'd won a role in a major motion picture. He sounded like he was being sent to prison. He hung up.

"What's going on?" She knew this man. She'd seen despair, anger, joy, satisfaction…everything. But this? This was new. She made her way over to him.

He didn't look at her.

He didn't say anything.

She sat down, letting him process whatever news he'd gotten. Honestly, she didn't have a clue what it could be.

Finally, he let out a breath. "I got the part."

A chill skittered across her skin, and her heart kicked into overdrive. It was confusing because, of course, she wanted to celebrate with him.

This is what we wanted, what we worked for.

He might not like acting, but it was the only profession that would deliver big money. Unfortunately, it hadn't happened, and all they had to show for their two years in Los Angeles was a whopping eighteen hundred dollars.

Which would go to her sister and the baby.

So, her rational self was cheering for the opportunity he'd worked hard for, but her heart was thundering. "Which one?" If he was worried that she expected him to settle down with her in Riverton now that they were married, he should know her better. They shared a vision for their future. "You can go back to LA, you know. If it pays enough, just shoot the commercial, or whatever it is, and then come home. If you start to get more calls…" She shrugged. "We'll figure it out." She sounded stronger than she felt, but truly, she wanted him happy. She wanted him to be proud of his accomplishments.

He shifted a knee onto the mattress to face her. "It's the clan war movie. The one in—"

"*Scotland?*" Her stomach dropped. "Wait, so it's a callback?" He'd auditioned once. Thousands had shown up for the cattle call.

"No. I got the part. It's mine."

"But it was only one reading." *Scotland?*

"I know, but they chose me."

No wonder he was so quiet. This job wouldn't pay much, and it would take him to another country. She couldn't go. Not after finding out her sixteen-year-old sister was pregnant. Their dad was great, but he ran the store. It took all his time.

No, she had no choice but to go home. "What does it pay?"

"That's the thing." He swallowed. "Nothing."

She felt bad for him. She really did. Hollywood's rejection had to hurt. "I'm sorry it didn't work out." She kissed his cheek. "If we'd had more time, you would've landed some good roles."

The money would've been nice, but the distance… *Well, let's be honest.* It wasn't that the job was in Scotland. They could handle being apart. It was the idea he'd be in a whole new world, surrounded by new people—*sophisticated* people—doing sex scenes with gorgeous women…

Maybe she wasn't too bummed it hadn't worked out after all. Now, if acting was his passion, she'd have an entirely different reaction.

But she noticed he hadn't moved a muscle. "Are you okay?"

"The actors get a piece of the box office. And as the lead, I'll get two percent of gross."

Oh. He's taking this seriously. "They want you to work for free in the hopes the film makes money?" That didn't make sense.

"I know how it sounds, but my agent thinks there's real potential here. She said it's got all the elements to make it a hit. Multi-generational, soap opera-style relationships… violence."

"You were going to blow off the audition, remember? You said it was a low-budget film with a no-name producer. When I asked if you'd go back for another audition, you said, 'No way in hell.'"

"I was wrong about the producers. My agent says they've been around a long time. They know what they're doing."

He couldn't possibly be considering this job. "I have to get home to my sisters. I mean, if it paid well, if it had real potential, then, yeah, sure…" But it didn't.

"I know it's a long shot, but Elz, it's our *only* shot. We have eighteen hundred dollars to our name."

"I'm confused. Two weeks ago, you said, 'Who wants to watch a three-hundred-year clan war in sixteen-hundreds Scotland?' and now, suddenly, it's the opportunity of a lifetime?"

But his jaw remained taut. "I took it."

"Took what?" She remembered his tone a moment ago

when he'd said, *I'm sure.* "You took the job without talking to me?"

"Yes." Finally, he broke into a smile. "Hey, we're outlaws, remember? We take risks."

"Trevor, this is not funny. You're going to Scotland when my family's in crisis?"

"That's *why* I took the job. Your sister's situation is just one in a long string of problems we're going to face. You know what life is like. A disease hits my dad's crop, and we're eating nothing but bread and tomatoes for a month. Weather fucks up your dad's deliveries, and he can't pay his bills."

"Okay, okay, hang on. Did I miss something here? In all your auditions and acting classes, did you somehow catch the bug? Do you actually *want* to be an actor? Tell me right now, because that will change everything. I love you, Trevor. And if this is your heart, your passion, then you should take it."

"*You're* my heart. You're my passion. I don't give a fuck about acting. But how can I make a life for us in Riverton? We'll be right back where we started two years ago with no money and no hope. This is the only opportunity I've gotten, and I have to take it."

"There's no pay, Trevor." Her voice rose, edging toward anger. "There never will be. It's a Scottish clan war. It's not going to be some runaway hit. You know that, right?"

"Elz, this is how it happens. Every movie star starts out taking shit jobs for no pay."

She'd met his agent before. Those were her words. "Look, I get it. We're going home empty-handed. It sucks. But we'll figure something else out. You know we will."

"No, you *don't* get it." He whipped a folded sheet of paper out of his jeans pocket and shook it at her. "I can't make this much money in ten lifetimes living in Riverton."

They'd made that list years ago in the Four Rivers diner when they were figuring out a plan to buy a ranch in Calamity. First, they had to pay off the farm's mortgage. Second was getting her dad out of debt. Third was setting up her sisters with college funds. And then, finally, they'd get to buy their property.

But even after checking all four off their list, they still needed enough savings to operate the ranch. The number circled in red at the bottom of the page was daunting, and Hollywood seemed the only solution for two scrappy kids from a farm community in Wyoming.

Her heart ached for the burden he'd placed on himself. "You've been carrying that around all this time?"

"Of course. It's my motivation. We've invested two years into this effort, and it's finally paying off. I just need to give it one more year, and I either get discovered, or it's back to Riverton, and we live hand-to-mouth like everyone else. But, Elzy, if I don't take this shot, we'll have debt up to our eyeballs and no future beyond doing the same boring jobs until we die." He shook the paper. "You bet your ass this is all I can think about."

He was an only child whose parents worked from dawn to dusk. She got it. That scarcity mentality was deeply embedded. "Hey, Wild Bill." She reached for his hand and kissed his knuckles. "You're not alone in this. I'm here, and I'm doing it with you." She gave him a gentle smile. "Don't forget the other list we made that day. It was full of business ideas. Working on the farm is not our only path. We're smart. We think outside the box. We're going to make something of ourselves—and it doesn't have to subject you to eight months of free labor in Scotland."

But he didn't soften his stance. He didn't crack a smile. "There's no better path to make that kind of money. If this movie takes off, there'll be a second one and a third. And even if it doesn't, it could lead me to another project. Don't you see? This is our only hope to make big money."

"Okay." She didn't believe that, but she wouldn't argue when he was so adamant about it. With the burden he carried on his shoulders, he needed her support, not her negativity. "I don't see it that way, but…" She'd just have to accept his decision. "Well, at least it won't cost us anything." She gave a bitter laugh. "They're not making you pay for your own costumes, are they?"

"No." His chin tipped up. "But they're making me pay for my travel expenses."

"Excuse me?" She shook her head. "Oh, come on. This is a scam. It has to be."

"It's not. My agent says it's legit. They'll feed and house the cast, but we have to get ourselves to Scotland."

"Trevor, we don't have any money." Now, she was pissed. He was taking this too far.

He gave her a steely look. "We have some."

His meaning kicked her right in the belly. "How much is airfare?"

"Eighteen hundred dollars round trip."

"Trevor, no. That's for my sister." She reeled away from him. "If you take it, how am I supposed to pay for everything she's going to need? A crib, diapers, formula… You can't do this. It isn't fair."

"Elz, I love you more than anything in this world, but you're thinking about right now. And I get it. You've been a mother to your sisters since you were eight years old. Yeah, that money can buy you diapers and formula, but how long will it last? Once we run out of it, then what? Then, you're back to working at the feedstore, and I'm working on my dad's farm."

It might make sense if this movie were going to be a blockbuster. But a clan war movie? With a budget so low the actors didn't get paid? *Come on.* "That baby will be here in five months."

"Yeah, I know. And we can get your sister a crib and a baby monitor, but this movie might lead to buying her a house and putting her kid through college. I'm willing to take a bet that has the potential to solve all our financial problems."

"Do you hear yourself? You're talking about gambling away the money I need for a baby." She could not believe this.

"The only thing that baby needs besides love is medical care which she'll get from the county clinic just like we did. All the stuff you want to buy is in your head. The baby doesn't need a fancy crib or highchair. And you know what? I'm not willing to sell out our goals because of your sister's mistake."

She reared back. Her stomach twisted into a knot. For the first time, they stood on opposite sides of a divide. "That *mistake* is my niece or nephew." *Calm down.* They'd always worked through their problems. They'd do it this time too. She had to remember he didn't have siblings. "I'm trying to understand your point of view… but this is my *sister*. And I get that you want to set up our future, but I don't know what that's going to look like if we don't take care of our families right now when they need us the most."

"If I walk away from this film and move back to Riverton, there won't be any more opportunities. Ever."

She hated to hurt him, but it needed to be said. "This is not an opportunity, Trevor. And guess what? There's no higher value than taking care of my sister, and if you insist on pursuing this *dream*, then you better understand that it's no longer *our* dream. It's yours. This is where our path splits."

Shock ripped across his handsome features. "What're you talking about? There's nothing more important than us." In one step, he was right in front of her. He grabbed her arms. "You and me, we're *home*."

"You're hanging on to some idea we came up with when we were kids, and I'm sorry, but reality's hit, and we need to be there for our family—" Awareness struck, and she wrenched out of his grip. "Sorry, *my* family. I thought we were in this together, but I can see we're not."

"Yes, we fucking are, and don't try to make me out to be selfish. The only thing I care about—the *only* thing that drives me—is getting us the life we want. And we can't do that until both our families are safe and secure. And that includes your sister. *My* sister. We're married, remember?"

She knew him. Their bond was solid. Their love had no beginning and no end. Yes, she was shaking like a leaf in the wind, but she looked him right in the eyes, knowing with absolute certainty he'd make the right decision. "If you go through with this, then there is no us."

He snagged his T-shirt off the bed and threw it on.

"You're the only woman in the world for me, and I wouldn't put our relationship in jeopardy for any reason other than to get us where we need to be. You have to trust that I'm going to make all our lives better." He started toward her—like he might hug or kiss her goodbye—but she glared at him.

Ignoring her defiance, he kissed her cheek. And then, he headed for the door.

He was leaving.

He was going to walk out on her.

This is impossible.

It didn't make sense.

"Trevor…" But her mind went blank. She knew that look of resolve. "You can't leave me."

"No, I can't. So, you know I'll be back."

"What if I don't wait for you?"

His eyes widened, and his voice went tight with emotion. "You have to. It's us. You and me." He held up his ring finger. "Forever."

"Not if you walk out that door."

"I have one shot, Elzy. One. And I'm going to take it." He threw open the door and stepped onto the concrete walkway. "I'll get a side job in a bar in town, and since my room and board is free, I'll send you every paycheck."

And then, he was gone.

She stood in the middle of the motel room, her skin bristling with static electricity.

Is this real? He'll come back, right? He has to.

She stood there while the fear spread like poison, until it hollowed her out. And when her legs could no longer support her, she sat on the edge of the mattress.

The smell of roses made her sick to her stomach, so she tossed the bouquet into the trash bin.

And still, she waited.

Because Trevor wouldn't do this to her.

He just wouldn't.

He'd come back.

He had to.

Chapter One

THIRTY YEARS LATER

IF JESSICA ELSWORTH DIDN'T OWN THIS PLACE, SHE'D BE doing a happy dance right there in the middle of the dining room.

Look at this. The holiday tea was sold out, and everyone was having the best time. Cheerful red berries brightened the holly garlands draped along the dark wood-paneled walls, and the plate glass windows exposed a winter wonderland of snowy pine trees and a frozen lake.

She was just so *relieved* at the turnout. The tables were filled with multi-generations of women, dads with little girls, whole families, and romantic couples. Everyone was dressed in their holiday finest and enjoying finger sandwiches, iced scones, and decadent treats from the Singing Baker Patisserie.

But then, she remembered, and fear reared up and locked her joints. Because while the tea was a hit, the New Year's Eve gala still hadn't sold out. And it was less than two weeks away.

The total spend for this month-long opening was two

million dollars—and she didn't get paid until guests checked out. At this point, she needed a full house to break even.

Okay, stop.

You're not spiraling.

You knew when you chose this swanky town there'd be competition for luxury resorts.

She also knew it took time to get established. But she trusted herself. She'd never failed before. She wouldn't this time.

Okay, back to work. She had a flight to catch and presents to wrap.

The moment she entered the kitchen, the sous chef spotted her and headed her way. The anxiety in his eyes had her bracing for bad news. "What's wrong?"

"Freezer's dead." A vein throbbed at the young man's temple. "I told Chef something was wrong. I kept telling him it's not keeping things cold enough. And now, it's dead."

This was the first she'd heard of the problem. "All right. Let me text maintenance."

Jessica: Freezer's lost power. Can you send someone over to fix it?

Bill: On my way.

Chef joined them. "Just put everything outside."

"No, don't do that," Jess said. "We can't risk the animals getting into it." She'd seen Big Joe, the moose who lurked in the woods, when she'd come in that morning. And he was hardly the only threat in the Tetons.

"Then, where do I put an entire freezer full of food?" the sous chef asked.

She considered the outbuildings. They had a garage for large equipment like snowplows and excavators, cabins, a dormitory for the staff, and—*ah*. "In the shed." *Yes, perfect.*

Relief softened his features. "Okay."

They'd built it to store extra linens and supplies, but at the moment, it was mercifully empty. She shot off a quick text to her sister, the property manager, to let her know the situation.

Once inside her office, she grabbed rolls of wrapping paper and pulled the gifts out of the closet. *Ugh.* She had no idea if these people would like what she got them. Unfortunately, she'd been so busy with the resort that she hadn't met her fiancé's family yet, so she didn't know their taste.

Normally, she wouldn't even consider leaving town during an opening, but she had to get used to dividing holidays. They'd spend the next three days in California with his daughter and grandkids, and then be back to Calamity in time for Christmas with her family.

A loud shout had her bolting out of her office to witness a server dropping two platters of pastries. All activity in the kitchen stopped as everyone watched shards of porcelain skitter across the floor amid splats of cream and dollops of ganache.

"That's it." Chef's deep, commanding voice bellowed. "You're fired." He pointed to the door. "Get out of my kitchen."

Jessica was on the move, stepping between the great bear of a man and the petite server.

While she understood his anger—there was no time to make new batches of gourmet French pastries—firing someone in the middle of service wouldn't solve the problem. So, she yanked the van's keys off the hook by the back door and handed them to the young woman. "Go into town and buy every pastry you can from Harley Lu Emporium. Then, drive to Wild Wolff Village and clear out the shelves of the Singing Baker. I'll call them both right now and let them know you're on your way."

The server nodded, cutting a glance at the chef.

"And don't stop for coffee," he shouted. "Don't text your mommy about what a piece of shit your boss is. Get the pastries and come back here." He glanced at the clock. "You've got thirty minutes before you tank the opening of this resort."

"I'm so sorry," the server whispered to Jessica.

"I know you are." She gave a comforting smile and touched her arm. "Drive carefully." Mid-December, the roads were snowy and crowded.

As the server headed out, Chef called, "Thirty minutes."

Once the door shut behind her, Jessica approached him. "This is your kitchen, but it's my world. Don't ever humiliate someone again under this roof. Are we clear?"

The man's jaw clenched, the muscle popping as he restrained himself. "We can't keep her. You know that, right?"

"Of course." The whole point of a soft opening was to work out the kinks with operational and staff issues and get feedback from guests who got to use the facilities for a deeply discounted price. By week three, a server should be able to carry a couple of platters. So, yes, she'd have to go.

"But there are ways to handle it and humiliating her in front of everyone is not one I'll tolerate. After the tea, we'll pull her aside and deliver the news privately."

He gave a curt nod. "I'll check how many pastries we have left."

But she stopped him. "You take care of dinner. I'll handle this." On her way into the walk-in refrigerator, she texted Grace at the Singing Baker Patisserie.

> Jessica: Hey, girl. I know it's a busy week with Christmas only a few days away, but we're in the middle of the tea and just lost two dozen pastries. What goodies can you sell me? I'll take everything you've got.

She'd run other properties, but this one meant the world to her. From the time she was a kid, she'd dreamed of living in Calamity, Wyoming, and she'd finally made it. She'd begun her journey with the lowest jobs in hospitality, and now, she owned a luxury resort.

Wild.

Of course, the original idea was to own a ranch, but she'd never known what that looked like. Would she and her ex breed horses? Run a B&B? Mostly, they'd imagined running wild on their land. Making love in front of a fire during a blizzard. Cooking together while their babies banged on pots and pans on the kitchen floor.

Damn you, Trevor.

He'd promised her forever, but he'd left and never looked back.

Even though she hadn't seen him in thirty years, it still hurt.

Isn't that crazy? That an old wound packs such a punch?

Ah, well. The power of first loves.

In any event, now was not the time to dredge up old memories. She had to text Lulu at the Emporium.

> Jessica: Hey, there. Sorry to bother you during the busiest time of year, but we've just lost two platters of pastries—right in the middle of the holiday tea! I'd like to buy as much as you can sell.

If she didn't hear back in fifteen minutes, she'd call them. She didn't want them ambushed by her server.

Checking the desserts, it looked like they had enough to last them another hour or so. Fingers crossed her friends would be able to fulfill her requests.

This can't fail.

It just can't.

She knew she had something good here. Something unique. She'd done her market research, of course, and she'd developed a concept this ritzy small mountain town didn't have—an exclusive, luxury wellness spa centered around a natural hot spring.

It had taken years of planning, saving, and researching, but when she'd discovered the thermal springs on a remote side of Lake Calamity, she'd known she had a winner.

From the moment she got her first permits, she'd begun the slow process of purchasing one parcel of land at a time. This was her baby. Her pride and joy.

And it *would* be a hit.

Her phone vibrated, and she quickly checked the screen. *Oh, thank God.* Grace responded.

Grace: I got you! And holiday or not, I'm always baking, so it's not a problem. I'll box up everything that's not in the display cases. Let me know if there's anything else I can do.

Jessica: You're the best! I can't thank you enough. But I can give you and Jaime a night of decadence on the house whenever you can get a babysitter!

Grace: I like how you think!

No matter how much her friend loved baking, it was still a matter of days before Christmas Eve. And Grace was not only a stepmom to an adorable little girl but pregnant with her first baby. It was a big ask, and Jess would pay her triple for the inconvenience.

She pocketed her phone just as her sister poked her head into the walk-in. She looked anxious.

"Everything okay?" Jess stepped out, closing the door behind her. "What's going on?"

"There's someone out there."

Shock blasted through her so fast the soles of her feet stung.

Because her sister wouldn't make a big deal over a random guest. Only if it were someone significant like... Trevor Montgomery.

Is he here?

No, that's ridiculous.

But her response highlighted how deeply she feared running into him. She knew he lived in town—it preoccupied her every thought—and she dreaded bumping into him at Calamity Joe's or while out hiking the trails.

How mortifying would that be? She could imagine his expression of pity, thinking she'd moved here to pursue him.

Uh, excuse me. Pity?

When he sees this place, he'll be blown away.

Now, shake it off. It's definitely not him. "Who is it?"

"You won't believe this." Her sister paused for dramatic effect. "It's Cole." And then, as if Jess didn't know exactly who she was talking about, she said, "Cole *Montgomery*."

For just one moment, the world stopped spinning. It lurched and rocked.

Trevor's son?

Is here? Now?

This is not happening.

Heat flashed across her body. "Who's he with?" *Please don't say Trevor.*

Do not say Trevor.

"It's just him and four little girls." Amber reached for her. "I can't imagine how weird this is for you. You don't have to go out there."

"No, no. It's fine." *Liar.* It wasn't fine at all. Disoriented, she didn't know which impulse to follow. Either she turned back into her office and shut the door or hurried into the dining room to see him.

"Do you think he knows about you?" her sister asked.

"No." Why would Trevor tell his son about some ex-girlfriend from thirty years ago? "He might've said something in passing. Like if he knew I opened this resort" —which, come on, would be impossible to miss considering the lengths she'd gone to promote it—"he might've said, 'Oh, someone from my hometown owns it.' But that can't be why his son is here."

Somehow, this was harder than seeing her ex. She'd thought the worst thing that ever happened was when he'd walked out the door of that motel room. But no. Seeing him as a father had broken her.

Because he'd gotten someone pregnant not even two years after abandoning her.

She'd never recovered.

Obviously. She'd never gotten married.

At least it had been the kick in the ass she'd needed to build a life for herself and stop waiting for Trevor to come back.

She owed this beautiful life to his cold, ruthless dismissal.

But her sister didn't need to know any of this. "Let's not worry about Cole Montgomery. We've got a broken freezer and a shortage of pastries to handle. Now, I've already heard back from the Singing Baker, so we should be okay. As soon as I hear from the Emporium—"

"Sweetie." Her sister set her hands on Jess's shoulders. "It's okay to be shook."

That simple statement broke the dam, and a rush of tears filled her eyes.

Oh, dammit.

Not here. Not now.

She was so used to being a mother to her sisters that she rarely opened the door to her own emotional life. But for thirty years, Trevor had been a hard knot of pain in the center of her heart.

So, now, to know his son and granddaughters were out there...

That he'd had a whole family...

Without me.

And as much as she wanted to be over it, she simply wasn't. Maybe it made her weak and foolish, but… *It is what it is.* "Yeah, okay. I'm shook."

Because that man out there in the dining room? That should be her son. Not some random woman's.

"You stay in the kitchen," Amber said. "I'll handle front of house."

But a sense of urgency took over, and Jess shook her head. "No." She had to see the boy—well, man. Cole was a father now. "I want to see him."

Her sister nodded. "Okay. You go on, and I'll handle the freezer issue."

"Thank you." She pulled her sister in for a hug. "I love working with you."

Watching her sister leave, Jess knew she'd made the right choice all those years ago. Helping her sister navigate pregnancy and motherhood and getting their youngest sister through college had formed an unbreakable bond between the three of them. It had been worth putting off her own career to get them on the right track.

As she headed into the dining room, she drew a deep breath.

Here we go.

As a hockey superstar, Cole Montgomery's face was plastered all over the news and social media. Until he'd married, he'd had a reputation for being a heartbreaker and a party boy.

Which, interestingly, his movie star father did not.

She steeled herself for the wallop of emotion she'd get from seeing Trevor's son.

But it didn't come. Because she didn't see her ex's lookalike. She saw a handsome, fit man sitting at a table with four little girls. Two were in highchairs. One of them patted her little hands on the tray, smooshing strawberry shortcake and bobbing her head along to a song only she could hear, while the other greedily shoved fistfuls of whipped cream into her mouth.

The other two were notably older—a definite age gap between the two sets. Cole sat perfectly at ease, handing a napkin to one daughter, offering a scone to the oldest, and chatting with them as though they were his buddies.

She couldn't take her eyes off him.

Wholly focused on his girls, he didn't seem concerned about being recognized. Which she appreciated. It meant he trusted this place. Given the level of luxury at her resort, she'd invested heavily in security. No one would be taking pictures of celebrities. Her highest priority was making her guests feel safe and at ease.

Watching him interact with his daughters, it was clear Trevor had raised a good son. A good man.

And dammit if her heart didn't squeeze so hard it beckoned a second flood of tears.

Because she'd wanted to be the mother of his children. The boy she'd grown up with would've made a great dad.

She would've liked to have seen that.

Once, she'd imagined having a whole passel of kids. Turned out, she'd had none of her own.

My God. You have to stop this.

She didn't usually wallow in the past. But being here in Calamity—where Trevor lived—dredged it all up. And now, seeing his son…

Enough.

Glancing around the room, she assured herself everything was going well. Her phone vibrated, and she blinked back tears to see Lulu had responded.

> Lulu: I got you! Boxing it up right now.

> Jessica: Oh, thank goodness! I appreciate you!

"Jess." Her fiancé's voice jerked her gaze up. Weaving around the tables, he made a beeline for her.

"What're you doing here?" But she didn't want to talk in the dining room, so she led him into the kitchen and over to an out-of-the-way spot. "Is everything okay?"

"Gabby's husband left her." He seemed frantic, and his salt-and-pepper hair looked like he'd raked his hands through it. But she understood. *This is his daughter.* "He just walked out the door."

"Oh, no. That's awful. What can we do?"

"I'm heading to the airport right now."

Dammit. Why did I put off wrapping the presents until the last minute?

Well, no time to think about that now. She'd stuff them in her suitcase and finish in San Diego. "Okay, no problem. I'm already packed. Just give me fifteen minutes to grab my suitcase and tie up some loose ends."

"No, no. I'm going by myself." He looked distracted, like he wanted to be three steps ahead of this moment— checking his luggage and heading through security.

She'd been in tough situations with her sisters too many times to count. She got it. "I'm not leaving you alone right now. Let me handle all the details. I'll call a car."

"No." He stopped her by covering her hand. "I've got one. It's waiting outside. I just came to tell you I'm leaving."

"Okay." It was no big deal. "I'll just meet you at the hotel. Let me know if I can do anything."

"I'm not staying at a hotel. We're all staying with my ex. My daughter, the grandkids. Me."

What? She wasn't so sure about that. "You want me to stay at your ex-wife's house?"

"Jessica, no." He pressed his lips together like he was trying to calm down. "Look, my daughter's devastated. That bastard insisted she stay home with the kids. He kept her shut off from their finances. And now, he walks out on her, leaving her with nothing?"

"Well, he obviously forgot her dad's an attorney because you're not going to let him take advantage of her." She rubbed his arm. "You're not alone in this. I'm here. Remember, I have two sisters who've been through a lot."

"Thank you for that." He softened, brushing his hand across her cheek. "I got lucky with you." He checked his watch. "Okay, I have to go. Your ticket's flexible, so you can use it for another trip. Just call to let them know you won't be on that flight."

"What? You don't want me to come at all?"

He shook his head. "She won't want anyone but her mom and dad." He smiled as though he knew she'd understand. "It's a family matter."

Stung, she reared back. *I'm not family?* "Okay." She followed him to the back door.

Before he opened it, he turned to hug her. "I'm going to

miss you." He cupped her cheeks and kissed her on the mouth. "I'll call you when I get settled."

She was too stunned to reply, so she just stood there.

"Oh. Also, I've canceled my return flight. I'm not sure when I'll be back."

"What are you saying? You won't be here for the New Year's event?" That was the resort's hard launch. It was the gala and the polar plunge.

It seemed trivial compared to what his daughter was going through, but she'd looked forward to sharing the special night with her fiancé.

"It's unlikely. I'll have to stay as long as she needs me." He kissed her cheek. "I have to run." He hurried off, his boots crunching in the snow.

Shaken, Jess stood there, letting the icy cold air wash over her.

Seconds (or was it minutes? Hours?) later, her sister pulled her into the kitchen. "What're you doing, you nut?"

The sudden warmth made her skin sting. "Joel left. He's going to California without me."

"You broke up?" Her sister sounded surprised.

"No. He needs to be there for his daughter. Her husband walked out on her."

"Okay." She studied her. "Are we happy or sad about not going?"

"I understand where he's coming from." That might've sounded a little flat. Well, frankly, she didn't know how she felt. Unsettled. A little…shaken, maybe?

Numb.

Amber made a circular emotion. "I don't know what's happening with your face."

"I guess I'm hurt?"

"Well, yeah, that's fair. I would be too."

"But I'm overreacting. His daughter's in crisis, and I've never even met her, so, of course, she wouldn't want some stranger there."

Okay, yes. This makes sense.

"Jess, it's *Christmas*. And he's icing you out? That's… I mean, his daughter's important, but you've been together a year. Aren't you important too?"

Good question. "Apparently not." She tried to laugh, but it came out a weird kind of honk. "I don't know. We'd better get back to work."

"Are you good?" Amber asked.

"Yes." Not really. She was still reeling. Unsettled.

"Great, because our server of the year hit an icy patch and ran off the road. But don't worry. She swears the pastries are fine, and I've sent someone out there to grab them. We're all good."

"You've got to be kidding me." Jess shook her head, but she wasn't entirely present. Her mind bobbed like a buoy on the ocean. "Well, you handled it, so… Perfect. Thanks. Okay." She started back to her office.

"Why are you talking like a robot?"

But she waved her sister off. "I have to cancel my flight."

"Do you though?"

Jess stopped. "What does that mean?"

Her sister caught up with her. "It means you've arranged this time off. Why not go and have some fun? Do some Christmas shopping in New York City. Hang out by the pool in Florida."

"Because it's the opening."

"And you've set it up so everything can't help but run smoothly. Besides, there's nothing between the tea and Christmas Eve. You deserve a break."

"Are you trying to get rid of me?" She said it with a smile, but the vise around her heart tightened, and she didn't know why.

"What? No." Her sister's tone turned urgent. "Jess, you've been working your ass off your whole life. And let's be honest, you didn't get a childhood because when Mom died, you stepped into that role. You raised us when you weren't even an adult yourself."

"I love you guys."

"And we love you. More than you know. But you've trained us well, and between me and Kelly and our husbands, we've got this place covered. Even if you don't want to leave, at least take a day or two off and go shopping. Enjoy the town you've wanted to live in your whole life. Visit Owl Hoot, take a spa day… go ice skating in Wild Wolff Village."

"That does sound nice." But something was niggling at the back of her mind. No, not just there. It ran like a current down her arms and legs. "Maybe I'll do that." She forced a smile and headed into her office.

Now, what was I doing? She tried to focus, but her vision swam, and she couldn't see anything beyond the blur of her laptop, her water bottle, and the boxes of shampoo samples she needed to try.

Ah. The presents.

Well, no need to rush wrapping them anymore.

She glanced at her phone to see if there was something

she needed to follow up on. As she scrolled, she noticed an unfamiliar name.

Chris Pullman.

Who's that? She read the last text he'd sent.

> Chris: Please! I'm desperate. I'll pay you double what you normally charge!

Oh, right. The consulting job. His family owned a hotel in Iceland, and he wanted to turn it into a luxury resort. Normally, she'd be all over a job like that. But the timing was off.

And yet… there went her fingers, texting him back.

> Jessica: Double, huh?

She didn't know why she'd done that. Nor did she know how he could offer to raise her fees when he didn't know what they were to begin with. She didn't list them on her website. Her consulting business was strictly word of mouth.

> Chris: Hello! Excuse me, I just choked on my wine. Let me go clean up my mess, and then I'll come back and incentivize you properly.

She smiled. *Who is this guy?* While she waited, she swiped to the start of the conversation.

Chris: Hello. My name is Chris Pullman, and I got your name from Leizel Ramos. I stayed at her Maldives resort and fell in love with her aesthetic (well, and her, but that's a story for another day haha. Fast forward to the ending: she didn't love me back). Anywho, my family owns this fabulous hotel in Iceland—well, I suppose if I want to work with you, I should be transparent. It's not so fabulous. But it can be. Can we talk?

Jessica: Thanks for reaching out, Chris. Normally, I'd be all over this project, but I've just opened my own resort in America and have to give it my full attention. Best of luck with your project.

Chris: Wait! Hear me out. What if you come out here right now (I promise to get you home in time for hot toddies by the fire on Christmas Eve) to walk the halls of this (potentially) glorious old dame, and then you can do the rest of the job remotely? Please? There's no one else I'd trust with this place.

The temptation surprised her. Why was she even interested?

Was it to show Joel that she was wanted somewhere? That she wasn't going to stay home and wallow in his rejection?

No, that didn't ring true. Whatever was niggling…it wasn't rejection.

Another text came in.

Chris: To be clear, I don't want just anyone for this job. I want you. And since I know it's a lousy time of year to ask for you to fly out here, I'll pay you double what you normally charge.

She watched the three dots dance as he composed another message.

Chris: What's the one thing you need for your resort's success that you don't have at this exact moment?

Jessica: Guests

Chris: Hahaha! I like you already. We're going to get on swimmingly. What's the deficit you're looking at right now?

Even though she couldn't possibly take this job, she was intrigued. So, she threw out a number he'd never be able to pay. Just because she wasn't ready to end the conversation.

Jessica: Two million dollars.

Chris: You thought that would throw me off, didn't you?! You underestimate my determination to make quitting my job and moving to Iceland mean something. I'll pay you two hundred thousand for the week, and if you decide to take the job, I'll pay you two million. How's that? Did I win you over?

It was a wild offer. Still, she couldn't take it. Not when she had so much to do here.

> Jessica: Christmas is in six days. I can't come for a week.

> Chris: Fair. How many days can I get?

She glanced at the calendar she kept on her wall. The next three days had red slashes marking them. She took travel into consideration.

And just like that, she wasn't playing with him anymore.

> Jessica: Four. I have to be back for Christmas Eve. My niece is getting married.

> Chris: Sold! But I'm carving your fee back to $199,999. So, when can you get here?

Would he seriously pay her two million dollars for this job? She kept her rates extremely high, not only because her time was valuable but to screen out people who weren't serious.

This man was serious.

And in that moment, the niggling stepped out of the shadows and took solid form.

I'm never anyone's first choice.

Trevor chose his career.

Her sisters loved her, but she wasn't an actual mother to them. She'd just stepped into the role. They had their own husbands and children, and as much as they loved her, she wasn't in the center of that.

And Joel, who was supposed to put her first, had locked her out when a crisis hit his family.

Were you ever really inside though?

You never even met his daughter.

She needed to think. And she couldn't do that here.

> Jessica: Sir, it's Christmas. Don't you have presents to wrap?

> Chris: Sadly, no.

Her heart pinched. She might be the fifth wheel in her family dynamic, but at least she had them. She had her sisters, her brothers-in-law, and her nieces and nephews.

> Chris: My assistant does that for me. LOL! But seriously, I'll get you home in time for Christmas Eve. All I want is for you to look around, get a sense of the scope of the project, and get your brilliant mind working on ideas. Then, we'll talk after New Year's. Sound good?

She shouldn't do this. Once she got into a project, she became obsessed. Her mind would start spitting out ideas, and she'd get lost for hours researching colors, styles, and drawer pulls.

God, she loved her job.

> Jessica: What's the urgency? Can it wait until spring when I'm clear of this opening?

> Chris: If I were a normal sort of man, then, yes. By all means, it could wait. But there's so much to do, and I want to honor the legacy of this place—

Ping. He'd just roused the part of her soul that yearned

for meaningful jobs like this. She loved history, loved family traditions… Yeah, he got her with that one.

Chris: Also, you should know, pretty much everyone in my family works in construction. We've got plumbers, electricians, architects, contractors…you name it. And they're all on standby, ready to go. So, what do you say? Are you up for an adventure?

Jessica: I am. But to be clear, I'm not committing to the project just yet. At the very least, I can write up a report that will guide you through every step.

Chris: Yes! I'm sending you a round-trip ticket right now.

Huh. Guess I'm going to Iceland.

Chapter Two

Trevor Montgomery never liked goodbyes.

Mostly, because he didn't get nearly as attached as the people he hung out with. That made it awkward.

He supposed something inside him was broken.

But Darby was cool. They were on the same page.

Together, they stood on the sidewalk of Concourse D waiting for the driver to pull the luggage from the town car. They'd met a month ago at a gala, and they hadn't been apart since. But their time was up, and now, she was flying to Iceland to spend Christmas with her family while he returned to Wyoming to spend it with his.

"You know, this doesn't have to end." She wagged a finger between them.

Oh, shit. Maybe not on the same page after all. He hoped he hadn't done or said anything to mislead her. He was pretty sure he hadn't. He tried hard to be transparent.

"All you have to do is sign the contract." She brushed her free hand down his chest. "And we can spend a whole year together."

Subtly, he took a step back. He didn't do public displays of affection. He'd learned early on if he wanted to preserve his privacy, he couldn't feed the media machine. "I'm not sure I can keep up with you." He grinned, resorting to humor. But it was true. They might be the same age, but they lived at different speeds.

The driver set Darby's suitcase down, and Trevor held up a finger. "I'm going to walk her in. I'll just be a minute."

But before they headed off, she pulled a hundred-dollar bill out of her pocket and handed it to the man. "Happy holidays."

"Oh, there's no need," the driver said. "The tip's included."

"It's Christmas." She pressed the money into his palm. "Surprise your partner with a bottle of champagne."

Her brilliant smile had the older man blushing. "Thank you."

As Trevor wheeled her luggage inside, she asked, "So, what, you're just going to sit on the porch wrapped in an old blanket when you could be watching NASCAR with me?" She bumped into him playfully. "Hey, I'll even let you behind the wheel sometimes."

A familiar burn at the back of his neck gave him a split-second warning of what was to come. After all this time, he'd become hyperaware of a fan's proximity. His intuition was confirmed when the cold metal of the selfie stick tapped his inner thigh.

When he spun around, the fan cried, "Boxers? Briefs? Or commando?" Her group of friends burst out laughing, and the woman said, "We love you, Trevor Montgomery. We're your biggest fans."

Even after three decades of the same movie franchise, people never grew tired of this game. Everywhere he went—no matter the country—people tried to find out what he wore underneath his kilt. Mostly, they were respectful.

"Thank you." He smiled, signed their autographs, and then turned his attention back to Darby.

"And that's why I want your signature on that contract," she said. "You've been retired for three years, and you're still the most beloved movie star in the world."

"I should probably stop wearing the kilts." But of course, he couldn't do that yet. When he'd passed the franchise onto the next generation, he'd committed to a small role in the first two films to ease the transition. His contract required him to wear the kilt in public until one month after the last movie's release.

"Oh, where's the fun in that?" Darby waited for the next available kiosk. "At least, I hope it's fun. Because if you do sign the contract, you'll have to wear that outfit for another year."

While he had no interest in continuing to dress in costume, his stomach pitched and rolled when he considered what the rest of his life looked like. "Let me think about it over the holidays."

"Okay, but don't forget. The season starts in February." She pulled her phone out of her messenger bag and pointed it at the ticket screen. "And it's going to be a damn good one." Her tone held pure confidence. "We're going to sweep the races this year. It's so much fun. You only got a little taste of it."

A celebrated driver, Darby had taken him around the track at nearly two hundred miles per hour. She was a high-octane woman, and they'd filled their every waking moment with meetings, dinners, antique hunting, and parties—which was in total contrast to the week she'd spent at his place in Wyoming, where they'd hiked, sat around the fire pit at night, and spent time with his four grandkids.

Needless to say, she'd been bored out of her mind.

"Okay, well, you go drink champagne on your luxurious private jet, and I'll slog it with the middle class." The woman had millions in endorsements, so he knew she was only joking. She got up on her toes to kiss him on the mouth.

But he turned just in time for her lips to land on his cheek. "Sounds good." All she wanted was his celebrity status to draw attention to her team, so he wouldn't need to do much but show up at the events.

Her love for her sport was infectious. Honestly, nothing was sexier than a woman who loved her work.

Mostly because, while he'd had a great career and achieved success beyond his wildest imagination, he'd never had a passion.

Well, not for a job or a hobby. For a person, yes. The garden in his heart grew nothing but Elzy flowers. But that wasn't the same thing.

And he needed it. Needed a project that consumed him, that he could throw himself into. He was lost without it. And the NASCAR season ran for ten months, so that would sure as hell be all-consuming.

Instead of heading off to her gate, she hesitated. "You sure you don't want to come with me?" Darby always dreaded going home. She said it was a whirlwind visit of family and friends who couldn't understand why she'd chosen a career in America over getting married and having kids who'd grow up with cousins, aunts, uncles, and grandparents back in Reykjavik.

He'd never been to Iceland and wouldn't mind seeing it. But it was Christmas. Family time. And thanks to a brutal filming schedule, he'd missed out on so much with his son. He was determined to be present for his grandkids. "Sounds fun, but I want to be with my family."

"You know, there's a simple solution to our problem." She had a teasing glint in her eyes.

"We have a problem?" he clapped right back.

"We do." She pressed a hand to his chest. "Wherever we go, we're both visitors. Guests. We don't really belong."

Though he couldn't deny the truth, it stung to hear it. He loved being a grandfather, but too often, he was in the way. In his son's household, it was always nap or bath time, or the girls were throwing a fit or racing out the door to dance class.

Trevor knew they loved and appreciated him, but his son and daughter-in-law were trying to wrangle order out of mayhem, and there just wasn't a role for him. Maybe when the kids were older it would change but not yet.

Up until a couple of months ago, he'd felt part of the family. So, when he'd heard his daughter-in-law's hushed, urgent voice behind the closed door of her bedroom, it had gutted him.

I can't handle one more person in this house.

He still visited, of course. He was there whenever they needed him to babysit or celebrate, but he was extremely conscious of overstaying his welcome.

"What's your solution?" Because he wasn't going to deny he had a problem. His life revolved around his family, but they were—necessarily—their own unit. His son was focused on managing four daughters, a wife, and owning a hockey team.

And now that Trevor was retired, he had no job. No hobbies.

He had no passion.

She gazed into his eyes. "We could belong to each other."

The suggestion blew through him like a brisk wind. They'd never talked about a future. Nothing serious at all. "We've known each other for a month. What do you mean?"

"Trevor, we've both had our great loves. There's not going to be another one for either of us. We also know how hard it is to 'visit' our families. And I don't know about you, but I'm so tired of dating apps—well, dating in general. It's awful. We could solve all our problems by being great companions for the rest of our lives." She reached for his hand. "Aren't you tired of being alone?"

He could say yes. It wouldn't be a lie. But there was a tug deep inside he couldn't ignore. Because on some level, he was still holding out.

For a woman he hadn't seen in thirty years.

One who'd moved on. Had a family of her own.

"Think about how we met," she continued. "We hooked up at a gala. Do you want to do that for the rest of your life?"

No. I want Elzy.

My Calamity Jane.

Her face popped up in his mind. Not the professional headshot she used on her website—that wasn't his sweetheart. But the way she'd looked when they'd exchanged vows in that Las Vegas chapel.

God, she was the most beautiful woman in the world.

And he'd ruined it.

Fucked it all up.

Sentenced himself to a life without love, passion… or true happiness.

So, yeah, he saw Darby's point.

"Trevor Montgomery?" Her eyes glittered with mischief. "Will you marry me and be my plus one for the rest of my life?"

Startled, he could only let out a laugh. "You're giving me a lot to think about over the holidays."

"Well, at least it's not a no, right?" Her gaze lingered, searching, no doubt, for a window of hope he couldn't give. Darby was determined. She got what she wanted.

Maybe she'd get her wish with him.

"It's not a no." He kissed her cheek. "Safe travels."

As he turned to walk out of the terminal, he got a text from his son.

> Cole: Well, merry fucking Christmas. All four girls are puking their guts out.

> Trevor: Flu?

> Cole: Yeah. So much for all the fun shit Hailey had planned. Looks like we're just going to hang out around the house.

The jolt that went through his body surprised him. Had he just been kicked out for *Christmas*?

His daughter-in-law had grown up as an only child, so

raising four kids had to be overwhelming for her. She had sick kids. It was a lot. He got it. He understood.

But Christmas?

He had only himself to blame. He knew that. Because he'd let his son be raised by nannies. Of course, he was a guest in Cole's house.

And, so, maybe Darby's invitation into her world would give him a chance to be part of something, give him a purpose. To belong.

Because Jessica Elsworth is not coming back.

And your son will never be close to you because you didn't form that bond when he was a child.

But Darby wants to give you companionship for the rest of your life.

His daughter-in-law's voice slipped into his thoughts.

I can't handle one more person in this house.

An urgency shot through him, and he turned around, darting between families, travelers, and airline employees to get to his friend.

"Darby," he called. "Darby!"

She turned around, concerned.

When he caught up with her, he cupped her elbows. "Let's do it."

Why the hell not? They both wanted companionship, nothing more. Neither could get hurt if it didn't work out.

"Let's get married."

Jessica got lucky.

A warm front hit Iceland, which meant there was very

little snow on the ground, giving her outstanding views both from the plane and the drive to the remote hotel.

Usually, when she traveled, she had an impression of the destination from movies or photographs. The canals in Venice, the grand, historic buildings of Paris, or the turquoise-blue seas of Bora Bora. But she hadn't known what to expect with Iceland.

And it was like another planet. Volcanic craters, electric-blue ice caps, black-sand beaches, and steaming hot springs made up the landscape.

Now, after a red-eye flight and a two-hour drive from Reykjavik, she sat in Chris Pullman's office. Judging by the streaks of gray in his thick, dark hair and skin roughened by sun exposure, the handsome man looked about her age. His wealth—as she picked up from the big, shiny watch, designer jeans, Gucci loafers, and Tom Ford flannel shirt—stood in contrast to a room that smelled like old paper and a hint of must. The furniture was dated and scuffed, and the chair cushions held deep impressions.

"Tell me about the history of this place." From the exterior, she could tell it had a great footprint. It might not be as much work to upgrade as he expected.

"My grandparents bought this land for pennies." He motioned toward the window. "It was largely unusable. How do you build on a thousand-year-old lava flow?"

She could answer that. "You work with it and not against it. Also, the quality of the lava's a determinant. You can't build on it if it's brittle, so I'm going to assume this field's strong and impenetrable."

Smiling, Chris sat back in his chair. "See that. Worth every penny."

"Well, it was a seven-and-a-half-hour flight. I had to do *something* to fill the time."

"Most people sleep on red-eyes." Mischief sparkled in his eyes.

"Most people don't get two hundred thousand dollars for four days of work." She'd also done her research on him. He'd made his fortune on Wall Street. Considered a maverick, he'd given countless interviews and closed massive deals, so she'd found enough information to form a solid impression of him.

"Very true." He laughed. "But that tells you how important this project is to me. So, yes. It's rugged lava, and my grandparents were able to build on it. Over time, they developed the geothermal features and wanted to share them with others, so they turned it into a B&B. With the help of an investor, they expanded into a hotel. The bones are solid, but it's never been anything more than a place to sleep for a night along the Golden Circle."

"And the inheritance battle? I read the hotel's been closed for a number of years."

"Correct. After my grandparents passed away, the property went to their children. They couldn't agree on what they wanted to do with it. Uncle Rat Bastard wanted to sell it outright. He wanted the cash, but my dad and aunt insisted on keeping it. They couldn't get a consensus, so it's just sat here."

"And now?"

"Uncle Rat Bastard died, and his siblings are too old to renovate this place." He lifted both palms. "The timing was good for me, so here I am."

"Just to be clear, how many voices have a say in the décor and, more importantly, the budget?"

"I own it outright, and I make all the decisions. And you should know, right off the bat, you have carte blanche to transform this place according to your vision. Do I want to see your choices every step of the way?" He nodded. "You bet. But I only reached out to one designer. There's no one I trust more with this place than you."

His confidence warmed her. "I appreciate that very much. And all this from one resort in the Maldives? What if you were love drunk because of the lovely Leizel?"

He laughed. "I've been to four of your properties. The Anabelle in St. Barts? That place is stunning. I've never seen anything like it."

She smiled. "Thank you. That was a lot of fun."

Truthfully? Even three decades into this career, she still felt uneasy about charging so much for doing something she loved. The little girl who'd never owned a single outfit that hadn't come from the church clothing exchange internally screamed when she sent off a proposal. But because of that, she took her work seriously and made sure she delivered value.

"That one took three years," she continued. "But since we're not changing the footprint, I don't think yours will take nearly as long. The biggest project will be adding a state-of-the-art wellness center and gym. Once we have our theme, it won't take much to turn the rooms into suites. But as you said in your text message, we've got all the time in the world."

He shifted forward, his features tightening. "You're right.

I did say that. But there's a new development that's pushing up the timeline."

She was unfazed. "Oh?" Most of her clients didn't understand supply and delivery issues, contractors who overbooked, and products that wound up being discontinued. "What's changed?"

"My sister called last night. She's getting married, and she wants to have it here. Childhood memories and all that."

"Okay, so what kind of timeframe are you looking at?" Didn't it take a year to plan a wedding? "Keep in mind the planning stage alone will take months. I can't guarantee it'll be done in time."

"I understand that, and I don't want to interfere with your process. I would, however, like to shift the agenda for your stay here."

She folded her hands in her lap. "I'm listening."

"My sister's a race car driver—well, retired now—but she owns a team, and the season starts in February."

The date landed in her gut like a brick. "If you're not joking, then you've just wasted two hundred thousand dollars. With a deadline like that, at best, you'll have time to slap on some paint and install new carpets. You can't transform this place into a luxury resort in two months. During *winter.*"

"No, of course not. But hear me out. A good part of what you do is interior design. For the short term, I'd like you to renovate the main part of the hotel—the entrance, the dining room, and some of the suites. Keep in mind, my family's in the construction business, so they can make it happen fast."

"You'll be throwing out whatever work I do. You

understand that, right? Because we don't even have a concept. I haven't studied the demographic, psychographic, or geographic characteristics of your target customer. It will take me months to find the right suppliers, the fixtures...to come up with a unifying palette of paint colors. We need a chef, a concierge—"

"I get it." He held up a hand. "And, yes, I fully understand what I'm asking you to do. That said, anything you can accomplish while you're here that can do double duty would be great."

"Does your sister understand what having it here will mean for you? The cost and effort?"

His gaze dropped to his black leather loafers. "My sister and I are the only ones who moved away. We were close growing up but living in America made us tighter." He sat back in his chair. "In my business, you don't make a lot of friends. You have colleagues and people you hang out with for a purpose." He shrugged. "You have ex-wives and kids you barely know." He shrugged. "But there's no one in this world I'm closer to than my sister. And this hotel… Well, let's just say it's the only place that has good childhood memories for us." With a look of resolve, he sat up straighter. "It has to be here. Can you help me pull it off?"

How could she say no to that? "Keep in mind, your family might have the expertise and connections, but they have no control over supply and delivery considerations. Especially in winter."

"I understand. But will you do it?"

She admired his determination. "Look, you're paying me. I'll do whatever you want. As long as you understand

I'm not a wedding planner. I've never even had one of my own."

Her stomach twisted at the lie. But hers was an elopement, and the marriage hadn't lasted an hour, so it didn't count.

Ugh. Why did it hurt to think about him after all these years? She wished so badly she could let it all go.

The way he had.

"Believe me, I understand. But she's marrying one of the most famous men in the world, which means the guests will be A-listers, and I can't have them staying in a shabby hotel."

"No, you certainly can't. And honestly, it'll be fun to spruce this place up."

His features broke wide open in relief. "Thank you. Excellent."

"Now, in terms of double duty, I can get started on the search for a chef, sommelier, and concierge. You'll need all of that for the wedding."

"That'll be easier than you think. You know how many people live here?"

"Three hundred and fifty thousand."

He chuckled. "She does her research. Right, and guess how many restaurants have Michelin stars?"

Now, that she didn't know.

"Three." He held up his fingers. "Which means you only have to interview three chefs. And there's only one master sommelier here, so there you go. I'll pay them more than they make anywhere else. See how much easier I've made your job?"

She smiled. "Only the CEO of a massive hedge fund

would think he could snap his fingers and complete a hiring process like this in four days."

He threw back his head and laughed. "Well, you only become CEO by working your ass off. I never ask anybody to do what I'm not willing to do myself. I made my money through hard work and sacrifice." His features fell, and he let out a heavy sigh. "At this point in my life, my sister's all I have, and I need to do this for her. She never thought she'd get married, but apparently, she's found the perfect man. You hear what I'm saying?"

"I absolutely do. I feel the same way about my sisters. I'd move heaven and earth for them, so yes, I get it." Her mind was already working on a plan of action. She grabbed a pen from her leather tote bag. "You've got three chefs and a sommelier in mind, so that's a great start. We'll need a concierge. Someone who was born and raised here and who understands Icelandic culture and traditions. I'll order new mattresses and bedding and get started on a kitchen renovation. Oh, and I'll hire a laundry service." She tapped the page. "We'll need to pull electricians, plumbers, and a contractor from their current jobs to get those rooms in shape." She glanced up at him. "Any idea about the guest list? How many rooms we're doing?"

He smiled warmly at her. "You said 'we.'"

She knew just what he meant. It was a solo climb to the top of any career, but once there, all the choices and results rested on the shoulders of the leader. "I did." The day her sisters referred to the business as, *We,* she'd taken her first full breath. "You're not in this alone."

"I'm glad for that. And no, I don't know the guest list, but I'll let her know the urgency in getting it to us."

"Now, do you have any thoughts on décor? Style? Colors?"

He shook his head. "I hired you for your vision. You have carte blanche to do whatever you want."

"Okay, well, I think we should reflect the environment with charcoal gray walls to mimic the lava and bathroom tiles in the deep blues of the thermal baths and greens of the moss that covers the lava. I love the idea of chandeliers and hanging lights that glow like the aurora borealis."

He shivered. "I just got a chill." He held out his forearm. "Do you see that? Wow. I love it." He flicked a hand. *Go on.*

"I think every aspect should be Icelandic. Which means bespoke artwork and sculptures, but"—she held up a finger in case he was about to warn her about the time factor—"for our immediate purposes, we'll visit art galleries and purchase what we need for the wedding. At the end of spring, I can come back and focus on the rugs and fixtures and the rest of the décor. Unless you need it sooner, in which case I'll have to find an interior designer who understands our vision."

"Nope. We're not hiring anyone else. After the wedding, you can work at your own pace."

"Okay, then." She shoved her notebook and pen into her tote. "I've got my work cut out for me."

"Aren't you exhausted from the flight? You didn't sleep."

"I'll sleep when I get home, but right now, I need to set up tastings and interviews. I can only do that during work hours." She stood up. "Do you want to come with me? Taste the food, drink the wine?"

"Taste the food of three Michelin-rated chefs? I think I could squeeze it into my schedule." His phone buzzed at that exact moment, and he read the screen. "That's her." He waggled the phone. "My sister's here." Excitement had him hopping out of the chair. "Let me introduce you to her and her fiancé. Come on."

"Great." She followed him out of the office. "Now, where can I set up shop?"

He tapped out a message on his phone. "Let me get my assistant. He'll set you up with everything you need. Sound good?"

"Perfect."

"Great. Come meet the bride and groom."

As they headed down the hallway toward the lobby, Jess's mind spun with ideas. Crisp white bedding to go with the charcoal gray walls. Mirrored nightstands to add a little sparkle against the dark—they'd echo the night sky of this remote location. Burgundy velvet couches in the lobby—with black, mirrored throw pillows.

No, no, no. Let's keep it thematically tied to the landscape and go with green velvet. The same color as the moss. "I'd like to get my hands on vintage photographs and historic maps of Iceland to go on the walls."

"Well, you're in luck because my grandfather was a collector. My assistant will take you to the owner's quarters, and you can have a look around. Take whatever you'd like for the resort. I really like that idea, by the way."

Voices in the entryway grew louder. From the conversation, she had a sense of the couple's dynamic. Where the woman was loud, bold, and had an infectious laugh, the fiancé was quieter, confident. He seemed to give her all the space her personality needed.

A good match.

And then, the man burst out laughing.

The sound hit like a strike to her funny bone. "Who's she marrying? I never asked."

But there was no way. *It's not possible.*

I've just been thinking about him a lot lately because of the move to Calamity.

There's zero chance Trevor Montgomery is in this random hotel in Iceland at the same time as me.

Chris gave her a mischievous smile. "I'm not sure whether to surprise you or warn you."

But before she could respond, a man in gym shorts and a tank top came hurrying toward them. "What?" He swiped the sweat off his face. "What's wrong?"

"Oh, good. You're here." Chris gestured to her. "Jessica Elsworth, this is my assistant, Jasper. When I asked if he'd make the move to Iceland with him, he gave me a list of demands—"

"Really?" Jasper clicked his tongue against the roof of his mouth. "A treadmill and weights are a whole list?"

"Let's not forget the granola." Chris grinned. "He'll only eat one brand and one flavor, so we have to special-order it. In any event, Jasper, this is Jessica, our resort designer."

"Hello," Jasper said. "Nice to meet you." Then, he turned to his boss. "You literally texted me, 'Where are you? Need you in my office ASAP.' I thought you were in crisis."

"I am. Jess is only in town for four days, so you'll need to get her whatever she needs to get her job done."

"Will do." Jasper smiled at her. "Whatever work you have is going to be a thousand times more interesting than picking up his dry cleaning and buying Christmas gifts for his family."

"Chris?" a woman called. "Where are you?"

"I'm here. Hang on." Chris touched her arm. "Come on. Meet my sister."

"If you don't mind, I'll meet them later," she said. "I need to make as many contacts as possible during work hours."

"Got it. Okay, I'll see you both at dinner." He headed off but called over his shoulder, "Jasper and I are the only two cooks around, so you'd better hurry up and hire that chef." And then, he was gone.

"This place has a nice atrium. Let's work there." Jasper led the way.

As she started to follow, a whisper of tension fluttered at the back of her neck. She glanced over her shoulder, certain she'd see someone watching her.

Weirdly, an image of Trevor's expression right before he'd closed the door of that motel room dropped into her mind.

Now, why would she think about that?

She checked, but the hallway was empty.

Chapter Three

ON THE PHONE WITH HIS SON, TREVOR TOOK IN THE view outside the window of his hotel room. In December, Iceland got about four hours of daylight, and since there were no city lights this far from Reykjavik, the sky was ablaze with stars. Moonlight hit the ocean and shattered.

It was wondrous and beautiful, and yet, somehow, it was hauntingly lonely.

Or maybe that's just me.

"Girls okay?" he asked.

"Put it this way, we've got trash bins stationed by each bed," Cole said. "And we've been giving them cool baths to get their fevers down."

"Damn. How badly do you wish you hadn't retired from hockey?" Trevor was only joking, but it landed wrong. Because what a shitty thing to say when he hadn't been there to soothe his own child's fevers. He hadn't taken him to the ER when his head hit the ice during practice.

No, he'd paid nannies to do that.

That familiar cold, hollow feeling came over him. But he reminded himself he had a new direction. A new purpose.

"I know it sounds weird, considering I'm ankle-deep in puke," Cole said. "But when my girls are hurting, I *want* to comfort them. Never thought I'd say it, but there's nowhere else I'd rather be."

They'd discussed it at length, so there was no reason to bring up his absence again, but still, Trevor couldn't help himself. "You're giving them the love you wished you'd had as a child."

His son's silence went on a little too long. Wind battered the window, and Trevor's breath fogged the glass.

Say something, Cole.

"Okay, darling." Behind him, Darby's heels clicked on the bathroom floor. "Your fabulous fiancée is ready. Turn around and tell me how gorgeous I look."

But he was suspended in time, waiting for his son's response. Not once had Cole pitched a fit or rebelled. He'd never railed at his dad for not giving him care and attention. He'd just…accepted it.

"I think you're right," Cole said in a low, quiet tone.

Relief shuddered through him. Just the acknowledgment, getting it out in the open, eased the massive weight of guilt.

"But, Dad, you know, the past is gone. You can't go back and make different choices. What matters is, since you retired, you've been there for me. I like what we have today. I chose you as the best man in my wedding for a reason. Outside of my wife and kids, you're the most important person in my life."

Which was saying something because Cole had a great group of childhood friends. "And you know you're mine."

"Yeah, I do. Which, I guess, is the point. You're a terrific grandfather to my kids. They worship the ground you walk on. Dad, we're good. *I'm* good."

Darby sidled up to him, putting her hand on his shoulder, urging him to turn around.

But he was still locked in this conversation with his son. Because he wanted to bring up the issue. He wanted to be *family*—not a guest. Not someone they felt they had to entertain.

Why did your wife say she can't handle one more person under her roof?

But now was not the time. Not when the girls were sick. Besides, it needed to be done face-to-face. "Yeah, okay. Keep me posted. If you need anything, I'm a plane ride away."

Once he disconnected, doubt grabbed hold of him.

Because his instincts had always been wrong. Obviously, since that was how he'd lost the only woman he'd ever loved. And they'd been wrong every time he'd signed a new contract to do the next film instead of coming home to raise his son.

Maybe they were wrong now. Maybe he should've stayed in Calamity and brought over soup and ginger ale. Done a few loads of laundry.

"What's wrong?" Darby's voice snapped him out of his thoughts.

He pocketed his phone. "Just checking in on my family."

"Yeah, I know, but you're just standing there. Is everything okay? It's just the flu, right?"

"Yep."

"That really sucks. Bad timing for them. But really, thank God, we're not there. I hate getting sick. Especially *this* Christmas." She got up on her toes and kissed his cheek. "Because I get to parade you around. No more pitying looks for the spinster Darby." She shook her head. "I've won more NASCAR races than any other woman in history, and the only thing I get from my family is, 'Did you know Emil is single again?' Or, 'I've got this guy you should meet. You'd love him.'" Her thumb rubbed off the lipstick imprint she'd left on his skin. "Well, not this year. Now, let's see what my brother's got cooking."

But he couldn't shake the feeling he'd gotten it wrong. And he very much wanted to get it right with his son. In fact, nothing was more important than knowing whether he'd made the right choice in leaving town for Christmas. "Go on without me. I'll catch up with you in a minute."

"What? No. My brother cooked for us."

"I know. But I'm worried about my family."

"They have the flu." She studied him. "What's really going on?"

They hadn't known each other long enough to discuss regrets and life choices. It had only been a month. But they *were* getting married. Eventually, they'd have to unpack a lot of history, and he might as well start now. "I have some guilt about the way I raised him."

"Oh, for God's sake." She gripped his elbows. "Look at me. Your son is happy, healthy, and living his best life. He was one of the greatest forwards in the NHL, and now, he's married with four children… He's good, Trev. Really good."

"He is. But I caused him a lot of pain."

"Well, that's part of the human experience, isn't it? We're flawed, and because of that, sometimes, we hurt the people we love. But let me tell you something. You were allowed to have a big career. You were allowed to follow your dreams and live out your passions."

Yeah, that was something else they hadn't talked about. How do you explain that the field you spent thirty years in wasn't your passion? How do you tell a woman who loves her career, who throws herself into life with such *zest*, that you don't feel passionate about anything?

Only some*one*. But at least, Darby knew about that. She understood she wasn't the great love of his life.

"You didn't abandon your son." Darby's confidence was empowering. "You didn't ignore him. You provided him with the best of everything. And when you look at what he achieved in life, you can see you were a great role model. Now, let him deal with four puking children. Believe me, the last thing he wants right now is a heart-to-heart with his guilt-stricken dad."

That was true.

"And we need to talk to our wedding planner, who's only in town for a few days, so come on." She sashayed away from him. Glancing over her shoulder, she said, "Show off your fiancée."

As they headed out of their room, he asked, "We're keeping this wedding small, right?"

"Oh God, no. It's a first for both of us. Let's make a splash."

She was good for him. She yanked his mind out of the past. He smiled and reached for her hand. "Whatever you want."

"How did you know those are my three favorite words?" She grinned at him. "I think we're going to get along just fine."

He'd met Chris earlier, so he recognized the man's booming laugh as they approached the dining room, but he hadn't met the assistant or the wedding planner since they'd spent the day working.

Just before they entered, he heard a woman say, "Hang on. Let me grab it. Be right back."

His pulse quickened, and he couldn't say why. There was something about that voice, something familiar, but in this context, this hotel in Iceland… It didn't make sense.

Curiosity had him pulling ahead of Darby, wondering if it was someone he knew. But that was impossible, of course. He didn't know anyone in this country, other than the Pullmans.

He didn't get to see her, though, because just as he entered, the woman he assumed was the wedding planner whisked around a corner. He caught a deep teal dress and miles of thick blond hair.

His blood roared in his ears. His reaction didn't make sense, but Chris was smiling at him and reaching out a hand in welcome. Trevor grasped it. "Thank you for making dinner for us. It's much appreciated."

"It's what my ex-wife used to call my 'creative outlet.'" Chris gestured to the empty chairs. "Sit, sit. We're eating family style." He grinned at his sister. "I made your favorite."

She scanned the offerings, and when her gaze landed on one dish in particular, she brightened. "Mac and cheese?"

Chris lifted the casserole lid. "Yep. But it's the grown-up version with lobster."

"Oh, my God. I haven't eaten anything that decadent in ages. Yum." She wrapped her hands around the porcelain bowl and dragged it toward her. "So, what're you guys having?"

Trevor laughed. "It's all yours."

"More of a meat man?" Chris asked.

"Totally. And he can't stand cheese." Darby shook her head. "Can you imagine? Who doesn't like cheese?"

"Well, hopefully, you like elk." Chris looked at him questioningly. "Not sure you've had that before."

"I'm Wyoming, born and raised," Trevor said. "If it's got four legs and a tail, we eat it."

Chris laughed. "Perfect." He gestured to the platters. "Help yourselves."

"Where's the wedding planner?" Darby asked. "I want to make sure she can pull this off in under two months. That's a big ask."

Chris shot his sister an irritated look. "She's not a wedding planner. I told you that. She's a world-renowned designer, and I hired her to turn Gapi's hotel into a luxury resort. Now, she's generously agreed to renovate the place in time for the event, but that's not her purpose here."

"Okay, I'm sorry. But, Chrissy, I'm getting *married*. Isn't that crazy?" She reached for Trevor's hand. "And look who I scored. Not only is he the most handsome man in the world, but he's a really good guy. I can't believe how lucky I got."

"I'm happy for you. I am." Her brother leaned forward and lowered his voice. "But I need you to understand how important she is to me. Please treat her with the respect she's earned in her business the same way you expect it in yours."

Darby's cheeks turned pink. "Okay, I hear you. So, where is she? When do we get to meet her?"

"She went to get her tablet," Chris said. "She's got some ideas to show me."

Trevor's phone vibrated, and he discreetly checked the screen in case it was Cole. It was. His son sent a photo of all four girls sprawled on the couch with blankets, stuffed animals, and big silver bowls at their feet.

He smiled and shot off a text.

> Trevor: Tell them we'll go on a sleigh ride when I get back.

"Okay, here we go—" a woman called.

The designer swept into the room, bringing a fresh, clean scent with her. It held notes of a familiar flower. What was it?

Wait, isn't that the same perfume my daughter-in-law wears?

It is. That's Iyantha.

But his son had responded, so he kept his attention on the screen.

> Cole: They'd love that. Paisley says she wants hot cocoa.

> Trevor: Her wish is my command.

A chair scraped back, and Trevor glanced up. His first impression of the woman was thick, buttery hair, a mouth made for kissing, and a teal dress that molded to lush curves.

A fireball of lust exploded from deep within, confusing the ever-loving hell out of him.

"Hello, I'm Jessica." She shook Darby's hand.

And then, her attention turned to him.

Their gazes caught.

Locked.

The world narrowed to the two of them, and the only sound was his heart banging in his chest.

Elzy?

My Elzy?

She's here?

How is this happening?

The designer was Elzy's doppelgänger, right? What other explanation could there be?

But no. From her reaction, it was clear.

Jesus. She's here.

Elzy's right fucking here.

"My Calamity Jane." He heard his voice as if it came from the bottom of a well.

But her expression—the agony in her eyes—tore him out of his shock and plunked him right back into the dining room of this old hotel in Iceland.

"You're the *groom?*" Elzy must've heard her tone because her eyes widened, and color spilled into her cheeks.

"You're the wedding planner?" The moment the words flew out of his mouth, tension gripped the room, and he understood his error. "I'm sorry. Designer. Resort designer."

"That's right." Her smile turned stiff.

"What're you doing here?" As soon as he asked, he realized how offensive that sounded. "I'm sorry. It's just such a wild coincidence."

"Yes. Small world." She stood there, frozen, the only

movement a slight tremble in the hand that clutched her tablet.

"What's going on?" Darby's voice cracked the shell of wonder between them. "How do you two know each other?"

It was obvious Elzy was having a hard time recovering her professional demeanor, so he slipped into his movie star persona. Now wasn't the time for a personal conversation. "Jessica and I go way back."

"To?" Darby seemed genuinely curious.

"We grew up together." Elz gave a smile he didn't recognize and took her seat.

"No kidding?" Chris laughed. "How long's it been since you've seen each other?"

"Not since we were kids. But Trevor and I can catch up later." Elzy tapped the screen of her tablet. "Right now, let me fill you in on the progress we've made today."

Trevor barely heard a word she said. Something about tastings, breweries…a trip up north to meet a man. A potential concierge.

But everything was a blur. Because he'd plummeted back through time.

To when he was four years old and kicking the back of his mom's seat. A moment he never would've remembered had he not looked out the window and seen a curtain of blond hair swinging, and a girl his age stomping her legs and pumping her arms. He'd been mesmerized.

Because in the middle of all the Saturday morning chaos at the feedstore, this girl was in her own world, doing a weird monster dance, with not a fuck given to anyone watching her. He'd asked his mom to open his window so he could hear the music. But it turned out, there wasn't any. The song played in her head.

In that moment, *he'd* wanted to be in her head. He'd wanted to hear the music. He'd wanted to know her.

He catapulted forward to when he'd tried to hold her hand for the very first time in middle school, and she'd smacked it away. As soon as she realized what she'd done, she'd laughed and told him she thought it was a bug landing on her.

The summer after her mom died, her dad sent the sisters to Illinois to spend time with an aunt. The moment she'd come back to town, he'd hopped on his bike and pedaled all the way to her house. He'd caught a glimpse of her through the open front door, so he'd jumped off the bike and run inside the house.

He'd slammed into her so hard, he'd knocked them both to the floor. But she hadn't pushed him off. In fact, she hadn't said a word. Just hugged him so tightly he'd lost sight of where he ended and she began.

On prom night, she'd come downstairs in a swishy, pretty dress, and he'd stopped breathing to the point that her dad had smacked his back. *You okay, son? You choke on an ice cube?* But he was so struck by her sultry-eyed, luscious-lipped beauty, by the fucking *honor* of this magnificent goddess choosing him, loving him, desiring him, that he couldn't believe it.

He just couldn't believe he got to be with Jessica Elsworth.

The girl who didn't give a damn what anyone thought of her. Who was fiercely independent. She was funny, rebellious, creative, sexy, and deeply compassionate.

And he'd loved her with every fiber of his being.

"All right then. We're all set." Elzy got up.

He sped to the present so quickly he grew dizzy and felt nauseous. "You're leaving?"

"Jet lag's caught up with me, so I'll see you in the morning." She waved, not once looking at him. "Goodnight."

Disoriented, he watched her go. How much time had passed? He hadn't touched his dinner, and her plate was empty. He wanted to grab some food and leave it outside her door. Make sure she had a full meal.

But she was treating him like an acquaintance from high school. Someone she'd barely known.

And, after thirty years, he supposed that was exactly what he was to her.

The longing, the yearning, the love that simply would not die, was all in his head.

Not hers.

Because he'd extinguished it long ago.

"Does that sound good?" Darby asked him.

He'd missed another conversation. But he didn't care. "Yep. I'm all yours."

He'd meant his schedule was all hers, of course, but from her smile, he realized she thought he meant he was all hers, body and soul.

And that was when it struck him—he'd agreed to *marry* this woman.

The day before he'd finally found Elzy again.

And now, she was planning his wedding.

Chapter Four

Jess awakened with a dull headache. She rolled onto her back, blinking in the darkness.

Groggy, she inhaled, expecting the soothing scents of lavender from the sheets in her suite at the Sweetwater. Instead, she got a hint of must in the air.

Wait, what?

She jerked over to flick on the lamp.

Where am I?

Am I late?

Shit, what am I supposed to be doing right now?

She traveled so much for work, and she lived in a hotel. It was often disorienting to wake up in a strange bed.

But then, she remembered. *Iceland.* And the pieces fell into place.

The design job.

And that was when it smacked her in the face like a slimy, wet fish.

With Trevor Montgomery.

She rolled back onto her side, burying her face in the pillow.

Helping him get married.

How is this my life?

She groaned. The jet lag and strange lack of sunlight didn't help.

Well, she was a professional, and she wasn't blowing up the reputation it took decades to establish for an old high school boyfriend. And really, that was all he was to her.

She'd do her work and get her butt back home.

Should be easy enough. It's only three more days.

Besides, it all happened so long ago. She was over it. Over him.

Liar. Moving to Calamity had pried open the box where she'd stored the pain and hurt. And now, seeing him all cozy and happy with his fiancée… It brought it all to the surface. And drove home the fact that, where she'd never been able to trust another man again, he'd come out of their breakup unscathed.

I resent him. I just do.

The experience was different for him. He'd gone off on his wild adventure, and she'd stayed behind, surrounded by memories in her hometown. Her high school friends would say things like, "Oh, no. I thought you guys would be together forever" and "I can't believe what a star he's become. Don't you wish you'd gone with him?" She'd had to see his parents pull up to the loading dock at the feedstore and make small talk with them at church.

None of that nonsense mattered anymore. *Just get your work done.*

Bunching pillows behind her, she reached for her phone to catch up on messages.

She smiled when she saw the photo her niece sent of her wedding gown.

> Bri: Picking this beauty up tomorrow! So excited!

> Jessica: You have to FaceTime me when you try it on!

Nothing from Amber. Hmm. It didn't seem possible that nothing had gone wrong in the last eight hours or so. She hoped her sister wasn't trying to protect her.

I'm not on vacation here.

> Jessica: Let me know how things are going. I'll be out most of the day but will be checking my messages. I'm here if you need anything.

Her phone vibrated not thirty seconds after she hit send. *Oh, dammit.* "I woke you up." With the time difference, it was one in the morning in Wyoming. "I'm sorry." She should've known her sister, as property manager, would keep her phone on all night.

"Oh, trust me, you didn't wake us. Because we haven't been to sleep yet."

"Uh oh. Sounds like you had some drama?" Jess settled into the pillows, ready to hear the story.

"You will not believe it. This is a soft opening, right? Which means most of the guests are comped. That's a *gift*."

"Yep. So, what happened?" She checked her phone and

saw she had plenty of time to get showered, dressed, and meet everyone for breakfast.

"So, I get a call from the front desk, telling me the couple in room twelve was making way too much noise and wouldn't cut it out." Amber's tone said, *Nothing new about that.* "So, I head over there and ask them nicely to keep it down. Guess what they told me?"

"'We're so sorry. We promise to be quiet as a bug in a rug.'"

"Ha. No, she goes, 'Get fucked.'"

"How demure of her. How elegant." Fortunately, they had a protocol for guests like that. "Is it resolved? Are they still there?"

"I had security remove them."

"I can only imagine what a scene *that* was."

"The woman said, 'We're influencers. We're going to tell everyone how awful this place is.' And I said, 'I hope you do. Because then, we'll have a reason to release the recording of you screaming at each other. We'll show photos of the damage you've done to the room.'"

"Wow. I'm really"—she stopped herself from saying she was proud of her sister because that would sound patronizing—"impressed." Amber had handled it perfectly. But then, Jess wouldn't have run off to Iceland if she didn't trust her sisters to stand in her place.

"Well, let's not forget I had the best teacher. You put so much time—"

"And patience," her husband called.

"Yeah, that, too." Amber laughed.

In the beginning, her sisters were busy raising kids, so they'd only worked with her part time and remotely. Over the years, though, their roles had become more specialized, and their husbands had gotten involved. The Sweetwater Resort and Spa marked the first time the family members were equal partners.

"You've had a rough night," Jess said. "I'm going to let you wind down with your husband."

"Well, wait. How's it going? What's Iceland like?"

"Hard to tell since I only get four hours of sunlight a day, and I used all of them yesterday to work. But from the little I've seen this place is like a whole other planet. I'd love to see more, but I've got a lot to pack in. For the next two days, I'll be busy with tastings and interviews."

"Okay, what's going on?" her sister asked.

"I just told you. What do you mean?"

"You've gone all Robo-sister again."

"*Robo*? Amber, I just woke up." And here she thought she sounded as normal as possible, considering she'd just run into the man who'd once told her she was his reason for living.

The man who only had two speeds of sex. One, slow, like he was translating the achingly sweet love in his heart through his body. And two, fast, hard, and absolutely feral, as if trying desperately to break through the barrier that kept their souls apart.

"Like you're constipated."

"Constipated?" Well, it wasn't like she could deny the low current of anxiety coursing through her. Because she would see him again in an hour. And she'd rather go back to working the front desk of a motel than ever look at his stupid, handsome face again. "Okay, fine. I'm freaking out."

"About what?" her sister asked.

"Trevor's here."

"What do you mean by 'here?' Do you mean there's a life-size cardboard cutout of him? Lars almost bought one of those. He was going to set an extra plate for Christmas one year and put it behind the chair. Fortunately, we share the same account, so I saw it and deleted it."

Jess broke into a smile. "Sisters forever."

"Right?"

"But no, as much as I wish it were the cardboard version, it's the actual man."

"You've got to be kidding me. What the hell is Trevor Montgomery doing in Iceland? Let alone in the same hotel you're renovating?"

"I've been asking myself the same question." She drew the covers up to her chin. "But it gets worse."

"No, it really doesn't."

"I'm not just turning the hotel into a resort. I'm getting it ready for a wedding."

"I will accept a wedding for the president of the United States," Amber said. "I will accept a wedding for Mickey and Minnie Mouse. I will not accept a wedding for the ex-boyfriend who shattered your heart."

"I'm afraid you have no choice. He's marrying Darby Pullman."

"Am I supposed to know who that is?"

"She's a race car driver."

"You ever hear of Darby Pullman?" her sister asked her husband.

"Highest finishes by a woman in the Daytona 500 and Indy 500. She's a NASCAR legend."

"Oh, awesome." Her sister came back on the line. "He

couldn't marry a recluse with yellow teeth? She has to be a freaking champion? Is she pretty?"

"I don't know. I was so shocked I couldn't even tell you what we had for dinner. I'm telling you, if you put ten women in a lineup, I couldn't pick her out. Basically, I gave them the agenda for the next few days and then skittered off to my room like a rat."

"Well, a beautiful, successful rat. But, man. This is awful. You want me to come out there? I'm coming out there. You don't have to face this alone."

"The only reason I'm here in the first place is because I have you guys running things at the Sweetwater. Besides, I only have a few more days of this."

"You know what I'm thinking?" her sister asked. "This might be good. It might be the closure you never got."

Uh huh. Sure. But she wouldn't argue it over the phone. "True."

"Maybe he's boring. He might only talk about himself and not ask any questions. Or he tells drinking stories. Like, dude, I don't care that you went car surfing after drinking twelve shots and a case of beer. Only for Trevor, it'll be stories from the set. 'This one time…'" Her sister deepened her voice. "'I was in the middle of a sex scene, and the actress farted.'"

"That would be a funny story," her husband said in the background. "I'd listen to that."

"Okay, fine," her sister said. "But maybe he smells like dirty underwear. Or he's one of those guys who picks scabs off at the dinner table."

"What do you mean one of those guys?" her husband asked. "How many guys do you know who did that?"

"Let's just say there's a reason I chose you." Amber and her husband laughed.

Normally, she loved the way her sisters bantered with their husbands. It made her feel good to know they'd found their forever people. Did it hurt sometimes to be the third wheel? *Oh, absolutely.* But most of the time, she didn't mind.

Right now, though, with the only man she'd ever loved snuggling in bed with his fiancée a few doors down…*No.* She couldn't handle it. "Listen, I have to go." When she sat up, the pain in her head traveled, stabbing the backs of her eyes. "I'm having breakfast with the bride and groom. Yay." Even though her sister couldn't see, she pumped a fist.

"Well, take your time getting ready. Use that Belle Starr body wash. Wear an outfit that makes you feel invincible. And remember everything you've done to reach this place in your life, the sacrifice you made to come home and help me through a really hard time. And that you're the reason Kelly and I graduated college. And never forget how hard you worked, scrimped, and saved, to become the resort mogul you are today."

I wish those accomplishments helped. But at that moment, when she hadn't heard a single word from Joel—and no, she was not going to reach out to him first—when Trevor was living his best life with an accomplished race car driver, and she had to renovate a hotel for his wedding, she just didn't have it in her. "Yep. I'm a real badass, all right."

"You put on those Veronica Beard flare pants that showcase your tight cherry ass, and you will be. You brought them, right?"

"Of course. But my ass hasn't looked like a cherry since high school." She threw off the blanket—a cute, folksy quilt that would, unfortunately, have to be replaced. "All right, I've got to get moving."

"You can quit this job, you know," her sister said quietly. "You don't need the money."

"You know as well as I do, we're not going to sell out for the gala. We need every penny of the two million he's paying me."

"I'm sorry. Did you say two million dollars?"

"Sure did." She headed into the bathroom and flipped on the light.

"Stay." Her sister adopted a stern tone. "Push through the pain. You're made of stronger stuff than that."

Jess laughed. "Don't I know it. Goodbye."

"Bye, Jess. I love you."

"Love you too." The moment she disconnected pain swept over her like a brutal wind.

Truly, she was so happy her sisters had love and companionship. It meant the world to her. But *she* didn't have it.

Isn't that why you chose Joel?

Because you never wanted another all-consuming passion like you had with Trevor?

That's right. She never again wanted to make a guy the center of her life.

So, there you go. The occasional bout of loneliness was the price she had to pay for that choice. *Deal with it.* She shook two pain relievers out of the travel-size canister. After swallowing them, she turned on the faucet and yanked off Joel's XL T-shirt.

Naked, she took in her body in the mirror.

What did Trevor see when he looked at her?

She'd never had cosmetic surgery, so she looked every one of her years. She'd laughed a lot. Cried plenty. A life of snowboarding and hiking, of swimming in the warm waters of the Caribbean and paragliding off the coast of New Zealand had contributed to every line around her mouth and eyes. She smoothed a hand over her cheek—yep, she'd earned a complexion that wasn't as soft and smooth as a girl's.

Which wasn't something she spent a lot of time thinking about.

But Trevor's a movie star. He's been around the most beautiful, fit people in the world.

How did she compare to them? One thing for sure, she looked tired. After working so hard to get the Sweetwater up and running and then not sleeping on her red-eye flight, she was exhausted. A little pale. She had some bruising under her eyes.

In all the times she'd imagined running into Trevor, she'd pictured herself glamorous and perfectly happy. She'd wanted him to see her living her best life. No, she wasn't a movie star, but she'd done well for herself.

And you know what? Screw it. Screw him.

I like who I am.

She jumped in the shower and washed away the self-doubt and resentment. All the negativity slid down the drain. And then, she did just what Amber told her to do. She blew out her hair and took time with her makeup. She dabbed perfume on her neck and wrists.

And then, she sorted through the small pile of clothing she'd brought. For sure, she'd wear the Veronica Beard pants. Did she wish she'd brought the blouse with the neckline that flirted with indecent but could still be viewed as one-hundred-percent work-appropriate? Maybe.

Yes. Totally.

But in the end, she felt good. Strong. Confident.

Ready, she grabbed her tablet, shoved it in the leather tote bag, and left her room. In the end, it didn't matter what Trevor thought of her. She was engaged, and he was marrying Darby.

And after Friday, she'd never see him again.

As she headed down the hallway, she breathed in the delicious scents of warm bread and bacon. Her stomach rumbled, reminding her she hadn't eaten dinner the night before.

Well, no more of that. Today, she would eat. She'd enjoy this opportunity to experience Iceland. Because really—now that she'd had some time to get over the initial shock of seeing him—she could see Trevor was nothing more than a first love.

So what if the relationship had meant more to her?

That's just the way it goes sometimes.

No harm, no foul.

But the moment she entered the dining room, she discovered her pep talk was as fragile as a bird's nest, made of nothing but twigs and string.

Because one look at the scene in front of her had her self-esteem collapsing in a flurry of dust and debris.

The four of them—Chris, Jasper, Darby, and Trevor—laughed like they'd known each other forever. With their plates loaded with eggs, toast, bacon, and fresh fruit, they looked like the best of old friends.

Her stomach twisted hard, and she stumbled. She'd only ever been part of a unit once.

Trevor and Elzy.

Wild Billy and Calamity Jane.

From the moment he'd walked out of that motel, she'd been on her own.

Daughter, mother figure, friend, aunt, business owner, boss.

Me. I.

Single servings.

One ticket, please.

Nothing drove it home harder than this moment when she was a total outsider.

But it was Darby's arm slung around her fiancé's shoulders, her head resting on his biceps—the absolute familiarity of a long-term couple—that scraped out her heart and left her hollow as a drum.

Stop it. Stop it right now. With her head held high, she approached the table. "Good morning." She had a job to do and a family to get home to. All eyes were on her, but she didn't focus on anyone in particular. If she did, they'd see her pain.

Why are you holding on to this anger? He'd been a twenty-year-old boy when he'd left. He'd barely experienced life. He'd gotten a better offer, and he'd never looked back.

Let it go.

My God, just let it go.

"Ah, there she is. Grab some food." Chris gestured to the counter. "I set up a buffet."

"Sounds great." She breezed right past him and headed for the counter. "Everything smells delicious."

Chris's chair scraped back, and he met her there. "What's your poison? Cappuccino or latte?"

Before she could answer, Jasper popped up. "Ooh, let me do it. I make an adorable foam flower."

"She doesn't drink coffee." The forcefulness of Trevor's tone had everyone turning to him.

"You haven't seen her since high school," Darby said. "You don't know the first thing about her anymore."

The simple truth of her comment knocked Jess off balance, and she reached for the counter.

I've kissed every inch of his skin. I know about the birthmark on the back of his right thigh and the constellation of freckles at the back of his neck.

I've touched every part of his body and know the two places that make him break out in goosebumps—just beneath his ear and the soles of his feet.

I've seen him cry during the movie Field of Dreams *when Ray plays catch with John, and I know it's because Trevor never had those father-son moments.*

She thought she'd been through the worst of it.

But in that moment, it took every ounce of strength to stay upright.

Because Darby had just driven home a terrible truth. The man she knew so intimately was a stranger to her now.

Her Wild Bill was gone. This movie star marrying a race car driver? He was nothing to her.

Nothing at all.

"You don't like coffee?" Chris asked, pulling her out of her thoughts.

She wanted to say, *Sure, I do*—if only to reinforce Darby's statement. But she wasn't about to make these lovely people go to the effort of making her something she wouldn't drink.

"I actually don't but thank you."

Jasper looked at her like she'd just knocked back a shot of bat blood. "How do you wake up?"

"With orange juice," Trevor said.

Jess wanted to swing around and snap at him to mind his own business. Instead, she grabbed a plate, eyeing the platters of food. The stress was making her hot and sweaty.

"I should've asked," Chris said. "I'll order oranges and squeeze some for you tomorrow."

"Dude." Darby smacked Trevor's arm. "Let her speak for herself." Smiling, she shook her head. "This is a side of you I haven't seen before."

"Hey, it's only been a month." Trevor grinned. "Imagine what other sides you haven't seen."

A month? What did he mean?

But she couldn't stand to see them tease each other, so she focused on the host. "Oh, please, don't go to the effort. I'm good with water."

"Bullshit," Trevor said. "She needs her OJ like the rest of the world needs caffeine."

Okay, she got it now. He was baiting her. Trying to force her to acknowledge him. But she wouldn't.

Not when she was working so hard to replace the boy she'd known—the one who'd knelt to tie her boots when her hands were frozen stiff from a snowball fight, and who'd booked a motel they couldn't afford because he didn't want her first sexual experience to be in a beat-up old truck—with the stranger he'd become.

Conversation resumed with brother and sister trading

jabs, the engaged couple teasing each other, and Jasper tossing in comments here and there.

And she was immobile, staring at a warming tray of eggs.

Get it together.

Do your job.

This Wall Street scion could hire anyone in the world, and he'd not only chosen her but said he wouldn't work with anyone else.

There you go. Her strength came rolling in.

See that? I'm fine.

I'm better than fine.

I'm excited about this project, and I'm going to kick its ass.

She scooped scrambled eggs—laced with glistening, melted cheddar cheese—onto her plate. The pain reliever hadn't kicked in yet, and her stomach was upset, so she didn't go for the chocolate croissant. Too bad. It looked flaky and delicious.

But really, she just needed protein.

As she sat down, Trevor asked, "So, what's on the agenda today?"

"She gave us the schedule last night." Darby looked at him like, *What in the world is wrong with you?* "Weren't you listening?"

"That's okay. I dropped a lot of information." Jess unfolded the napkin and draped it across her lap. "Chris has an interview this morning." She glanced at her phone. "Actually, he should be here any minute now."

"Right. Better finish up my breakfast." Chris sat back down.

"We've got three chef tastings today." She cast a smile at him. "Do you want the good news first or the bad?"

"I'm built to take it." Chris tore off a piece of croissant before putting it in his mouth. "Give me the bad."

"Two of your Michelin star chefs declined the invitation."

"But the good news is one of them said yes?" Trevor asked.

"You got it." She stabbed a clump of eggs to avoid looking at him. "And I've got two others for us to visit with in the city. I think you're going to like them."

"Which is the one who's interested?" Chris asked.

"The one from Westman Island."

"That's fine, then." Chris nodded. "He's the one I want the most."

"His food is divine." Jasper set espresso cups in front of his boss and Darby.

"Ooh, look at that." Darby grinned at him. "That *is* the prettiest foam flower I've ever seen."

"I know." Smugly, Jasper sat down and picked up his croissant.

Chris tipped his chin at her. "Go on."

"He'll be here at ten today, and we'll meet the other two chefs this afternoon in the city. Tomorrow, we've got an appointment with the country's only master sommelier, who'll connect us with liquor distributors. And then, on Friday, my last day, I'm heading to Snaefellsnes to meet a guy who runs sightseeing tours."

"That's so far," Darby said. "When's your flight home?"

"I've got a red-eye Friday night, so that'll give me the

whole day to drive there, visit with him, and then, go straight to the airport."

"I hope you'll make it home for Christmas Eve with your family." Darby seemed genuinely concerned.

"I'm lucky I came during a warm front. The roads are clear, there's no snow… I think I'll be okay."

"Well, that's the thing." Darby and Chris shared a troubled look. "There's a storm coming in. And honestly, in Iceland, you never know. The weather here changes on a dime." She snapped her fingers.

"But that's not forecast until Christmas Day," Trevor said. "So, she should be okay."

"Yes, I'll be long gone by then." Jess hoped no one noticed that she wasn't looking at her ex.

"Instead of driving so far, why not do a video call with him?" Darby asked. "Just to be safe?"

Jess wasn't sure why the woman was so concerned. She guessed some people were afraid of snow. But she lived in the mountains, so she was used to it. "A concierge can make or break a resort. He has to be patient, informed, and willing to do just about anything to accommodate the guests. For that kind of thing, I have to meet him in person, watch his mannerisms, and get a feel for him."

"Makes sense." Darby sipped her espresso.

"But also, you're having a destination wedding. Remember, we won't have a gym or spa ready, so you're going to need things for your guests to do. He'll arrange all of that."

"I hadn't thought about the details, but you're right," Darby said. "Ooh, what about a cake tasting? Can we fit that in?" She smiled at her fiancé. "What's more important than the cake?"

"The dress," Jasper said, not looking up from his plate.

"I told you. She's not a wedding planner." Chris offered an apologetic look to Jess.

"That's okay." Jess didn't take offense. She didn't expect anyone outside the field to understand her job.

"What does a resort designer do, exactly?" Trevor asked.

"I'm involved in every aspect of creation. I plan the layout and work with architects and landscape designers. I handle menus and uniforms… Even the music you hear while wandering around the grounds." She spoke directly to Darby. "The pastry chef will be important, but I won't be handling that on this visit."

Darby nodded to indicate she understood. "Your job sounds like an interesting mix of creative and technical."

"Yes, exactly. That about sums it up." She smiled at the woman but only to keep from staring at Trevor's arms. It was impossible not to notice the way he'd rolled the cuffs of his flannel shirt to his elbows, exposing tanned skin, ink, and sexy muscles.

Her stomach lurched. Because those weren't the arms she remembered.

These were even better.

And given how much she desperately wanted to explore those tattoos, she forced herself to look away.

"So, basically, you give a resort its vibe?" Darby asked.

"She gives it its soul." Chris beamed at her. "And I'm damn lucky she took me on. Did you know she just opened one of her own?"

Jess jerked as if someone had pinched her. She wasn't ready for Trevor to know she lived in Calamity too. Which was stupid considering the town had ten thousand permanent residents, and she was very involved in the business community.

"Really?" Darby asked. "Where?"

Fortunately, her phone buzzed, and she checked the screen. "Ah. Our nine o'clock is here. Let me go get him." She raced away as if the room had gone up in flames. "Be right back."

She knew she was being ridiculous. Of course she was. But she couldn't get a hold of herself.

All those years spent thinking about him, the countless internet searches.

I mean, come on. I held off buying property in Calamity because of him.

And now that they were finally in the same room, seeing him blissfully happy with another woman and getting married, it made all the time and emotional energy spent on him seem…

Embarrassing.

Because he hadn't thought about her at all. Not once. Not even a little.

You knew that. He had a baby two years *after he said his vows to you in a Vegas chapel.*

How many reminders do you need before it sinks in that he doesn't care?

Well, she couldn't let the landscaper see her like this, so she ducked around a corner and leaned against the wall. Closing her eyes, she willed herself to let Trevor go. More than anything, she wanted to free herself from his grip on her.

"I don't know how," she whispered. Tears scalded, and she blinked them back.

Despair threatened to pull her under.

Why did it still hurt? Why couldn't she fully move on?

Come on. Use this as the kick in the pants you need to finally let him go.

It had worked twenty-six years ago when she'd seen him with his son.

Let seeing him with his future bride be a permanent fix.

And maybe, instead of blaming Joel for excluding her from his Christmas plans, she should take a hard look at how she guarded her heart from him.

Of course you don't love him.

How can you when you keep him at arm's length?

Sure, she'd been preoccupied with the resort, but she could've made more of an effort.

I mean, really, in all this time, how have you not met his family?

And that's my answer right there.

She resolved to let down her guard and spend more time with her fiancé. She'd give this relationship a real shot.

Right. Good.

Okay, I got this.

She pressed her hands to her belly, drawing in a deep breath.

In her mind's eye, she called up an image of her and Trevor at the altar with the cherubs and the roses and the officiant in the bolo tie. Standing at the shore, she set it on a rowboat and pushed it out to sea.

There you go.
She smiled.
A Viking burial.
See that? I'm good.
Now, let's get this interview going.
And forget all about Trevor Montgomery.

Chapter Five

Jessica carried on to the lobby, where she found a tall, lean man wearing a dark-red beanie and an unzipped puffy coat. She shook his hand. "Hi, I'm Jessica. Thanks so much for coming out here."

"Emil." His voice was gruff, his demeanor reserved. "It's no problem."

Well, we're not hiring him for his personality. "I thought I was asking for the impossible, looking for someone who understands the topography of the area and comes with outstanding recommendations, so I couldn't be happier to find you."

As his gaze wandered around the dated lobby, he seemed uncomfortable, almost like he expected ghosts to float by.

"We're excited about the renovation," she continued. "This place has a great layout, and when we're finished, it's going to be spectacular." *In other words, you'll want to be associated with this resort.* "Would you like me to give you a tour of the property?"

"Not necessary." His gaze swung back to her. "I've been here before."

"Okay, well, let's get that interview started."

Instead of following her, he stayed rooted in place. "I need to know who referred me. Was it Chris? Did he ask you to call?"

She studied him for a moment, trying to figure out what was going on. "No. I'm the one who found you. Do you have an issue with him?"

"Not at all. Chris is a good guy." He seemed conflicted.

"Then, what's the problem?" She needed to get to the bottom of this. "Have you worked here before?"

"No, but I spent time here in the summer when I was younger."

Every single person she hired impacted a guest's impression of the resort. One bad interaction could prompt a scathing review. This man's broodiness and clipped answers were unacceptable. "Emil, I have a very small window of time to hire the right people. If you're not interested in this job, let's not waste each other's time."

"Is this a family project?" He seemed too preoccupied to hear her. "Are all the Pullmans in on this?"

In on this? Did he think he was being pranked? *This is bizarre.* "This is Chris's project, though his family will handle the renovation. If that's not going to work for you, you need to tell me now." His attitude was concerning, and she wouldn't subject the owner to it. She'd walk him right back out the door if there was even a hint of an issue.

"Yeah." Shame crept across his features. "That's fair." His shoulders pushed back, and he wiped his face clean of broodiness. "I'm interested in the job. You won't find anyone better."

She was still uncertain, but he held strong under her scrutiny, so she decided to move forward with him. "Okay, let's go meet Chris." She led him down a wide hallway. "So, as I said in our text exchange, they're hosting a wedding at the end of January, so we're going to spruce up the original B&B section of the hotel. I'd like you to think outside of the box and see what you can come up with. I'm looking for elegance but also drama that fits the surroundings."

"I can do that."

"Great." She swept into the dining room and approached the table. "Everyone, please welcome Emil Birgisson."

A bizarre chain reaction unfolded. Chris shot a look of concern to Darby. Darby's gaze snapped over to Emil. And the landscaper went stock-still.

"Did you do this?" Darby asked her brother in a choked whisper.

"What?" Chris asked. "Of course not. I've left everything to Jess."

Brother and sister turned to her as if she understood the past dynamics of this family. "He's the most celebrated landscaper in the country," Jess said. "I've seen his work. He's a true artist. I don't think we're going to find anyone better." *And this is why rushing a job is problematic.* She didn't have time to learn about relationships. "I'm sensing we have some personal issues to work out."

"No, we don't," Chris said. "Darby lives in North Carolina, so I don't see how hiring her ex-boyfriend matters."

Oh. Now, she understood the pain in Darby's eyes. The vulnerability pierced Jess's heart because, so far, this woman had been nothing but confident and strong.

"She won't even be back until the wedding." Chris wiped his mouth with a napkin and stood up. "Come on, Emil. Let's go into my office and talk."

With every step the landscaper took away from her, Darby grew more anxious. It was like her spirit was tethered to him. She watched him with an almost desperate need for him to acknowledge her, but he just kept going.

While Darby remained silent, her eyes screamed, *Look at me. Talk to me.*

Jess felt for her so deeply. She could hardly catch her breath with Trevor sitting across the table from her. She couldn't think. Couldn't eat. She could barely function.

When Emil was two steps from turning the corner, he paused. His chest expanded as he drew in a breath. Darby's expression opened, hope burning in her eyes.

The tension was unbearable.

But then, the man continued on. And in two steps, he was gone.

Darby deflated, and Jess wanted to hug her. She wanted to say, *It'll be all right. Whatever this pain is, it'll fade over time.*

But she'd be lying. Because she was living proof it thrashed like a living beast inside her.

"Come on," Jasper said to Jess, flicking her seat with his napkin to brush away imaginary crumbs. "Take a few bites. You've got a busy day."

She sat back down and picked up her fork, but no one was eating. Everyone was watching Darby.

"You okay?" Trevor asked his fiancée.

That simple question, spoken with such gentle concern, broke something in Jess.

It was so much easier to think he'd become a vain, entitled movie star. But that gentle tone and concerned expression? That was the man she remembered. The way he patiently waited for his fiancée to answer, the way he never turned his attention from her, that was the same kindness he'd always shown her as a teenager.

It hurt worse to know he hadn't changed.

That someone else got to be the recipient of it.

"I don't know." Darby said it with a laugh, but she was clearly upset. "I haven't seen him in twenty-six years." She pressed a hand to her heart. "Whoo. I did not expect this reaction."

Trevor gave her hand a gentle squeeze.

"Remember that great love we talked about?" Darby asked as if no one else was at the table. "Emil was mine. He was my first everything. I thought he'd be my last. We were going to America together, but at the last minute, he bailed on me. Never even told me why." She glanced up at Jasper and Jess. "I'm sorry. I know you don't want to hear any of this. I'm just…rattled."

"It's okay." Jess understood better than Darby would ever know.

"I thought I was over him. I thought…" Darby waved her hand as if flicking away dust motes. "I was so sure I didn't have any feelings left."

And that was the moment Jess couldn't help herself. She finally looked at Trevor.

And found him watching her. He looked ravaged. The stark desperation in his eyes was almost too much to bear.

Had she gotten it wrong? Was he as shaken about seeing her as she was about him?

"I feel so foolish. I'm sorry." Darby shook her head. "I think it's just too much at once. I'm jet-lagged, newly engaged, and the last thing I expected was to bump into Emil in my grandparents' hotel. Okay, enough. Let's go over the schedule again." She let out a strained laugh. "I'm a race car driver. Trust me, I normally have better focus than this."

She could see how badly Darby needed to recover, so she clicked the side button of her tablet, awakening the screen. "So, like I said, our first tasting is here at ten. Hákon Björnsson's a chef on Westman Island, who's looking to move back to the mainland. Considering the name he's made for himself on an island that gets so little business in winter, I'm looking forward to seeing what he can do. After that, we head into the city to meet with two other chefs."

But Darby's napkin had become an origami project, and a storm of emotion clouded Trevor's eyes. Neither was listening. Neither cared.

Jess set the tablet down. "It's a busy day with four hours of driving, so you certainly don't have to participate. I think your brother was hoping you'd choose a chef for the wedding weekend, but I can work that out on my own if you'd rather not make the drive."

"Oh, I'll be happy with whoever you choose," Darby said. "I'm not a foodie at all."

But Trevor is.

"We're going," Trevor said definitively, looking Jess right in the eyes. "To all of them."

"Of course." Darby patted his thigh. "He's particular about his food."

It was more than that though. Trevor ate with gusto. As a kid, he'd take a huge bite of watermelon, close his eyes, and declare, "Damn, that's good." Or she'd make him cookies, and he'd gobble them up, telling her she was magic in the kitchen.

Of course, he'd devoured her the same way he did a slice of watermelon. He did everything with gusto.

So, maybe that was his nature. It wasn't about her specifically.

Oh, man. That hurt.

Her hand pressed on her chest, but nothing could soothe the ache. So, she forced her thoughts back on business. "Next on my list is, do you know how many guests you're inviting? We need to know how many rooms to renovate." She figured—between Hollywood and NASCAR —they'd have a lot. This might be a bigger project than Chris realized.

"I don't know." Confident, badass Darby Pullman was now uneasy and a little lost. "We talked about it, and we can't agree. Trev wants it small."

Trev? He used to hate when people shortened his name. *"How hard is it to go for the second syllable? Is it so exhausting to add the or?"*

"And I want it huge." Darby rallied with a smile. "But then, I'm over-the-top on everything."

"Don't let him fool you. He loves the attention." Only after the words came out did Jess realize how unprofessional she'd sounded. *Really? Making fun of your client's future brother-in-law?* But she'd said it, and she had to turn it into humor. "Mr. What-Am-I-Wearing-Under-My-Kilt is notoriously over-the-top."

Jasper and Darby laughed, but she wanted to slink under the table. Way to let him know he was getting to her.

"Oh, that's for show," Darby said. "He's not really like that."

But Trevor watched her, head tilted as if trying to figure her out.

She was being immature and petty, and it stopped right then and there.

No doubt about it, planning his wedding to another woman was the cruelest job she'd ever had, but her reputation was on the line, and she wouldn't let Chris down. "We'll need to figure that out as soon as possible. I've found a hotel supplier, so I'll start ordering things as soon as I get a number from you."

"Trev?" Darby nudged him. "How many people are you inviting?"

"Inviting?" He looked like he'd just snapped out of a fugue state. He sat up and tossed his napkin down on the table. "We have some things to talk about." When he stood up, he addressed Jess. "We'll see you at ten for the tasting."

He waited for Darby, and together, they left the dining room.

He didn't even look back at her.

After a moment of silence, Jasper said, "Well, that happened."

She'd made a total fool of herself. "I shouldn't have made the kilt comment."

"Oh, that's not the issue." Jasper seemed amused.

"You think he's jealous about Emil?"

Jasper broke into a slow grin. "No, I'm not thinking that's the issue at all." He pushed back his chair. "I'm thinking you two might've been more than just pals in that little ole town of yours."

"We might've been a thing." She attempted a teasing tone, but she couldn't play. She was devastated. Confused. Her entire world had turned upside down, and she was shaken. "But that was a very long time ago."

"Are we going to pretend that handsome hunk of man flesh wasn't staring at you so hard he was literally willing you to pay attention to him? And really, good on you for not giving it to him."

"Why?"

"Because you just played him like a fiddle."

She shook her head. "Believe me, I'm not playing. And now, you and I have work to do."

And if she didn't dive into it, she'd be obsessing over everything Jasper just said.

Because the last thing she wanted was to play games with her ex.

She wanted to finish this job and get out of there.

She wanted to get as far away from Trevor Montgomery as she could.

He'd made the decision yesterday, the moment he'd laid eyes on her.

Since then, his mind had been revving, his thoughts spinning, but it was the mention of a guest list that snapped him into focus.

Because he couldn't waste anyone's time with something that would never happen.

He had to end this engagement, but it had to be done privately.

Unfortunately, they didn't make it halfway across the lobby before Darby stopped and turned around. Distress carved deep lines in the skin around her eyes.

"You okay?" he asked. "You forget something?"

"No." She let out an uncomfortable laugh. "Well, yes, actually. My mind."

In the month they'd known each other, she'd been full of energy and confidence. She ran her business like a pro, taking no shit and yet rewarding her team with praise, encouragement, and a good deal of autonomy.

But right then, she seemed lost and confused, haunted by her ex.

He could relate. "Do you need to go talk to him?"

"No. He's in an interview."

"You can wait for him in the dining room." It would put off their conversation, but she wasn't going to be able to focus on anything else.

"Yeah. That's probably a good idea."

In his peripheral vision, he caught a flash of red and black—the colors of Elzy's blouse. Anticipation exploded in his chest.

Is it her?

Shit. Yes.

It's Elzy.

He could not let her go. "Meet you back in the room?"

"Sure."

He took off, his boots smacking on the hardwood floor.

He had no idea what he'd say, no plan for what to do. He only knew that his Elzy was there, and he had to be with her.

But the moment he caught up with her in the hallway, her eyes flared. She looked trapped.

And that confused him. How could she not be as excited by the outrageous alignment of their paths crossing here in Iceland?

Of being together again?

Her steps faltered, and her path arced around him like he was a feral animal or a steaming pile of crap in the middle of a sidewalk.

Holy shit.

He hadn't expected that reaction. *What do I do?* He didn't want to make her uncomfortable. He should back off, leave her alone.

She strode past him, leaving him in a soft, subtle cloud of her perfume.

But he couldn't let her go. Not when he'd just found her. "Elz." His voice came out a hoarse, raw whisper. And yeah, maybe he sounded a little hurt.

But she wouldn't even look at him. She just hurried past.

He had to fix it. He had to make it right.

He took off after her. "Elzy." He said it sharply this time, demanding an acknowledgment. "Can you stop for a minute?"

"I'm afraid not. I'm really busy right now." She tossed it over her shoulder as if he were a stranger on the street asking for a handout. "I'll see you at ten." She stopped outside her door, pressed her key to the pad, and slipped inside.

Did she plan on spending the next couple of days

avoiding him? *No.* Without thinking, he kicked his leg out. His boot slammed against the door, stopping it from closing.

He was pretty sure her alarmed expression mirrored his.

She stood there wild-eyed, confused. "What are you doing?"

"I don't know." He really didn't. He wasn't a violent man. He wasn't aggressive. He just… *This is Elzy. My Elzy. I have to see her. I have to talk to her.* "But that fucking door was in the way."

"You're not James Mackintosh, leader of the clan, you know. This isn't a movie set where you drag me back to your lair." She flapped her hand at him. "Just go."

"Not until we talk."

"Well, I guess that answers my question." She sounded exasperated.

"What question?"

"About whether being a movie star turned you into an entitled jerk."

"Entitled? Elzy, we haven't seen each other in thirty years and seven months, and you don't think it's crazy that we both wind up in this exact hotel in Iceland at the same time?"

"Where I get to plan your *wedding*? Yes, Trevor, that *is* pretty crazy."

The stark pain in her eyes gutted him, and he crashed. The rush of adrenaline, the compulsion to see her, it all just burned out. "It's not what it—" But he shut his mouth. Because he couldn't tell her the truth until he talked to Darby first.

Fine, but there was zero possibility he'd walk away from

this opportunity to be with his heart. "How are you?" The question landed lamely, as it should have.

She gave him a dull look. "If I answer, will you leave?"

"Probably not."

"Look, I don't know what you want from me. We've been apart more than twice as long as we were together. There's nothing left between us."

"There sure as hell is. At least for me." He reached for her but lowered his arms when she recoiled. "Elz, there's not a day that goes by that I—" *Shit. Fuck.* Again, it wasn't fair to Darby to confess these feelings to his ex.

"That you what? Don't regret the choice you made to abandon me forty-three minutes after we got married? After that neat speech you gave about me being your inspiration, your motivation, the love of your life? You took the money I needed for my sister, and you never looked back."

Shame hit him square in the chest. "That's not fair. You know I came back for you. And I tried getting a job, but the director told me it was a violation of my contract." By the time he'd scraped up the money and sent it to her, it was far too late. Her niece was eighteen months old by then.

"I don't care. I really don't." She lifted both hands in surrender. "I handled it. And you know what? I'm so glad I did because my sisters have turned into wonderful women. They're married, they're moms, and we all work together. I like the way my life turned out. And clearly, you're living your best life. So, what else is there to say?"

"I'm glad things turned out well. But we're here, Elz. We're right here, together."

"So? Did you think we'd reminisce? Pull out the scrapbook and laugh about old times? Well, guess what? I don't have time for that. Besides, your life's been well documented in the media."

"That's not my life—"

She held up a hand. "I don't care. I'm here for work, that's it." And then, she tipped her head. "Oh, okay. I get what's really going on here. You want me to say the magic words to release you from the pesky guilt that keeps rearing up when an image of me alone in that motel room drops into your mind."

"You're right." She'd nailed it. He did live with that exact image. "I do have guilt. And that memory comes up a lot. But that has nothing to do with why I'm happy to see you. Because Elzy, I have *never* forgotten you. I've thought about you every day for thirty years."

"Were you thinking about me when your son was born *two years* after we eloped? How about when you proposed to Darby? Or were those just the two moments in your life when you forgot about the high school girlfriend you *married* and then walked out on?" She pressed a hand to her forehead. She let out a frustrated breath. "Listen to me. I sound so bitter. Well, look, I don't hold you accountable for something you did when you were just a kid. And let me assure you, I have a great life, and everything worked out the way it should. Okay? Are we good now?"

Once, they'd been filming along the River Spey. It was an action scene. He was charging after the clansman who'd run off with stolen booty, but it had been raining heavily, and he'd sunk into the mud. There was a moment of panic when he couldn't move. He was trapped, and everyone was relying on him—cameras were rolling—actors were running —and he couldn't lift his feet.

That's what this feels like. She stood there, fiery, explosively angry, expecting a response from him, but he was stuck, and he couldn't get his brain to function well enough to answer.

Because for the first time, he was hearing it from her perspective, and she was right.

But she didn't know the whole truth. How could she?

Tell her. Talk to her.

He had the chance to clear things up, but his brain was sluggish, and he couldn't kick it into gear, so he said the only thing that came to mind. "There has never been anything better in my life than you."

"Except the woman you slept with a few months after you got to Scotland?" She waved a hand dismissively. "Forget it. This conversation's going nowhere. We were kids, living some kind of Bonnie and Clyde fantasy. It was a lifetime ago."

"It doesn't feel like it. It feels like it was yesterday."

"Well, *today*, your fiancée is waiting for you, so you really shouldn't be in another woman's room."

But you're not another woman.

You're the only woman.

He couldn't say any of that, though. Not until he ended things with Darby.

And yet…

Now that she's back in my life, I can't walk away. I can't be anywhere in this world except with her.

"Why are you just standing there? Go." Her tone turned imploring. "God, Trevor. What do you want from me?"

Everything. From this day forward, I want everything with

you. "I handled this all wrong, and I'm sorry for upsetting you."

I have to clean everything up.

But I'll be back, and I'll make it right.

I will fix this.

The moment he turned away the door slammed so hard it jarred his bones. He knew, if she had her way, she'd never talk to him again.

But she wouldn't have her way. She was his other half, woven into the fabric of his soul.

He'd lost her—and that was one-hundred-percent his fault. But now, by some crazy miracle, their paths had crossed.

He finally had a shot to win her back

He wouldn't blow it.

Chapter Six

Trevor burst into the room. "Darby?" When she didn't answer, he checked the bathroom. *Dammit.* She wasn't there.

You've got to calm down. Jamming his hands into his pockets, he gazed out the window at the black-sand beach. As daybreak neared, a fiery ring of orange around the horizon was capped by a crown of midnight. It was stunning. Unlike anything he'd ever seen.

And yet… He couldn't focus on it. Rattled, he held his hand out in front of him, watching it tremble.

Why did you come on so strong? He dropped to a crouch, lowered his head, and jammed his fingers through his hair, remembering how he'd kicked her door. *Jesus.*

I'm out of control.

But she's here. My Elzy is right fucking here.

He *had* to talk to her. They'd never hashed anything out.

Wind whistled through the window, and he stood up. He needed a plan.

"Were you thinking about me when you had a son two years after we eloped?"

He should've answered her. He should've said, "Yes. Hell, yes. I never stopped thinking about you."

He should've reminded her that he *had* come home. He'd bought a plane ticket the very first break he'd gotten from filming. He'd tried to talk to her, but she'd blown him off.

The second time, though… She didn't know about that one. He'd had money in the bank. He was ready. He'd planned on winning her back.

He would never forget that feeling, the happiness… the anticipation… the fucking *hope*. He'd been soaring because he'd be with her again. The gnawing pain would finally end.

Even before getting on the plane, he'd felt the relief of being in her arms. Having her back, skin to skin, mouth to mouth. Making him feel whole.

The pride that he'd finally gotten a paycheck and could deposit money in her dad's account. That he had enough money to buy their freedom.

He remembered—clear as day—the moment he'd headed out of his apartment. He could still feel the cold plastic handle of his suitcase in his hand. He'd done a quick check for his ticket, his wallet, and the gifts he was bringing —a Nessie stuffed animal for her niece, shortbread cookies for Elzy's dad who had a sweet tooth, and luxury bath products he'd found in a shop on the Isle of Arran for her sisters.

But just as he'd stepped out of the door, his phone had rung. Back then, it had been a landline. He'd had plenty of time to get to the airport, so he'd gone back in to answer. Just in case. The studio still owned him, after all.

Remembering the news he'd gotten still had the power to shock his nervous system.

He'd had no choice but to miss his flight.

With the turn his life had taken, he couldn't go get his Elzy. He had a new priority.

He had a son.

Tipping his forehead to the cold window, he closed his eyes.

He'd fucked up so badly.

He guarded his personal life fiercely, so only three people knew the truth about Cole: the man who'd raised him for two years, Trevor's agent, and Cole himself.

He couldn't wait to explain it to Elzy. It wasn't what she thought. Not even close.

But first, he had to end things with Darby.

He pulled out his phone and texted her.

Trevor: Where are you?

He waited for an answer, but nothing came. *Fuck it.* He'd go find her. But just as he turned around, the door opened. *Thank fuck, you're here.* But he didn't say it because Darby looked shattered. "Hey." He met her in the middle of the room. "You all right?"

"I just talked to Emil." She kicked off her heels, set down her key card, and crawled into the unmade bed. "I saw your expression, you know? The way you looked at Jessica, the way you ran after her, and I knew she was more than a high-school friend."

He nodded. "Much more."

But she wasn't really talking to him. She was lost in her own thoughts. "And it made me realize how I do the exact opposite. You face your fears, and I run away. That's something I really admire about you. You're willing to fix things—even when it might hurt. Like with your son. You're brave, and I want to be brave, too. So, I waited for him to finish his interview." Her gaze snapped over to him. "Just for the closure, of course."

He couldn't let her think they were going through with this marriage. It might hold her back from her own reconciliation. He stood at the edge of the bed. "Darby, that woman? She's not just an ex. She's the love of my life."

She went still. "Jessica's your great love?"

"Yes."

She drew the covers up to her chin. "Emil was mine."

Yeah, he got that. "I can't marry you." The way she flinched told him he could've been less blunt. Should've eased into it. But he wasn't in subtle mode. He was all fired up, and he knew they had to deal with this issue head-on. "I've had a lot of fun with you this past month, but seeing Jess made me realize I'm only stepping into your life to avoid building one of my own."

"But this could *be* your life. We're a great team."

"Maybe, but you've already got your path. I haven't found mine." He wouldn't tell her he'd found his when he was four and saw a girl doing a monster dance outside the feedstore.

My path is Elzy.

He'd known it all his life. He'd just never allowed himself to embrace it because it wasn't what a man did.

He'd been raised to work hard and provide for his family. His dad used to say, "A woman needs to feel safe. If you want to win her heart, show her you can provide for her." His dad's definition of a man was someone who led the family, put food on the table, and cared for his community.

And it was such a reasonable, *good* perspective, how could Trevor have questioned it? Falling short meant he was a selfish asshole. So, he'd tried—so fucking hard—to live up to his dad's vision. But all along, the truth kept whispering around him.

My path is Elzy.

And the truth of it got slammed home yesterday when, just by being near her, he had the first sense of peace, of *home*, he'd felt in thirty long, lonely years.

"I've been at loose ends since retiring." How did he explain what he was just beginning to understand? "Without the structure of a filming schedule, I don't know my place in the world or within my family. And the idea of joining up with you seemed…well, it was a relief. You have a mission, a passion… I admire you. But Elzy's here. And I'm not going to let her get away a second time. I'm going to do everything in my power to win her back."

"I'm not sure it works like that," Darby said quietly. "There's a lot of water under the bridge."

"Right, but that's because we never talked. Which means she's made up a story from the bits and pieces she's heard over the years. Now, I have the chance to explain my side and listen to hers. She needs to know I never stopped caring about her. I never wanted to lose her."

"Trev, sit down." She patted the bed.

He couldn't do that. He was too amped up. Too desperate to see Elzy. To make her understand.

"I'm the woman who got left behind," she continued. "So, I'm here to tell you, her experience isn't the same as yours."

"What do you mean? *You* left Iceland. Not Emil."

"Right, but we were supposed to leave together. He bailed at the last minute and didn't give me an explanation. At least not one that made sense. And I had to piece together a story over many, many years from the information I got from family and friends."

She had his attention.

"Take it from me, she's not going to hear your side of the story and throw herself into your arms. Not with the fortress of resentment she's built around her. She needs to get to know you again. You think, after thirty years, you can say, 'Oh, I never stopped loving you,' and she'll believe you?" She shook her head. "Not a chance. I promise she's going to be even angrier. Why didn't you come back a month later? Two years? She probably would've given you five years to get your shit together. But thirty? Forget it."

"You don't understand—"

"I don't need to understand the details. Trust me. They won't matter to her. Actions matter. Especially when the first time she sees you, you're *engaged*. And *she's* planning the wedding."

Anxiety tightened his chest, and he found it hard to breathe. "I'm going to tell her we broke it off."

"And then what? If we're not engaged, why are you here? Why would you show up at a tasting if we're not getting married?"

Fuck. Shit. "You're right." He couldn't think clearly. He was powered by need, desire… Desperation.

Darby sat up, pressing her hands flat on the mattress. "The thing is…when I was talking to Emil—and believe me, he's a man of few words. He's all broody, dark energy…big, deep feelings…fire-in-his-eyes kind of guy. But as I was talking to him, I thought, 'What exactly do I want from him?'"

"He lives here, and you live in North Carolina. Is either of you willing to move?"

"Well, we haven't gotten that far." She let out a bitter laugh. "But, yeah, it's more than that. The relationship I mourn is gone. And that's probably true for you and Jessica too. So, maybe the best we can hope to get is closure."

No. The best was to have her back fully.

"I guess what I'm saying is, I'd hate for us to end our engagement only to find out there's nothing there with our exes. Nothing but memories of a first love."

"Everything you say makes sense, but it's different for Elzy and me. There will *always* be something there. It's more than love with her. It's…" He tapped his heart. "She's in here. She'll never be anywhere else."

"If that's true, then why did you stay away for thirty years?"

Desperation clawed at him. Every instinct in his body screamed to be with her, but Darby was making him think things through. If he had one shot at winning Elzy back, he couldn't go crashing through her door.

So, he sat on the edge of the bed. "I didn't. The first time I tried to get her back, she ignored me. The second time, a crisis came up I had to deal with. And the last time was six years after we broke up. I found out she was working at a resort in Idaho. I flew out there with a ring in my pocket, but I saw she had a husband and a kid, and I knew I'd be a piece of shit if I tried to break up a marriage. A *family*."

He'd been broken. His dreams, his hopes… Everything he'd wanted had been irretrievably destroyed. *Because of me.* It had been the hardest time of his life.

"Okay, so, what's changed—other than her children might be grown now? If she's still married, are you willing to rock her entire world in the hopes of rekindling something?"

"That's a fair question. If she's happily married, then no. I'll walk away. But I have to find out and there's nothing about her personal life on social media. She's very private."

Darby smiled. "Well, you two have that in common."

"But I hear you. I get it. I'll go slower." *Go. Talk to her.* Every second he wasn't with her was a wasted opportunity. He got up and headed to the door, his blood pounding in his ears.

"What's your plan?" she asked. "If you want to win her back, we need to stay engaged."

He cut her a look. "Darby, I can't marry you. Even if she's happily married and can never forgive me, now that I've been in the same room with her, it's…" He let out a breath. "There's a reason I've never gotten married."

She raised a hand to stop him. "I'm not holding you to anything. It was a crazy, impulsive idea. I get it. But you have to think about this. Jessica's a busy woman. She owns a resort and travels the world for consulting jobs. What will you do?" She smiled. "The offer to work with me is still on the table."

If he could choose how to spend every day of his life,

he'd be in bed with Elzy. Cooking for her, riding horses, or hiking on their ranch. Even just sitting quietly reading books together while holding hands. When her career took her to places like Iceland, he'd go with her. He'd carry her luggage. Refill her water bottle.

But he understood that wasn't a viable plan. *She owns a resort and is tight with her family. She's busy.* She might not need a provider, but she'd certainly want a man who was active and pursuing his own goals. "I hear you, and I'll figure something out." He headed for the door. "To be clear, I'm not going to lie to her. I'll participate in the tastings, but I'm not going to say we're engaged or deceive her about us getting married. I've done enough damage—I won't lie to her face. And when the opportunity comes to tell the truth, I'm going to do it. Are you okay with that?"

"Yeah, of course." She smiled at him with a look of admiration. "You're something else, Trev. Your determination's got me all fired up. I don't know what can happen with Emil, but I can't help wondering if something might come of this. So, okay. I won't lie, either. And I won't make it sound like we're planning a wedding. I'll just give my opinion on the best chef for the resort." That gleam hit her eyes again.

"What? No games."

"Maybe a teeny one." She put two fingers together with very little space between them. "Does she know how to drive a stick?"

"She didn't back then. Why?"

"Well, how's she going to get up north? We don't have trains and hiring a driver to come two hours out here, four hours to Snaefellsnes, and then another two back to the airport isn't exactly feasible. And she doesn't need us to meet the concierge, so she won't be asking for a ride."

"So, Chris will offer her the use of a car." He grinned because he might not be thinking clearly, but Darby sure was. "I like the way your mind works."

"I doubt she'll find a rental a few days before Christmas, so the only car she'll be able to use is my grandpa's old Land Cruiser."

"Which is a stick."

"Yep."

"And you wonder why I said yes to your proposal." Smiling, he pulled her into his arms for a hug. "In another world, we might've been great together." Except there was no other world. *There's only the one with me and Elzy.* In every universe, across every space and time, there was only her. "Thank you."

She shrugged. "I didn't really do anything."

"You've stopped me from screwing it all up, and I appreciate it." He headed for the door.

"Where're you going?"

"To find her. I have to be where she is."

Smiling, she shook her head. "You've got it bad."

"She's the only woman I'll ever love."

And nothing would stop him from winning her back.

Jess dropped into the chair by the window. "He's such an asshole."

Oh yeah? Then, why is your heart still pounding from the way he kicked the door open?

When would she ever get over this man?

"Okay, but that does sound kind of hot," her sister said.

"What?" Jess couldn't even pretend to be outraged because it really was. The thrill of that moment still rang through her body.

"Sorry. I mean, it's bad." Amber faked a stern tone. "He's a very bad man. Shame on him."

"Who the hell does he think he is?" *Turning me on like that?*

"He's a man who lost the love of his life. And it sounds like he's going for it."

"Going for what? I'm *engaged*." She popped up. "And for God's sake, he's here to plan his *wedding*." Every muscle in her body clenched, and her skin flashed hot, then cold. "If he thinks I owe him a second of my time, then he's an entitled piece of shit. I'm here to do a job. Not go frolicking down memory lane with him."

And yet, instead of checking out light fixtures and paint chips online, I'm freaking out about some dickwad who walked out on me a lifetime ago.

When her sister didn't respond, Jess asked, "Are you there? Are you even listening?"

"Hang on a sec. I'm picturing you frolicking. Like, are you two holding hands and skipping down the street? Are you giggling, riding bikes downhill with your feet off the peddles? I mean, either way, it's really cute."

"*Amber.*"

"Fine. But can I just say something?" her sister asked, all humor gone.

"No."

"*No?* Then why did you call?"

"To check on the resort." There was some truth in that. But boy, did she need to vent.

"Uh huh. Okay. Well, it's going great. Chef fired Miss Butterfingers, which puts us in a bind, so Kelly's called a few of the servers from the first round of interviews to give them a second chance. So, yeah. That's it. Okay, bye."

"Wait." Jess chuckled. "Don't leave me yet."

"You know, it's okay to come to me for advice. I'm only three years younger than you." Her sister paused. "You're not my mom, you know. You never were."

"Yeah? Then, why do you and Kelly send me Mother's Day cards?"

"Because it's funny. And because you were like a mom when we needed it. But, Jess? We don't need one anymore. The three of us need our sisterhood. And part of that code is brutal honesty, so I'm going to tell you something. If you want to move on—and I mean finally let this whole traumatic thing go—then, you have to talk to him. Get the closure you never got. It's wild that you guys were so in love you got *married*, and then, he left, and neither of you ever even tried to work it out. I mean, make it make sense."

"I did try." *I just never told you. Because, yes, I did want to preserve that boundary between a parent and a child.* "His mom told me he'd bought a place in Calamity, and I went to see him." Even though it killed her to know he was living their dream without her. "It was four years later, and I still lived at home, but I'd grown up enough to know I'd handled it all wrong." She remembered it so vividly, that sense of purpose, of rightness. She was going to get her man back, and everything would be all right. She'd reclaim her equilibrium instead of moving through life like the earth's axis had tipped at a hellish angle. "I had this whole movie in my head about him seeing me and breaking into a run."

"Am I going to need a stiff drink to hear this?"

"Probably."

"Oh, God. What happened?" Her sister sounded wary, like she wasn't sure she could handle the answer.

"Well, first of all, there was a fancy security gate. So much for the running into my arms scenario." He'd bought the great, big ranch they'd always wanted, and she half-believed he'd done it with her in mind. *Ha. What a fool.* "I didn't know what to do, so I just sat in my little junker of a car for a minute, trying to figure out a plan. I'd come all that way, and I was determined to see it through. And then, this huge SUV pulled up. All black and shiny with tinted windows. I thought, Oh, my God, it's him. He's here." The memory kicked an old bruise, so she steeled herself against the pain.

"You don't have to finish telling me. But also, you kind of do. *What happened?*"

Her sister's quirky sense of humor eased the tension. "I had…" Her voice came out strangled, so she swallowed. Took a breath. "I had all these presents for him. Those gross sour gummies he liked so much." He used to say, "Oh, but the punishment feels so good." She hesitated, finding it hard to be so vulnerable. "A pair of boots."

"Boots?"

"Yeah, I know. It sounds weird, but Trevor and I spent a lot of time imagining our ranch in Calamity. I mean, we knew the color of the kitchen cabinets." *Slate blue.* "And one thing he always wanted was a pair of good cowboy boots." As a kid, Trevor never owned new shoes. But the farmhands' kids sure did. They also had gas in their trucks. Which was a beautiful thing. Truly. But it also sucked for Trevor when he couldn't get to school some days.

"If you tell me you've kept those boots all this time, I'm going to bawl my eyes out."

Since she moved so often, she had a storage unit for all the things she dragged from one resort to the next. They were somewhere in there. "Put it this way, as long as you keep sending me Mother's Day cards, you'll never be privy to that kind of information."

"You do. Oh, God, you kept them. Go on. Finish the damn story. I can't take much more."

"Anyhow, I got all my gifts together, and I was just about to open the door." She would never forget sitting there like a total lovesick moron. "When Trevor got out of the car in his stupid kilt and combat boots."

"And you said, 'What a tool' and then floored it back to Riverton?"

"No. He went to get the mail, but something in the car kept distracting him, so he opened the back door and leaned in. He pulled out this little kid who was crying and wailing, and…" Her heart wrenched. "The boy clung to him like he was the last safe harbor in the entire world." She would never forget the sight of those little arms and legs clutching, digging in. "And Trevor…" She swallowed past that painful knot. "Hugged him. He held him until the boy quieted down. And I knew right then, it was over. For good. Because he was a dad." And a good one.

"Oh, God, Jessie. I'm so sorry. That's awful."

It broke me. "It was. But it kicked my butt into gear,

right? There I was, waiting for us to get back together, and he'd moved on." It had only been four years later.

That's all it had taken for him to erase me.

God, it hurt.

"You know, I admire you," her sister said. "You took something that could've destroyed you and used it to build a great life for yourself. I just wish you'd told me this before. I couldn't figure out why—after a lifetime of being single— you'd choose to marry a guy like Joel."

A guy like Joel? "What does that mean? He's a good guy."

"Maybe for someone else. But you don't love him. Come on, this can't come as a surprise."

"No, but—" She wouldn't bother defending herself because what she'd accepted as normal now sounded sad coming out of her sister's mouth. "We're fond of each other." Amber laughed so loudly Jess had to pull the phone away from her ear. "Oh, cut it out." But she quit grumbling because her sister wasn't wrong. "I *know.* You think I don't know? I've barely thought about him since I left town." It was a relief to say it out loud.

"Well, I guess it doesn't take a genius to figure out fondness is a lot safer than the kind of love you and Trevor had."

"I like Joel. We have fun together." When they'd started dating, she was in the permitting stage and hadn't broken ground yet, and he was still a partner in a law firm. They'd both worked crazy hours. Then, six months ago, he retired. With his first taste of freedom in years, he'd wanted to play. Bad timing, since she'd been hiring and ordering supplies. "I think we just need different things."

"You're not hurt that he blew you off for Christmas?"

"Oh, I am." She gave a bitter laugh. "But I haven't made him a priority, so how can I fault him for not making me one?"

"That's a fair point. And sad that you've spent a year with a guy, and you're nothing more than pals."

"Please, Amber. Don't hold back. Tell me what you really think."

"Oh, I'm sorry. Is now the time you need me to soap your ass?"

"No." Jess laughed. "It's not. And you know what I keep remembering? After he told me he was leaving, I didn't argue. I didn't yell. I just let him go to California without me."

"Which is the same thing you did with Trevor."

A memory dropped into her mind. She was jammed into the utility room—a bar of light underneath the door, the smell of ammonia from the cleaning products—and listening to Trevor's voice when he'd come looking for her on a break from filming.

She could've confronted him, yelled at him.

Instead, she'd hidden. "I don't know why I did that."

"I do."

"Fine. I was a coward. You can say it." Uncomfortable, she crossed an arm over her stomach.

"Nope. You're the bravest woman I know."

"So, what, I'm stubborn?" Jess asked. "A big, dumb cow?"

"I mean, yeah. Maybe not the cow part, but you're stubborn as all get-out. That's a good quality, though, because it meant you never gave up on me, and it helped build a very successful business."

"Okay, then what?" Jess asked. "Just go on and say it."

"Do you remember Miss Martha?"

"Uh, she brought her pet chicken every time she came into the store. That's not a lady you forget. What about her? Don't tell me she talked about me?"

"Everyone talked about you. When Trevor came back to town to get you—"

Get you. The very idea drove a stake through her heart.

Because, if she hadn't been so immature, would they have been together all this time? It was unbearable to even consider it.

"He was not quiet about it," Amber continued. "And neither were you with the way you kept hiding from him. It was like watching the worst reality TV show play out in our little town."

"Are you serious? Everyone knew? I thought I was so discreet."

"Yeah, it was super discreet when you wedged yourself behind the diner's dumpster. Honey, everyone saw. Anyhow, she said when Mom died, you fell apart. You were crying your eyes out, just inconsolable. And she thinks it made you feel so powerless over loss that you just shut down. You learned you can't make people stay."

You can't make people stay.

She let the words sink in. "I was eight when she died, so I don't remember a lot of that, but I do know the powerlessness I felt when Trevor left. I was…devastated."

"I know."

"I thought I was doing such a good job of pretending."

"Sweetie, I lived under the same roof. You think I didn't hear you crying at night after we all went to bed? I think the biggest reason I got my shit together was because I felt so bad for you." Amber drew in a breath. "But you're not powerless, and he's right there. So, it would be a real shame if you didn't talk to him. He's in Iceland, for God's sake. He's there for a reason."

"Yes, and the reason is a woman named Darby."

"And here's the bad side of stubbornness. If you really want to give Joel a fair shot, it'll only come after you get closure with your first love."

Jess sat up straighter. "You're right. How did you get so smart?"

"I had the best older sister in the world. She guided me through some really messy times in my life. You ready to let me return the favor?"

"I think so."

"Good. Then, go talk to him."

"All right. I'll do it." But it was easier said than done.

Because she'd only ever known him as the boy who'd looked at her with devotion and lust.

And now, he was in love with another woman.

She didn't think she could bear being in the same room with them.

Chapter Seven

JESSICA COULDN'T SAY WHAT THE CHEF PREPARED. SHE didn't know if the food was too salty or not flavorful enough.

She was overheated, overstimulated, and about to lose her mind.

Because Trevor was working her last nerve trying to get her attention.

He wasn't being rude or childish. No, he was charming and funny. He was delightful.

So much so that no one noticed what he was doing.

Except her. Because that man knew exactly what to say to stir her up, to engage her. Even worse, every time their gazes collided, sparks flew.

Ignoring him was exhausting.

Yeah, she got it. She should've moved on long ago. Getting closure should've been a simple thing, just two friends talking through what went wrong.

He explains his side. I explain mine.

We hug it out, and all is peachy.

But she just couldn't do that. Not in front of Jasper, Chris, and Darby. Her emotions ran too high.

Besides, she was *working*.

This is a job.

My reputation's on the line.

For the past hour, the others raved about the food and listened with rapt attention as the rosy-cheeked chef described his cooking ethos and told stories about each dish. He was as captivating as he was talented—and he even had a great temperament. Which was rare for a chef.

After the servers brought out a selection of side dishes, the chef stood in front of the table and rubbed his hands together. "How's everything so far?"

"Couldn't be better," Chris said.

"I'll be honest. Food's always been more like fuel for me, but this..." Darby gestured to the plate in front of her. "Your cooking might turn me into a foodie."

"We appreciate you coming out here," Jess said. "I know it wasn't easy." He'd had to pack up his food and knives, travel by two different modes of transportation—car and ferry—and cook in an unfamiliar kitchen.

"For this opportunity, you bet I'll take my traveling tasting show on the road." Hákon grinned. "Now, you said no dessert because you're looking to hire a pastry chef..." Both servers came out of the kitchen with platters loaded with treats. "But my wife trained at the Cordon Blue in Paris, and she threatened me with a month of sleeping on the futon if I didn't offer you a taste of her magic." He looked at Jess questioningly. *Is this all right?*

She smiled. "You should've mentioned she was a pastry chef when we talked. We'll add her to our list."

"Does she have her own bakery?" Chris asked, but his attention was on the array of pastries the servers set down in the middle of the table.

"Oh, wow." Jess took in the Napoleons, lemon tarts sprinkled with confectioner's sugar, slices of chocolate mousse cake, and colorful petit fours. "These look amazing."

"No, she works with me." The chef's smile expressed how proud he was of his wife and how much he enjoyed sharing a space with her. "Our kitchen's tiny, so she does her work at night and in the early mornings, and I do mine during the day. She's the yin to my yang."

Chris bit into a creamy éclair, and his eyes squeezed shut. "Unreal."

"You like?" Chef asked.

Chris made sounds of pure delight, and everyone laughed.

"I'll be sure to tell her." When the two assistants came out of the kitchen, loaded with insulated bags, the chef swiveled around. "Now, I don't mean to be rude, but we have to skedaddle. There's a storm coming, and we need to make the ferry back to the island."

Chris got up. "Let me walk you out. I've been so busy eating I haven't had a chance to talk about my vision for this place."

After the group left, Jasper said, "We should hire him."

"He's definitely got the attributes we're looking for." *Notice how I didn't address the quality of his food? That's because I couldn't taste anything.*

I'm obsessed with Trevor Montgomery.

You couldn't help but look at him. The combination of charisma and physical beauty… The man was magnificent.

He'd filled out so much over the years. Broad shoulders, muscular chest, arms, and thighs. Tattoos that made her want to pull up his sleeves and explore.

His greatest appeal, though, was his sincerity. Because that smile was not fake. Deep inside, this man was a well of happiness. He radiated all the goodness brimming over in his soul.

But he belonged with someone else. He hadn't been hers in a very long time. "He's the real deal. I talked to his staff."

"You did?" Jasper asked.

She nodded. "You can't hire someone until you get the dirt. References are curated, so they don't carry much weight. We want to hear from people who've worked for him."

"How do you find them if they don't work there anymore?" Darby asked.

"You follow the trail. Putting his and his restaurant's name in search engines always leads to conversations, reviews, and people who used to work there. And Hákon is beloved by everyone and produces outstanding food."

"What about the pastry chef?" Trevor asked. "Do you trust a husband and wife working together?"

She knew he didn't care about the answer. He just wanted her to acknowledge him. Which was unfair. Cruel, actually. "If they've done it successfully so far, I don't see why not." Because looking into his eyes unearthed so many damn memories.

When he'd smile at her from across the classroom. A look of anticipation for the fun adventure they had planned for that afternoon. Or, later, after they'd become physical, a promise of what his hands, mouth, and tongue would do to her.

Of him bracing his hands on either side of her head, watching her intently as he drove into her.

Oh, damn him. She had no choice but to look away. It was just too painful. "But I leave those decisions to Chris. All I can do is source options."

"You're good, you know that?" Jasper asked.

"Well, thank you. That's very nice of you to say. Of course, I've had lots of experience. There's nothing more important than who you hire. The wrong vibe can sink a resort."

"How long have you been doing this?" Trevor asked.

And bingo. He'd asked just the right question to get the direct eye contact he wanted. "I got my first job in hospitality twenty-six years ago." She watched him make the mental calculation.

Yes, that was the same year you bought a home in Calamity —our dream—and moved your two-year-old son into it.

A son who wasn't mine.

So, let's stop pretending we can ever be friends, okay?

But her attempt at a withering look didn't pan out as she'd hoped. Because he nodded and said, "Do you spend your time traveling from one job to another?"

Darby nudged him. "She just opened her own resort. Chris told us at breakfast."

"That's right," Jess said. "But to answer your question, no. I rarely take consulting jobs."

Darby seemed subdued, and she couldn't help wondering if it had something to do with Emil. It had to be, considering the woman wasn't touching her fiancé this morning.

Jess didn't see any flirtatiousness at all.

"Where's your resort?" Trevor asked.

And here it comes. She had no choice but to say it. "Calamity, Wyoming."

His fork clattered on the plate. "Are you serious? You live there?"

His shock was almost insulting.

Did you think you were the only one who got to live our dream? "I do."

"I live there too."

"Yes, Trevor. I know." And with that, she was done with the conversation. "Anyhow, I hope you got some ideas for your menu from this tasting." She stood up. "Try that lemon cake. It looks delicious."

As she fled the dining room, her heels clacked on the floor, and white noise filled her mind. A flurry of conflicting emotions made it impossible to identify exactly what she was feeling. Anger, definitely.

No, it's not anger.

It's hurt.

I'm hurt.

And she couldn't stand carrying this pain anymore.

Of course I know where he lives.

I've searched the internet countless times, greedy for every morsel of information I could get.

And him? He's been filming movies, raising a son, and getting engaged to race car drivers.

I stopped existing to him the moment he walked out the door.

As she neared the lobby, Chris and the chef's voices grew louder, and she didn't have the composure to talk to them. So, she made a quick turn down a hallway. Out of sight, she leaned against the wall and closed her eyes.

Shaking, she crossed her arms over her chest in a hug-like gesture.

How did she stop feeling this pain?

I beg you to release me from it.

"Elzy."

Dammit. She didn't hear his footfalls because this section was carpeted. She lowered her arms and pushed away from the wall. "What?" Unfortunately, her tone came out more plea than exasperation.

Trevor's scent filled her senses. And no, it was nothing like the boy she remembered who'd only used bar soap and deodorant. This version of him smelled expensive—and she didn't know why because it wasn't cologne.

"Let me guess," she said. "You bring your own fancy soap wherever you travel?"

"My what? *Soap?* No. I use whatever's in the hotel."

"This hotel hasn't operated in ten years. There are no supplies in the rooms."

"I don't know." He grew flustered. "I used whatever was in the shower. It must be Darby's."

We're talking about soap now. Awesome. "What can I do for you, Trevor?"

"Nothing. I just…want to be near you." He stood there as jittery as a boy finally talking to his crush. "I want to…" Grabbing the back of his neck, he blew out a breath. "Can we just talk?"

She sighed. *Here's your chance to get that closure.* And yet…

She just couldn't do it. She couldn't look into his eyes and not see devotion and lust. For whatever reason, she needed to preserve that part of her past. Hold on to it. *It's all I have of him.* "I'm afraid this trip is all business for me. Maybe when we get back home, we can meet for coffee, okay?" *Over my dead body.* But hopefully, it would make him go away.

"No." He stepped closer. "Look, for whatever reason, we both wound up in this hotel in Iceland, and I'm not going to waste the opportunity. I get it. You've moved on. It was a long time ago. But I don't believe for one second the hurt I've caused you is entirely healed." He came so close she could feel the heat of his body. "Call it guilt—call it whatever you want—but this is my chance to make things right."

"You can't do that, Trevor." It was his vulnerability that did it. Made her stop running. She'd always had the sense he'd moved on and never looked back, but there was no denying this man was as upset as she was—and that meant something.

It meant it hadn't been easy for him. That he had regrets. And she wanted to hear him out. She just did.

Okay. You win, Amber.

I'll get the damn closure.

If it would get this trauma out of her body, she'd talk to him. "But if you have something to say, please. Go ahead." She gestured to him. *Talk.*

But he didn't do that. He watched her with a strange expression. Was that yearning? Or was she imagining it?

Of course you're imagining it, you idiot.

My God, you're a hot mess.

He lifted a hand, as though he might touch her.

No. She froze. Fight or flight kicked in.

Because she longed for his touch. More than anything, that was what she missed.

Come on. They'd been inseparable. They couldn't keep their hands off each other.

I miss that.

I need that.

But he wasn't hers anymore, and if he touched her right then, she would hurl herself into his arms and beg for more.

And that snapped her out of it. Because she would *never* do that.

But he seemed to sense her turmoil as he pulled back and rubbed the back of his neck.

It left her feeling as disappointed as she was relieved.

No, relief is good. We don't want to unearth longing.

We just want to let him go.

He was just so…*familiar.* Beneath skin that had aged from years of filming under a Scottish sun and dark hair now threaded with silver, she still saw the boy she'd loved with all her heart. The boy she'd thought was her soulmate.

And she couldn't stand it. "Why are you just standing there? You wanted to talk. Talk."

"You're so different."

He'd dropped a lit match at her feet, and she burst into flames. "You *think?* You mean I'm not the same girl who trusted with her whole heart? Who *loved* with her whole heart? Who believed every word the man she *married* said to her? Wow, Trevor, I'm sorry if I somehow changed when, forty-three minutes after hearing my *husband* tell me I'm his best friend, his lover, his peace, his motivation, his inspiration, his North Star, and the love of his life, he walked out the door and never talked to me again." She punched the air with her fists. "You think that might fundamentally change a girl?"

Anger sparked in his eyes. "I tried to talk to you again, remember? And you blew me off." He held up both hands in an apologetic gesture. "That doesn't change what I did, and I'm sorry, Elz. I'm so sorry for the way everything turned out."

"You're sorry for the thirteen movies you made? For the son you had with another woman?"

He shook his head with conviction. "No. I can't be sorry for my son. He's the best thing I've ever done. But I am sorry for the way he was conceived, and I'm sorry for hurting you." He reached for her, but she jerked away. "I'm *sorry.*"

That was it? After exposing herself so completely—letting him know she'd memorized his stupid, empty vows—all he could say was, "Sorry?" "Well, cool. Apology accepted." She shouldered past him.

But he caught her upper arm. "No. You're not running away." He was so close the warmth of his breath gusted on her cheek. "In all these years, our paths haven't crossed. Not once. Until *now.*" Gripping her shoulders, he turned her to face him. She allowed herself to be handled as easily as a rag doll. "Listen to me. I have missed you every minute of every day. I dream about you at night. You have never, *ever* left my heart. And now that we're together, we have a chance to—"

"To what, Trevor? You're getting *married.*" She wrenched

free of his hold. "Does Darby know I'm 'still in your heart'? Does she know you dream about me? If not, you should tell her. She deserves to know this little fact about her future husband."

The man looked tortured. *Well, good.* Because it was killing her to stand this close to him and hear him say things like *You have never, ever left my heart.*

With a fiery cocktail of rage and desperation burning inside her, she didn't know whether she wanted to beg him to tell her how he could've left her so callously or punch him in the balls so hard he dropped to his knees.

But the bastard had a steel rod for a spine. "No," he stated firmly. "She's not part of this. We need to talk, just the two of us. When I left, I knew I'd hurt you. I knew you were angry, but I never thought it would end us. Do you think I'd have gotten on that plane if I'd known you'd never speak to me again? I thought you'd yell at me, but that we'd get through it."

"Well, then, you were delusional."

"Maybe. Or maybe I was desperate to manage the kind of problems a twenty-year-old had no business fixing."

"Oh, you figured that out, huh?"

"I realized it after my parents died. And believe me, that was a tough lesson to learn. I fucked up, Elz. No question about it. But we're here now. We have a chance to—"

"No. The only thing we can do is dredge up a past we can't change. Nothing you say will ever fix the pain I live with every single day of my life."

His eyes turned glossy, and his lips pressed together. "You're the only woman I've ever loved, and to know I hurt you that deeply..." His eyelids fluttered shut, and he took a slow breath. But when they opened, he radiated a steely resolve. "I think you're wrong. I think talking can heal us both. Can we start by getting to know each other again? I want to know how your life turned out. There's nothing about your personal life on the internet."

"That's because it's no one's business." He didn't get to know anything about the life he'd chosen to leave. "My story is a privilege for the people close to me, who've been there for me. You are not either of those things."

She would never expose herself to this man again.

"This isn't going to work," he muttered.

"Now, you're catching on." She sounded so snarky, so detached, when really, it made her unbearably sad that he'd give up so easily.

"That's not what I mean." His tone was strong, confident. "When I left, I believed I was doing the right thing. I thought you'd get it when I paid off the farm and your dad's debt. That everything would fall into place when I bought us a ranch in Calamity."

"You bought that ranch for yourself. And your son."

"If I wanted what was best for my son, I would've built a house in Riverton so my parents could help raise him. But I chose Calamity because I never gave up believing we'd find our way back to each other."

"How, Trevor? By magic? Don't feed me bullshit lines from a movie. Because I never heard from you."

"That's not true, and you know it. I wrote you letters. I flew back home. You know that. You know how hard I tried to talk to you."

Mortification washed through her as she remembered how childishly she'd behaved. "I don't know what this has to do with having a baby two years after we broke up. Can you see how your words sound empty when your son is out there in the world? You said I never left your heart, but Trevor, you had a *baby*." *While I was still curled up in my bed bawling my eyes out.* "You had sex with another woman." Her voice sounded raw, but that was because each word came tearing out of the deepest reaches of her soul.

"You want to know that story?"

"More than anything." She regretted the words the moment they came out of her mouth, but being around him threw her back to the girl she used to be.

Honest, blunt.

Reckless and impulsive.

"Okay." He gave a curt nod. "I borrowed money to come home after the first film wrapped. When you wouldn't talk to me, it broke me. I only had a few days before I had to get back on set, and I was out of my mind. I *needed* to talk to you, Elz. I had to make things right. Living without you was unbearable."

She wished she'd been mature enough to talk to him back then.

But she hadn't been.

"I thought if I could give you back the eighteen hundred dollars, you'd see I was doing this for us. For our future. But you refused to see me so, the minute I got back to Scotland, I took a job in a bar. The cast was still living in a guesthouse at that point, so I had to sneak out, but I did it. About a week in, I got hammered."

"You don't even drink."

"I know. But you'd blown me off. I didn't know if you'd *ever* talk to me. I couldn't..." He let out a huff of breath, pain ravaging his handsome features. "I was in agony, Elz." With a shake of his head, he got back on track. "Anyhow, these women came in for a hen night."

"A what?"

"A bachelorette party. They recognized me from the set. It's a tiny town, so it wasn't a big surprise. I don't know how I thought I'd get away with working there. They were all having a great time, flirting with me like crazy, but I wasn't interested. This one woman didn't want to party, so she hung out at the bar, and we started talking. I told her my story, and she said I was an absolute fool for putting money over love."

You were.

"She told me eighteen months was too long, and that I should quit filming and go back home. I couldn't stand it, the pain of knowing I'd made a fatal mistake, that I might've lost you for good, so I took a shot, and it dulled the ache. And then, I started pounding them. I got obliterated. And somehow, during that night, I had sex with her."

Hearing it was like a fist punch to the heart. "That's my point. You had a girlfriend eighteen months after we broke up."

"No. I never saw her again. I don't even remember hooking up with her."

It didn't relieve the ache, not one bit. Because he'd still touched another woman. He'd still made a baby with her. "Okay, but you didn't quit filming, and you didn't come back to me."

"Oh, but I planned on it. First, I had to finish out my contract. After that second film, I was going to quit and come home to you. In fact, my suitcase was packed, and I had my boarding ticket in my hand. I was walking out the door to head to the airport when I got a call from my agent. A man claimed his wife had slept with me and had my baby. They'd planned on raising the kid as their own, but since she died, he didn't want it."

"*It?* He didn't want *it?* That boy was his son."

"Believe me, I know. In any event, I had to stay and take the DNA test."

"Of course."

"And that's how I found out I had a son."

"You never saw her again after that night? She didn't come back to see you?"

"Never saw her again. Didn't know she was married." He sighed. "Barely remember the night."

"Well, I don't know what to say." He'd altered their history, and it was disorienting. Because one slight shift readjusted the entire picture. One tug unraveled a fabric of emotions she'd stitched together over three decades.

He must've seen it in her eyes because he grew excited. "We have so much more to talk about. I know you're busy, but what about tonight? After dinner? Can we sit down and talk?"

"I just don't see the point. Trevor, stirring up all these memories—"

"But they're not memories. We're clearing up the stories we've told ourselves to make sense of things. Now, we can get to the truth."

"Okay, but then what?" she asked. "You're still getting married."

"Elz." The pleading in his eyes confused her. He had something he wanted to say.

What? What is he not telling me?

"I don't want to talk about Darby right now." He said it urgently, like he was dodging something. Sidestepping. "We need to stay focused on us."

"There is no us. And as long as you're still engaged, I'm not comfortable talking to you."

He was hiding something from her, and she didn't like it.

She didn't like any of this. Because being this close to him stirred up memories and feelings. She was susceptible to him in a way she couldn't explain.

Trevor was compelling. He was *exciting*. Reckless and impulsive. He got a call from his agent, and he walked out the door. And right then, after bumping into her in Iceland, he declared she'd never left his heart.

He got so carried away he forgot all about his fiancée.

Joel would never do that. He'd remained on such good terms with his ex-wife that he was staying with her for Christmas, just to take care of their adult child.

Joel's a good, steady man.

I'm in a good place. I like my life.

And I'm not going down this road with Trevor Montgomery again.

She put her mask of professionalism back on. "I'm glad we cleared the air, but I have to make some calls."

"Elzy, don't go. Just wait. Talk to me."

And that was it right there, wasn't it? All the years of pining for this man, and for what? "Sorry. I don't wait for people anymore."

Chapter Eight

TREVOR CAME BACK FROM A WALK ALONG THE BEACH. He was cold, damp, and frustrated. And somehow, he'd managed to push Elzy even further away.

As he entered the suite, he found Darby facing the mirror, slicking on her lip gloss. She looked like she was attending a premiere.

"We're just going to tastings, right? Am I missing something?" The warmth in the room loosened his joints.

"Yes, but these are two of the fanciest restaurants in Reykjavik." She eyed his sandy boots, jeans, and parka. "Hurry up and get into your kilt." She popped the lid back on the tube.

Hell no. Dressing in costume would only remind Elzy of the reason he'd left her. "Not necessary. We're eating in the kitchen."

She lowered her arm. "That's what you talked to her about? *Business?*"

"No." He lifted his phone. "Chris sent a group text." He sat on a chair and untied his boots. "Our conversation lasted all of fifteen minutes. I brought up my son, but that was it. She didn't want to talk about anything else."

"Why not?"

"Because I'm engaged. She thinks it's shitty of me to be alone with her behind your back." At least he'd gotten to tell her how Cole was conceived.

Fuck.

All this time, she thought I'd fallen for someone eighteen months after leaving her.

He couldn't stand it.

I've never loved anyone but her.

"I love that she's a girl's girl, but yeah, it's a problem. What should we do?"

Good question. After pulling off his socks, he unbuttoned and unzipped his jeans. "If I tell her the truth, I'll have to leave, and I'm not willing to do that." But he had to stop coming on so strong. "I need to back off. Just hang out with her and be friendly."

"You don't have much time."

"Believe me, I know." He remembered the heat, though—the longing—in Elzy's eyes. The way sparks danced on his skin when he'd moved closer to her. "It's there. The chemistry. Attraction. Whatever you want to call it. It's still there. And if I can just hang out with her like a friend, I think, eventually, she'll let down her guard. I think…" *It'll all come rushing back.* "I don't think there's any other way to approach this."

"Oh, I can think of another way."

"Yeah?"

"Nothing works faster than jealousy. Say the word, and I'll be the best fiancée you've ever seen."

"Absolutely not." He cast her a warning look. "Don't stir the pot, Darby."

She grinned. "Where's the fun in that?"

He knew she was teasing, but he wasn't in the mood. He didn't think he could explain the urgency in him. He would not fuck up his chance to win her back.

Her phone buzzed, and she glanced down. "Oh." Her eyes widened. "That's Emil. He wants to have coffee with me." Her fingers shook as she typed a response. "I can't believe it."

"You haven't talked to him in all this time?"

"Not once. Every time I come home I find myself looking for him. I see a car drive by, and my heart jumps into my throat because I think, *That's him. That's Emil.* But it never is." She dropped the lipstick into her black leather purse. "I thought I was ready to see him. It's been long enough, and my life is so good that I convinced myself I didn't care anymore."

That was not the case for him. He'd never stopped loving Elzy. Wanting her. Missing her.

For years, he couldn't understand the loneliness that plagued him. He was on a set with dozens of people, living in a friendly, welcoming town. He had his son, a daughter-in-law, and grandkids. What was wrong with him?

But now that he was back in the same room with her, it was clear the sense of emptiness came from missing the other half of his soul.

"Well, it's not like I've spent the last twenty-six years and five months hoping we'd get back together." She laughed, and he knew it was because she could recite the exact date they'd broken up.

But it wasn't funny. Because he *had* spent the last thirty years and seven months missing Elzy so ferociously that vivid dreams about her regularly woke him at night.

Darby's smile faded. "But having him appear out of the blue like that…being so totally unprepared…"

"You didn't know he was a landscaper?"

"I did. But the wedding was the only thing on my mind. I was thinking caterers, contractors, painters… And most of that crew is my family. It never occurred to me that my brother would be interviewing landscapers when he only hired the designer a day ago."

He pulled a dress shirt from the closet. "How long were you together?"

"Oh, you don't want to hear the whole story." She batted her hand. "It's not a good one."

"Up to you." He chose a pair of black slacks. "But if you want to talk about it, I'm right here." Anxiety had him fumbling, and the pants slid off the hanger.

Damnit. It sucked knowing Elzy was a few rooms down the hall, and he couldn't be with her.

The fear he'd never get a chance to talk to her was suffocating.

"He grew up east of here in a place called Hofn. It's a seaside town, and his parents owned a gift shop. They didn't have much money, and Emil had a big appetite."

"Are you saying they couldn't pay for his food?" he asked.

She laughed. "No, I meant an appetite for learning, for experiencing things…" She caught his gaze. "For sex. And his little town wasn't enough, so when he was sixteen, he spent the summer in Reykjavik. My mom's retired now, but she used to own a little café where I worked every holiday. Emil got a job there too, and we started dating. The connection was…" She shivered. "So much passion." Her eyes clouded, and her features pinched with pain. "So much love."

"What happened?"

"Oh, you know. Teenage drama. We fought all the time. He went back to Hofn for the school year, and it was hard to communicate. Back then, we didn't have cell phones, and the whole family shared a computer. One time, he'd grown distant, and I was convinced he was sleeping with another girl, so I stole my mom's car and drove out there to surprise him." She had a wistful expression. "Turns out, he was working extra jobs so he could buy a car to come see me more regularly."

"What made you finally break up?"

"It's so embarrassing." She opened a travel jewelry box and pulled out earrings. "We'd come up with this idea of slow traveling the world. We'd live off whatever we could earn from odd jobs here and there. His parents didn't think it was a great idea, but they knew he had to figure it out on his own. My parents wanted me on the college track. They made me apply to all the top schools in England, France, and America. I did it to keep them off my back, but I had no intention of going."

He sat on the bed to put on his socks and black leather dress shoes.

"Anyhow, the summer after high school, when we were earning money for our trip, he told me he couldn't go." She tipped her head to put on a diamond stud. "Keep in mind, I'd turned down all the universities that had accepted me, so this was really upsetting news. But his dad had a heart attack, and he had to go back home. I figured he'd help out at the store, and then come back, and we'd be off on our adventure. But he didn't come back."

"Was his dad okay?" He tied the laces.

"Yeah, he was fine, but Emil decided, just in case something *did* happen, he couldn't be thousands of miles away and leave his mom alone. And I guess… I don't know. Something just felt fishy about the whole story."

"Maybe there was more to his dad's diagnosis. Some people are private about medical things."

"Where were you twenty-six years ago?" She laughed. "Not that my teenage self would've listened. Oh, no. That girl had her mom drive her out to visit him. And I was about to go into the store when I saw him talking to the same 'friend' I thought he was sleeping with. She was pregnant." Her fingers fisted in her sweater. "I stood there watching them—I mean, they didn't touch or anything. He was just so…concerned about her. So *invested.* I don't know. Anyhow, my mom dragged me back to the car, drove me home, and got me out of the country a few days later. Turns out, my parents had paid the deposit on three of the schools —one in New York, one in Los Angeles, and one in—"

"North Carolina."

She smiled. "Exactly. So, I left and never looked back."

Finished dressing, he got up, grabbed his wallet and room key from the dresser, and slid them into his pocket. "Ready to go?"

She nodded, and they headed to the door.

"Neither of you reached out over the years?" he asked.

"He sent two letters. The first one said it wasn't his story to tell, but that he wasn't the father, and he'd never slept with anyone but me. The second basically told me to go fuck myself."

He closed the door behind them. "That was harsh." He couldn't help checking the hallway for Elzy and went hyperalert for sounds as they passed her room. "Did he actually say that?"

"No. He said he was sorry for putting that girl's secrets over our relationship, that he regretted it, and that if I gave him a chance, he'd make it up to me. But then, he ended it with, 'And I'll work on trying to forgive you for bailing on me without even a conversation.'"

"Ouch." Though he had to respect the guy's stance.

"Yeah."

"You didn't respond?" he asked.

"No, because nothing had changed. He still couldn't leave Hofn. What kind of life would that have been for me?"

A beautiful one. A perfect one.

Elzy had once told him the film wasn't their only hope for making money. That they could create a business together. At the time, he didn't have her vision, so he'd signed the contract without talking to her.

Once he'd figured it out, he'd have done anything to go back to that motel room and reject the offer. By that point, of course, he'd found out about Cole, and it was too late.

As they neared the meeting point, his pulse pounded. Was Elzy there? He quickened his pace. "But you thought about him over the years?" He rounded the corner to find the lobby empty.

Fuck.

All right. It's fine.

It's not like she left town.

You're going to see her.

"Well, I have this neat party trick. When I have a negative feeling—anger, hurt, whatever—I immediately drown it with a justification. So, every time I thought about Emil, I'd tell myself our relationship was too dramatic, that we'd have been miserable together, or that it was impossible since neither of us could compromise." She shrugged. "It's my superpower."

"And now?"

"And now… I wonder what my life would've been like if I'd answered his letter. If I hadn't been so prideful."

"So, you'll go to coffee, and you'll talk to him."

"I'm never moving back here. And who knows if we'd even still get along. We were kids."

"Darby. Talk to him."

Her gaze wandered, unseeing, across the empty lobby, and then, she gave a nod. "Maybe. I'll think about it."

"Where is everyone?" It was a two-hour drive into the city. He wanted to be sure he sat next to Elzy. His blood went hot just thinking about being near her.

She pulled her phone out of her clutch. "Let me check the group chat."

One of the things he missed most—that he'd never had with anyone else—was the way the world disappeared when he was with Elzy. When their bodies were pressed together, when her scent filled his senses, and he was wholly consumed by her. By *them.* That was peace. That was when he felt his best self. Complete.

Happy.

And without it, he was just wandering the earth.

It sounded dramatic, but it was true. He didn't feel connected to anything, didn't have a passion for anything.

But Elzy.

"They left." Darby sounded surprised.

"What do you mean? They said we're leaving at noon."

"Jessica wanted to hit some shops in town, so they went early."

"And they didn't tell us?" Of course not.

She wants to leave me behind.

She didn't know what it did to him, how it drove him back to the worst time in his life. That first time he'd gone home, so sure he'd get to see her, talk to her, *explain.* But she'd hidden from him. It was like racing through a maze that had no exit. His frustration had blown up into a wild, panicked desperation as he looked for her everywhere but never once found her.

Well, fuck that. She's not putting me through that shit again.

"How're we going to get there?" he asked.

"How are you with driving a stick?"

"I'm a farm boy. I can drive anything. Let's go."

You want to play, Elz?

Game on.

She was not going to make this easy.

Trevor sat across from Elzy at a small table in the corner of a busy kitchen. She seemed determined to treat him like a stranger.

Fine. But her indifference didn't match the fire in her eyes when they'd talked privately.

So, which is it, Elz? Is the love dead and gone, or is there hope for us?

A server approached the table with a white porcelain pitcher, leaning over Trevor to pour soup into a bowl. "This is a cold tomato consommé."

Elzy's hand shot out to stop him. "No. No tomato for him." She went right back to her conversation with the chef as though she hadn't just defended him from the dreaded fruit like she would've done when they were teenagers.

And that was his answer. Her instinct to protect him was all the confirmation he needed. The connection was still there. It wasn't one-sided. All he had to do was calm down. Stop trying so hard. Give her the time and space to let down her guard.

"Are you allergic?" Darby asked.

The comment snagged Elzy's attention.

"No, I just can't stand them." Even the smell made his stomach tighten and his throat close.

"What about tomato sauce?" Darby asked. "Wait a minute. When we had that pizza party in Marco's trailer, I noticed you didn't eat anything. What's up with that?"

"Let's just say I've had my fill of them." When he cut Elzy a look, he saw a ghost of a smile crossing her face. "But please enjoy the consommé."

"Cooked, raw?" Darby asked. "Or just tomatoes in general?"

"Oh, this smells so good." Elzy watched a different server approach with a tray of small plates.

He appreciated her attempt to distract Darby, but it didn't work. "Just tell me. What's the deal with tomatoes?" she asked.

He'd never told stories about his life because he didn't want to shine a spotlight on his parents or anyone from his community. They were good people, and they didn't need media and fans descending on him.

His parents might be gone now, but he'd still preserve their integrity. "My mom had a garden, and in lean times, we'd eat whatever she'd grown that season."

"The infamous tomato season," Elzy said.

Everyone smiled, and he nodded. They seemed appeased, and conversation resumed. He gave Elzy a subtle nod of thanks.

But his mind kept replaying the way her hand shot out to cover his bowl. Because she'd always looked out for him. And he'd needed it. His parents were good, hardworking people, but the farm took up all their time and energy. In bad times, when weather or disease got the crops, food was scarce.

One summer, they lived off two ingredients: tomatoes and bread. His mom tried hard to be inventive. Tomato soup, tomato pie, tomato salad…marinated, baked, broiled… Everything she could think of to make it palatable.

By July, he was so sick of it, he couldn't even come to the table for dinner.

And what did Elzy do? She'd ride her bike over to his house with a sandwich. She'd pack a slice of pie into her lunch bag. Every time he'd come to visit, she'd have cookies for him, still warm from the oven.

She'd looked out for him—and what had he done with her love? Her devotion? He'd cast it aside for some ingrained sense of duty.

Only when Darby tapped his thigh and asked, "What's yours?" did he realize how lost he'd gotten in memories.

He had no idea what they were talking about, so he was grateful when Elzy stepped in. "I'll tell you mine. As a college graduation present, I took my sisters to Italy. We had the best time. All the pasta and gelato. Yummy. But then, we went to a little town called Siena, and we found a restaurant on this narrow, cobblestone street. It was the most perfect meal I've ever had."

"Do you remember what it was?" Trevor asked because he wished he'd been with her. He wanted to merge their memories, experience hers as if they were his own.

He'd missed out on so much.

Fierce determination gripped him. Because while he couldn't get that time back, he could make sure he didn't miss one more second with her.

"You bet I do. I had the lightest, freshest gnudi with the most delicious sauce to ever get in my mouth. It was so good we splurged on dessert, and it was hands-down the best tiramisu I've ever had in my life. I remember every detail to this day."

He wanted to share that taste memory with her. Wanted to stroll down the cobblestone street with her, hand in hand. "My best meal ever was when I was fifteen."

Elzy tensed. Her gaze sharpened.

"Fifteen?" Darby laughed. "Let me guess. It was a burger at Hooters."

"Nope. As we headed into the fall harvest, I had to miss a couple of football games, and my coach kicked me off the team." And that right there—the way their smiles faltered—

was why he didn't share stories from his past. Because they made people uncomfortable.

What they didn't understand was that his childhood had made him into the man he was today. It made him strong and relentless.

"But my best friend invited me over, and when I got to her house, she had a big family dinner for me." Even as kids, they understood their differences. Where Elzy needed to be quiet when she got upset, Trevor, as an only child of parents who constantly worked, needed to be surrounded by people who supported him.

"Her?" Darby asked. "Your best friend at fifteen was a girl?"

He nodded. "She made mac and cheese, burgers, chips and dip, and ice cream sundaes for dessert." He could still see the bright red maraschino cherry sitting on top of the pile of whipped cream. "Best dinner ever."

Elzy watched him, giving no clue what she was thinking. But through a tiny crack in her façade, he saw a glimmer of softness.

Hope roared through him. And there wasn't a damn thing he could do to contain it.

Because he saw it. The connection. It was still there.

It was just covered by a mound of hurt and anger that had hardened with every passing year.

That was on him.

So, he'd keep digging down to the heart of her. And he wouldn't give up.

He'd die trying.

"That's really nice." Darby gave him a warm smile. She rubbed his thigh.

And just like that, Elzy stiffened. She turned her attention to the servers. "Ah. Great. The next course."

Darby figured out her mistake and removed her hand, but it was too late.

The connection broke, and there was no restoring it.

Dammit.

Now, he had to wait for another opportunity. Preferably, time alone with her.

But the day after tomorrow, she'd leave for Snaefellsnes, and she didn't need him or Darby to accompany her.

He was running out of time.

Chapter Nine

After the third and final tasting, they stood outside the restaurant.

The night was over. They'd be in the car with two other passengers, so Trevor would have to wait until they got back to the hotel to talk to her.

While her brother handed the valet his ticket, Darby huddled up with him. "It's cold as balls out here. Why didn't you wear a coat?"

Because he'd been preoccupied. "I wasn't thinking." His breath left his mouth in cloudy bursts, and his fingers were stiff.

"I'm sorry about touching you during dinner," she said.

"I'm not sure it matters. As long as she thinks we're engaged, I don't have a chance with her."

"She's badass," Darby said.

Throughout the tastings, Elzy had ignored him, talking about her ideas for the resort and the stores they'd visited earlier in the afternoon. She'd gushed to the chefs about their food, the ambiance of their restaurants, and the kinds of events she thought would be great when they opened.

She was brilliant and animated, and she captivated everyone.

Sitting across from her, he'd basked in her warmth. She was the sun, and he'd happily orbit around her for the rest of his life. He didn't care what he did as long as he could be in her life.

"And pretty," Darby said.

"She's the most beautiful woman in the world." Even as he watched Elzy and Chris waiting for their car, he could feel Darby studying him.

"Okay." She pulled out her phone and muttered, "Don't mess this up." And then, she sucked in a dramatic breath. "Oh, my God."

Her brother called, "What's wrong?"

"It's Dad."

"What's Dad? What're you talking about?" Chris whipped out his phone.

Of course, Trevor stood close enough to see Darby's blank screen.

"He fell." To her credit, Darby delivered an Academy Award-winning performance. "They're on their way to the hospital."

"I didn't get a message." Chris joined them, features tight with concern.

Trevor didn't like the deception, but before he could say anything, the black Range Rover pulled to the curb.

"You guys," Darby said. "I'm so sorry to do this to you, but we have to go."

"Of course. Go take care of your dad." Elzy had her hand on Chris's arm. "Is there anything I can do?"

"I don't know." The man looked lost. "I don't even know what's going on."

The only reason Trevor didn't blurt out the truth right then and there was because he knew Darby would explain it to her brother the moment they got in the car.

As Chris got into the passenger seat, Elzy leaned in. "Text me if you need anything at all."

They both watched as Darby drove off, a white cloud of exhaust lingering in the frigid air.

"Do you think he's okay?" Elzy asked.

He said he wouldn't lie, so he had to come clean. "I'm sure he is."

"How do you know?"

"Because I saw the screen of her phone. She wasn't looking at her text messages."

"What're you saying? Why would she lie about something like that?"

When the Land Cruiser pulled up, he gestured to it. "Here's our ride. I'll explain everything on the way back."

But she was tapping away on her phone, an obvious ploy to keep from talking to him.

That's fine. He had two hours alone with her.

The valet came around the car, and Trevor handed him a good tip. "Merry Christmas."

The guy grinned. "Thanks, man."

Trevor held the passenger door open for Elzy. "Ready?"

She waved her phone. "Oh, that's all right. I'm going to stay in the city tonight. There are a few more stores I'd like to see. And you know, it's Christmas. It's pretty, and all the shops stay open late."

He sighed. *This woman.* She was stubborn, willful, and clever.

All good qualities when you're on her side. But when you're not, she's one formidable opponent.

Well, if she thought he'd give up, she was wrong.

Twinkling white lights wrapped around streetlamps, and festive garlands draped across crosswalks. In the courtyard of a city church, a Christmas tree was all lit up, its branches heavy with ornaments. "That sounds like a good idea. There better be a store that sells coats because I think my organs have frozen solid."

There it was. That break in her composure. Just the hint of a smile.

If he was lucky, there wasn't a hotel or B&B with a room in the entire city. "Might be hard to book a hotel though." He gestured to the pedestrian traffic. "Seems like a popular time of year to come to Iceland."

"No, I got one." She waved her phone. "I'm good."

"Cool." He caught his spirits before they crashed. Because he'd just turn this into an opportunity to hang out with her. "I'll walk with you."

"Trevor—" But her jaw snapped shut, and she pocketed her phone. "You really don't have to do that." Abruptly, she walked off.

He loved her fiery nature and couldn't help wondering what it would take to steer hate to love. What were the magic words to clear anger and resentment? That would make her understand he was a kid who'd made bad choices but with the very best intentions? "Let me take care of the car." In the time it took to pay the valet to park it in the lot behind the restaurant, she'd gained some distance, forcing him to jog to catch up.

And no, it didn't warm him up. It made his throat sting and his eyeballs burn.

Jesus, it's cold.

In a silence that was anything but companionable, they made their way down the crowded street. As they passed restaurants, conversation hit them in bursts. Music from a second-story club filled the air.

"So, you're going to hire the Westman Island chef?" he asked.

"We haven't talked about it, but that will be my recommendation. Why? Is that the meal you liked the best?"

"No." He couldn't remember a single thing he'd eaten all day. "It was the only one you tasted, so I just assumed it would be your choice."

She smiled. "You always were too observant. Usually, I'm pretty good about moving food around my plate so it looks like I'm tasting everything equally, but I just couldn't eat that fermented skate."

"That was clear to me when you gagged."

"I did not…" She looked worried. "Was it that obvious? I only threw up a little in my mouth. Did everyone notice?"

He laughed. "Not at all. You kept the conversation going like nothing happened."

"The conversation was about the *uric acid* a skate secretes through its skin. They wanted me to eat *urine*. That's—"

"Piss. Yeah, not appetizing."

"I mean, my God. That smell. Did you notice it? What was it? Ammonia?"

"Yeah, it was pretty bad."

"You ate every bite," she said incredulously.

"What was I supposed to do?" He laughed, and it felt so good, like the bindings had broken free. "The chef was right there watching me chew. I thought I had to eat everything."

"Yeah, I know what you mean. You have to learn the tricks of moving your food around and making it look like you're taking equal bites of everything. But also, the older I get, I'm more like, 'Screw it. This is Chris's resort. He has to like the food.'" She gazed up at him with a smile, and she must've felt the same zap of electricity as he did because she quickly looked away.

But that was okay. That one single moment was enough. For now.

She stopped outside a store. "I'm just going to pop in here and grab some gifts for my family and staff. You might as well head back. It's a long drive. I'll be fine on my own."

She was cute when she was trying to get rid of him. "You know, I'd like to bring home some gifts too. I have four granddaughters."

He regretted the words the moment they left his mouth. The stark pain in her eyes nearly took him down. But he had to keep moving forward. He couldn't pretend his family didn't exist. So, he reached around her and opened the door. "Come on. Let's see what we can find."

Unfortunately, her stony look told him he'd lost whatever ground he'd gained. "Trevor, I don't want to be your friend. Do you understand that? I don't care that you were only twenty when you abandoned me. I don't care that you thought you were acting out of some misguided sense of purpose. You left me alone in Las Vegas, and you never looked back."

"Oh, trust me. I looked." He caught her arms and moved her out of the doorway. "I came back to town to apologize and win back my *wife*, but you refused to see me. My second attempt was cut short when I had to take a DNA test. And by the third time I came for you, you were married with a child. So, don't say I never looked back. I absolutely fucking did."

She reared back. "What are you talking about? I never married, and I don't have any kids."

Why was she saying this? He'd seen it firsthand. "You were working at a resort in Idaho, and I came to talk to you, but when I saw you carrying a child, I asked the girl at the desk if you were married, and she said you were."

"Well, I don't know who you talked to, but it wasn't true. And if I was carrying a child, it was probably for one of our guests."

"No, you had the baby in one of those slings." He motioned across his chest. "And a man came up and put his arm around you. I watched the whole thing. There's no way that man was a guest. And I saw the way you were rubbing the top of the baby's head. That kid was yours."

"Idaho?" She glanced at the street in contemplation. "That would've been seven years after Vegas."

The bright lights from the store exposed her rosy cheeks and red-tipped nose. Those lips that had given him so much pleasure looked ripe as fresh raspberries.

"Okay. That was Carly. My niece. There are six years between Amber's daughters."

Fuck. Fuck. Fuck. "The girl at the desk told me you were

married. You looked like a family." If only he'd gone over there and talked to her. If only he'd said hello.

"So, what, you came all the way to Idaho, saw me holding a baby, and gave up?"

"You'd moved on. You were happy, and I figured the best thing I could do was respect your new life."

"That girl you talked to probably got minimum wage to check guests in. I doubt she even heard your question." She drew in a breath. "Do you see how this trip down memory lane only makes things worse? I don't want to know that you tried to find me. I don't want to know how close we came to seeing each other. Because, ultimately, neither of us tried hard enough. And that's what matters. Go back to the hotel, Trevor. We've said all we need to say." She brushed past him and entered the store.

He followed. Of course he did. He didn't want to hurt her, but they had to talk it through. There was no other way to get back to each other but through the pain.

Because one thing was absolutely clear. The high color in her cheeks, the sparks in her eyes, and the emotion in her tone told him she cared. If she truly didn't give a shit about him, she'd be neutral. Flat.

Okay, but you have to calm down. Just be friendly.
Nothing more.

He entered the brightly lit store to find knit sweaters imprinted with the Icelandic flag, mugs and T-shirts with a Viking emblem, and tables stuffed with lava cheese and black volcanic salt. He joined Elzy in front of a bookcase crowded with slippers. They ranged in style from playful wool socks to high-end leather. He held up a pair for babies. "I'm going to get these."

"Oh? Are you and Darby expecting?" She had a cool tone, like she was pretending not to care.

He burst out laughing. "Nope. They're for my granddaughters. Cole, my son, adopted two little girls after his high school friend passed away. He married the co-guardian, and now, they have twins."

She studied him for a moment, and he must've passed some kind of test because she let down her guard. "You'll need to know their shoe sizes. Those are for newborns." She picked up a pair of slipper socks with reindeer on top. "So cute." She grabbed four pairs. But her gaze kept wandering to the suede slippers.

He slid a hand into the thick, shearling footbed. "These are nice."

"I have a whole collection of slippers. I'm obsessed with them."

"Yeah?"

"I wear heels most days, so the only thing I can think about when I get home is getting into my slippers and sweatpants."

"Get them."

"Believe me, I don't need another pair." When she moved on to a table of skincare products, he followed.

Other than the words vegan, herbal, and volcanic, he barely noticed anything. *Because this is Elzy.* And he was standing next to her in a store in Iceland.

It was surreal and, strangely, perfect.

For all the scents swirling around him, the only one that connected with his very core, that excited his molecules into a frenetic dance, was the one emanating from her. It was a mix of her shampoo, her rich perfume, and the essence of Jessica Elsworth.

My Elzy.

He wanted to wrap his arms around her and hold her close until their hearts beat in sync.

"My sisters will love this." She held up a basket of bath products.

Maybe he didn't deserve the privilege of asking about her life, but the only way to earn it was to be consistent. "How are they? Are they still in Riverton?"

Distracted from sniffing a bar of soap, she said, "Oh, no. They've all come to Calamity with me."

"No kidding? That's great." He got a strange pinch in his heart. Without his parents, he rarely returned to his hometown, so he'd lost that community. "You always understood your priorities."

She stopped sniffing to look at him. "Yes, I did."

Towering over her like this, seeing the indignance in her eyes, he wanted to cup her cheeks and tell her how pretty she looked, how she was always right about everything. Because it was clear—the barrier between past and present was as thin as a butterfly's wing.

At least in his mind. So, instead, he gave her a soft smile and said, "You always were smarter than me."

"Oh, I don't know about that." She reached for a bottle of lotion. "But somehow, I managed to convince my sisters, their husbands, and their kids to get into the hospitality industry. We're all co-owners of the resort."

"Your mom would be so proud of the way you've kept your family together."

She gazed up at him, and he saw the moment awareness

hit. Everything about her softened, and she broke into a radiant smile. "Thank you for saying that. You know, it's funny. In my mind, I did it because my dad died while my sisters were in college, and since I'd already moved away, they didn't have a home base anymore. My whole motivation for getting out from behind the reception desk was to give them a home for the holidays. But I don't think I realized until recently how much the loss of my mom impacted me."

"Sounds like you worked your ass off to get where you are today."

"I'm not going to lie. It wasn't easy. But isn't that true for all of us?"

It sure as hell was. For thirty years, he'd filmed in driving rain and blinding snow, he'd had to reshoot physically grueling scenes dozens of times, and he'd played therapist and negotiator to all the difficult personalities who made it so damn hard to get anything done. "How many nieces and nephews?"

"Six. Both my sisters have three kids." She sniffed a candle. "I love having all of them with me."

"And both husbands work at the resort?"

"Yes."

He noted the hesitation in her tone. "But?"

"I don't think Kelly's husband wants to be in Calamity. Well, maybe that's not the issue. He's a farmer, you know? He likes physical work. He likes to be outside."

"What's his role now?"

"He's our director of operations. Which is a big relief for me because I've always had that role."

"Ah, okay. So, a desk job. What if you made him a tour

guide? He could organize fly-fishing trips. Hiking. Heli-skiing. Things like that."

Holding a stick of incense, she gazed up at him. "We don't have a role like that." It only took a moment for her to flash him a dazzling smile. "But we should. That's a brilliant idea. It'd be great for us, and I know he'd love it." She took a moment to appraise him. "Thank you." Then, she moved on to a table of T-shirts. "Of course, that puts operations back on me."

"You can hire someone to do that."

"Well, that's not going to happen until we're in the black. Fingers crossed that'll happen sooner than later."

"How long've you been open?"

"Oh, we're brand-new. Not even a month. Our hard launch is New Year's Eve, and we're not sold out yet. So, that makes me nervous."

"Yeah, people have their traditions. It might take time, but eventually, through word of mouth, they'll choose your place."

She gave him a funny look.

"What?"

"Nothing. Just… That's exactly what I was thinking yesterday. Calamity has a lot of great events on New Year's Eve. Mine has to be so unique, so special, they'll be fighting to book a room."

"What's your plan?"

Excitement lit up her eyes. "It's a mix between a black-tie party and a polar plunge."

"I'm not seeing a connection between the two."

"Well, everyone shows up in tuxes and gowns for a fancy

dinner. Then, at eleven, they'll change into swimsuits and go into the lake."

"No wonder you haven't sold out. I've done a lot of crazy things in my life—"

"Like driving off-road and winding up in the mud flats?" It was barely noticeable, the way she leaned toward him like that.

But it stirred him down to his very soul. *Here she is.* All of her. Not the brittle, angry part—which he deserved—but the soft and warm parts. "Hey, I was a dumb kid. But yes, like that. Even I wouldn't do a polar plunge in the Teton mountains in winter."

And it felt fucking fantastic.

"Would you do it if the water was warmed by a natural hot spring?" She had a mischievous grin.

"Are you saying your resort has thermal features?"

"Yep. It took me years to convince the town to give me permits, but they did. And the springs flow into the lake, so the temperature's bearable. But after, we'll all sit in the specially designed hot tubs and watch our very own fireworks show."

"That's brilliant. Where can I buy tickets?"

"Oh, I'm sorry." She moved onto a table of glassware. "We have a very strict dress code."

"And what is that?" he asked, amused by the smile she was fighting.

"No kilts or combat boots."

He burst out laughing. "I deserve that, I know. But I hope you believe me when I say it's not my choice. I don't get off on people shoving a selfie stick between my legs."

"Then, why do you do it?"

He moved closer. "Can you keep a secret?"

"We don't exactly move in the same circles, but sure, your secret's safe with me."

"You know how we thought the producers were newbies and didn't know what they were doing? Turns out, they were extremely savvy."

"Just cheap."

He shrugged. "I think they were smart. They went with first-time actors who would take their offer, which meant they could put their money into production and marketing. But anyhow, as soon as the franchise took off, the media descended. None of us were prepared for it, and I had a son at that point, so they helped me broker a deal. In exchange for my privacy, I had to give the paparazzi something publishable."

"I get that, but what about all the random people who happen to catch you drunkenly making out with your co-star in a pub or leaving a married woman's home at four in the morning? You can't have deals with everyone."

What she really wanted to know was how debauched Hollywood had turned him, and he was glad for the opportunity. "You're right. And there's a foolproof solution for that."

She waited for his answer, working hard to conceal her interest.

"If you don't want to be caught doing bad things, don't do them."

"Oh, come on. You never did anything bad? In *thirty* years?" She wanted to believe him.

He heard it in her voice. "I never did anything that would embarrass my son or my parents." He hesitated on saying more but screw it. He was taking his shot with her. *Balls to the wall.* "And to be perfectly honest, I never wanted to give you a reason to turn me away."

"Why would you even think like that? We weren't in each other's worlds at all."

"I never gave up believing we'd find our way back to each other. It didn't seem possible that I'd never see you again."

She studied him for a moment. "You must've had a lot of temptations over the years."

Good. Push me for answers. Because I'm ready. "I think we're born with a bent, you know? You've either got a kink or addiction, or you don't."

"And you don't?"

"I've got a bent for you." He said it matter-of-factly. "None of those temptations, as you call them, really interested me."

"Okay, you're being ridiculous. In all this time, you've never had a passionate fling or a wild hookup? You've never gotten blind drunk?"

"Did you hear my story about how I came to have a son? Trust me, that was my one and only hookup, and I haven't been drunk since." But he'd said enough, and it was time to go back to the plan of being friendly and not pushing. So, he picked up a mug with a Viking design and wooden handle and pretended to consider it. "Your event sounds great."

She seemed lost in thought and didn't move for a moment. But then, she said, "Yeah, I'm looking forward to it. Even better, my oldest niece is getting married on Christmas Eve."

"That's a strange choice. Won't their anniversary take second place to a big holiday?"

"We tried to warn them, but they met at a Christmas Eve party, so it means a lot to them. They were on the same team for a gingerbread house competition and spent the whole night talking and drinking cocoa, so the table decorations are—"

"Gingerbread houses?"

"You got it. And we've got an elaborate hot chocolate station, so yeah. It's really sweet. Also, they jokingly like to say it's a date they know they'll remember."

"I get that. My parents never remembered their anniversary."

"Well, no. They probably did. They just didn't believe in celebrating themselves."

A prick of awareness sent a shot of adrenaline through him. Funny how he'd never seen it like that before, and yet, it was so obvious.

"You look like I just rocked your world. You were the one who complained they had no joy."

"Yeah." He clamped a hand at the back of his neck. "But I never thought about it like *that*." *How fucking sad.* "You know, I don't have a single memory of them laughing."

"Or celebrating you. Your mom would bake cakes for the farmhand's kids, but she never once threw you a birthday party."

Sometimes, she'd make him a special dinner. A chicken casserole and lemon meringue pie. But no parties. Not even for graduation. "But you did. You celebrated all my victories."

"Well, sure. I felt sorry for you." She flashed him a

teasing look before picking up a travel mug. "Oh, look. Puffins. How cute is that?"

"Hey, now. No need for pity. I got my mom's special chicken casserole."

He could see her try to fight it, but the laugh broke free. "I loved your mom. I really did. But she was the worst cook." She held his gaze with true compassion. "I'm sorry for your loss. Losing them so close together had to have hit hard."

"Couldn't have been more fitting for them though, right?" His dad died of a heart attack, sitting in his tractor, alone in a field, and eating a ham sandwich. His mom passed away less than a month later. She just didn't wake up one morning.

It was unbearably sad.

Elzy's arms were loaded with gifts, so he jerked a thumb over his shoulder. "Let me grab you a basket." He moved quickly, lowering his head to keep from being noticed. He'd expected to spend his time in cars and kitchens, so he hadn't bothered with a disguise.

He didn't see any baskets by the entrance, so he bought several large recyclable totes and a wool beanie. Bumping into Trevor Montgomery in a tourist shop in Iceland was out of context, so he wouldn't need more than a hat.

After pulling it down over his ears, he held a tote open for her and jammed the others under his arm. "Here."

"Perfect. Thank you." She dropped her items into it but kept her gaze on him. "You're hilarious if you think no one will notice you in that hat. You're a movie star with one of the most recognizable faces in the world. There's no disguising it."

"I've been retired three years."

"Okay." She rolled her eyes. "Stay humble."

"What? I'm in Iceland. No one would expect to see me here."

"Are we really going to do this?" She gave an exaggerated sigh.

"Do what?"

"You're an unusually handsome man. Even if you didn't star in the *Clan Wars* franchise, people would still notice you."

He broke into a grin. "You think I'm handsome?"

"Says the guy who was chosen Sexiest Man Alive a record-breaking three times."

Without thinking, he wrapped an arm around her and pulled her close. "You counted. I'm touched."

Laughing, she shoved him away. "Yes, because those were the only times I've ever had to abandon my cart to go throw up in the parking lot. They really shouldn't put magazines at checkout counters."

"But you bought them, right? Now, if I look under your pillow, which one will I see? The one with me shirtless in a kilt? That one shows my rippling muscles."

"Did I call you humble?" She shook her head. "What I meant was egomaniac." She dropped four insulated tumblers into the now-full tote bag. "These are perfect for my nieces."

"Here. I've got another one." He handed it over.

"Oh, thank you." At the next table, she picked up a box of crackers and read the ingredients. She stared long enough that he figured she wasn't really paying attention to the list.

And then, she looked up at him. "I'm sorry I didn't go to their funerals."

He wasn't prepared for the intimacy of direct eye contact, and heat exploded in his chest. "That's okay."

"I was still in my petty phase. It took me a while to get over the fact that you had a son."

"I don't blame you. That would've destroyed me."

"It almost did." She set the box down and picked up a saltshaker. "Are you sadder that your parents died alone or that you weren't closer to them?"

He let out a bitter laugh. "No one's ever asked me a question like that." Someone bumped into him, so he moved closer to the table. "I hate that they died alone, but you know, that's the life they chose. As for not being closer to them…" Years of training had him crafting an acceptable answer, but it was Elzy, and he didn't need to do that with her. "They wouldn't let me be close to them. I took care of them as best I could…" He shrugged.

"You paid off their farm, and they still continued to work."

"Yep. They were set for life, and other than buying a new couch and some farm equipment, their lives didn't change. That was a real wake-up call for me. So, yeah, I made peace with my relationship with them."

"Do you miss them?" She asked it casually as she picked up a box of cookie mix with a mini whisk attached.

He doubted she was in the market for any of it, but if this was the only way she could talk to him, he'd take it. "I wish I could say I did." He had to speak truthfully. "But I don't." His relationship with them was centered on duty and obligation. "There was no affection in my house."

"No, there wasn't."

But I got it from you.

All those mornings when she'd slip a note into his hand on their way to homeroom. The Saturdays when he'd back his pickup to the loading dock, grab her hand, and tug her into the storeroom so they could make out. She breathed life into him. She was his happiness. His home.

His entire heart.

She returned to a display of bath products. "I'm going to get two of these. My sisters will like it."

"Your sisters or you?"

"Yeah, you're right." She unscrewed the lotion and sniffed. Pleasure suffused her features, but she tightened the cap and set it back. "Scent is so personal. Who knows if they'd like it?" She looked into the bag. "But I do need a few more things for them. I'll keep looking. You can go if you want. It's a long drive back."

"That's okay." He pulled a third tote out of his back pocket and snapped it open with a flourish. "I'm getting gifts too, remember?"

She shook her head with a smile. "Tenacious."

I just want you so damn much.

But instead of responding, he returned to the glassware table and grabbed a couple travel mugs with puffins on them. "The older two grandkids will like these. I'll get slippers for all the girls." He headed back to the bookcase display.

"Size, remember?" Elzy called with a laugh in her voice.

"Yep." But he wasn't there for the kids. He was there for the shearling slippers. Did women's feet change in size? Because she used to wear a seven. *That's what I'll get.*

On his way back to her, he watched her touch and scrutinize every single item, taking such care with each purchase. And that was one of the things he'd loved about her. She remembered what you said, what food you liked, what colors you favored. She gave a hundred percent to the people she cared about.

But who made her feel special? The moment she moved past the bath products, he grabbed the basket she'd liked. And actually, why not get the same scent in a candle? Before she could find out what he'd done, he quickly headed to the cash register. He snatched a wool scarf off a table and included it in his purchases. He'd make sure no one recognized him tonight.

He wouldn't let anything pop this bubble with Elzy.

When they headed back out into the icy cold night, he tried to take the heavy bag from her.

But she resisted. "You have enough of your own stuff to carry. I got it."

"You'll need your hands free for the other shops." He paused outside a boutique. "Like this one."

She took in the window display. "You're not wrong." Laughing, she shoved the tote at him and headed inside.

Right away, she went to town, buying T-shirts and sweaters. "Oh, my God. Look at these." She stood before a wall of slipper socks with puffins, reindeer, Vikings, snowmen...all kinds of winter and Icelandic designs. "They're one-size-fits-all, so I'll buy a pair for my entire staff."

As she went to the desk to arrange the purchase and shipping of the gifts, he found a few more things he thought she might like. At the counter, he showed her a knit hat with a white puff ball on top and a braid hanging down on either side. "This would be cute on the girls."

"It's adorable. They'll love it."

"Don't you need a hat?" He set it on her head and gently tugged the braids until it fit her head. "Oh yeah. That's the one."

Her grin was pure light, piercing the darkest parts of him and warming him to the soles of his feet.

Until she yanked it off. "Oh, I don't need one. But you should definitely get it for your granddaughters."

He did, but he also bought one for her.

As they continued down the street, he noticed the streetlamps were decorated with old-fashioned candleholders. Most of the stores on this street were for tourists and sold similar items, so they didn't need to go inside.

But when they passed a jewelry store, something caught her eye. "Look at that."

He pressed closer to the window to see bold, heavy pieces. "You like them?"

"I think Chris would, don't you? They're made of black lava. What a cool present for a man living on a lava field." She headed inside, flagged down a salesperson, and got into a conversation about the Nordic symbols on the sturdy silver jewelry.

As he wandered around, a case of diamond rings caught his eye. They'd married on an impulse, so they'd never exchanged real wedding rings. He didn't know her taste anymore, and it certainly wasn't his place to buy her jewelry.

And yet...he carried two large tote bags filled with silly stuff. Nothing real. Nothing meaningful. And she'd just spent the last hour thinking of everyone but herself.

He shouldn't do it. He knew that, but while she was

preoccupied with buying something for her client, he found another salesperson to help him.

Because he'd found the ring. The only one in the world Elzy should wear on her finger.

"Can I see that one?" he asked.

"Way to pick the nicest ring in the store." She pulled out her keys and unlocked the case, setting the stunning diamond on a velvet pad. "It's actually three rings." She showed him each band separately.

He held them in the palm of his hand. "I've never seen anything like it."

"That's because each piece here is one-of-a-kind."

"Like her."

The woman smiled. "Yes, that's the idea."

In the center, the beveled oval diamond glittered. The three diamonds in the top ring formed a crest. Altogether, it was designed for a queen. "I'll take it."

"Don't you want to check the certification? This totals five carats of diamonds."

"I don't care." If the stones were shitty, he'd replace them. But he'd never find a band so intricately carved. The rose gold was unusually pink and shiny. It was undoubtedly made for Elzy.

"Okay. And what about you? Do you have your wedding band picked out?" She reached for a display at the other end of the case.

He cut a look over his shoulder to make sure Elzy wasn't listening. It was more than presumptuous of him to buy rings for an event that might never happen.

She'd given no indication of any interest in even talking to him, let alone sparking a relationship.

And yet, he was driven. Because a world where they weren't together didn't make sense. If they didn't get back, it would not be because of him.

When she set the rings down, his eye was immediately drawn to a dark band.

"What's this one made of?"

"Oh, good. That's the one I was thinking about for you. This is sandblasted palladium, and the inlay is genuine Gibeon meteorite."

He grinned. "I'll take it."

"You'll need to try them on."

Elzy was wrapping up her purchase. He didn't have time. "They can be sized, right?"

"Of course." Shaking her head, she laughed. "You're the easiest customer I've ever had." She glanced at Elzy. "I've been doing this a very long time, and I know you've made the right choices. If you give me your credit card, I'll get everything handled in the back room, and she won't notice a thing."

"Perfect." Was it presumptuous? Hell, yeah. But he'd never find anything better. He was sure of it.

Once outside, she said, "Did I see you buying something?"

He wouldn't lie but hoped she didn't ask for specifics. "Yep."

"I noticed Darby's not wearing an engagement ring. Did you get her something?"

His heart galloped. As much as he wanted to tell her the truth, it was only thirty minutes ago that she'd told him to go back to the hotel.

But he could lead her to some insights. "We got engaged

the day before yesterday, and it was a spur-of-the-moment thing."

"That seems like the most romantic way to do it." She used her professional voice. "When you're overcome with feelings."

Ha. If by feelings *you mean loneliness and a lack of purpose, then, sure.* He was overcome. "We were saying goodbye at the airport. She was at the international gate, and I was headed back to Calamity."

"And you couldn't bear to be apart from her, so you proposed?"

She was probing, and he was here for it. "Well, like I said, we'd only known each other a month. You'd have to ask her what went through her mind."

"She proposed to you?"

He nodded. "It was either that or never see each other again." As they passed a restaurant, he inhaled the scent of roasted meat. "Hungry?"

Her features softened, and the tight lines at either side of her mouth slackened. "I'm starving."

Chapter Ten

WAIT, DARBY PROPOSED?

Jessica stared at the menu, seeing nothing but a sea of letters.

Now that she thought about it, Trevor hadn't touched his fiancée. Not once. He'd shown concern, sure, but never affection. In fact, he treated her like a friend.

Is Darby his Joel?

The thought sped through her like a bullet, shock waves splintering every molecule in her body.

Because it opened the door to possibility, and that was as terrifying as it was exhilarating.

The past two days with Trevor only confirmed the obvious. She and Joel didn't have chemistry. She liked him. Joel was a good, decent man, but he didn't provoke her, challenge her, excite her… His touch didn't set her on fire.

He wasn't Trevor.

Damn, if he hadn't shut her out of his holiday trip, if she hadn't had this distance, she might not have seen the weak foundation of their relationship. How many times had she reminded herself to call or text her fiancé? And still, she hadn't done it. Neither had he. She could chalk it up to them both being busy, but the truth was...she didn't miss him.

Of course, she was preoccupied with Trevor.

Even more so now that she understood his engagement wasn't a love match. She had no doubt about that.

"You know what you want?" Trevor's voice busted through her thoughts, returning her to the moment.

She tuned into the Christmas music and lively chatter and breathed in the smell of roasted meat and warm bread. "I have no idea." She scanned the menu. "What looks good to you?"

"I'm getting the sushi festival." He wore a beanie and scarf, thinking no one would recognize him.

And, sure, maybe they wouldn't know it was Trevor Montgomery, the movie star, but they'd still take a second look. They'd stare. Because he was dashing. Those blue eyes set against tan skin and dark hair, that expressive mouth...

God, the way he used to kiss her. From her earlobes down to the soles of her feet, those lips had traveled every inch of her.

Rattled at the direction of her thoughts, she said, "I'd expect nothing less." Which made no sense whatsoever.

"Oh yeah? How's that?" he asked with a lift of an eyebrow.

"You lead a glamorous life." She scrambled to force the words coming out of her mouth to make sense. "You go to galas, travel the world. Your life's one big festival." *You really need to stop talking.*

"I think, if you're only looking at photos of me at the Oscars and screenings, you could get that impression."

"But in reality?"

He nodded as if willing to give her a peek behind the curtain. "In reality, I spent thirty years away from my other half, and it was the loneliest goddamn experience you could ever imagine."

His fervent tone, the fire in his eyes, snatched her up in his thrall.

I can imagine it because I lived it.

Knowing he did, too… She wanted more.

She wanted this window into his soul.

"I spent twenty-eight years phoning it in with my son. My *child*. I'm trying to make it up to him, but without the foundation, it's hard. It sucks. I focused on things that didn't matter to me and lost the only things that do. And to be honest, I don't know how to fix anything. But I'll sure as fuck die trying."

Her heart pounded. Her palms went clammy. She loosened the scarf around her neck and pulled at the top of her sweater. She was listening with her whole body.

Because he wasn't the happy-go-lucky movie star who laughed when people looked up his skirt. He was a human being who suffered guilt and was tortured by his failures.

It was humanizing, and it was heartbreaking.

"What a waste of a life." He yanked off his beanie and scraped his fingers through his hair, scraping it back from his forehead. "Everyone else on the set loved making movies. For them, it was their passion. For me, it was a means to an end." He jammed the beanie back on. "I've only ever fit in one place, and I lost that. I lost *you*. And yes, you can say it was my choice, but I believed I was doing the right thing. So, fuck the money, fuck the glamour, fuck the magazine covers. None of it matters because I lost you." He shoved his chair back and got up so quickly the water glasses shook. "And the worst part is knowing it's entirely my fault." He balled up his napkin and tossed it on his chair. "Excuse me." He had to move around the server who'd just shown up to take their order.

"Uh, should I come back?" the young man asked in his distinctively Nordic accent.

Distracted, she forced a smile. "That might be best." Everything in her screamed to follow Trevor. Be with him. She got up. "Excuse me." She hurried across the crowded restaurant.

She'd gotten it all wrong, hadn't she? He really had missed her, longed for her, the way she'd done for him. Blood roared in her ears, and she found it hard to catch her breath.

He was hurting, and she had to get to him. She felt his pain as if it were her own.

She saw his form in the narrow, dark hallway. It was unmistakable. Those broad shoulders, that muscular frame.

And that was when self-preservation kicked in.

Because what did she think would happen when she caught up with him? Did she think she'd comfort him? Soothe him?

Kiss him?

No. No.

This is all wrong.

And what the hell are you doing spending an evening with him anyway? You should check into your hotel.

You're here for business. Chris is paying you to do a job.

Not to get closure with an ex.

In the dark hallway, she caught up with him. "Hey." Her smile felt rubbery, but she forced it to stay in place. "I just wanted to let you know that I, uh…" She jerked a thumb over her shoulder like a moron. "I'm going to head out. I'm pretty beat, so I'll just grab some room service. You know, take a hot bath. So, I'll just, uh, I'll see you tomorrow." With an awkward wave, she spun around.

But just as she took off, a big hand grabbed hold of her arm and pulled her back against a strong chest. Intense, dark eyes captured her. "What just happened?" Trevor asked.

"I just told you I need to check into my hotel."

"Okay, but in a weird voice."

"Oh, my robo voice?" She gave a weird laugh. "Yeah, my sister accuses me of that a lot. I think jet lag's really caught up with me. I'm going to go."

"You're running."

Oh, enough of this crap. Enough letting this man take control of her emotions. "Well, yes, Trevor, I am. And I'm sorry, but I've made it clear I don't want to do this with you. You don't understand how hard it is for me to hear you say you missed me, you were lonely without me… I don't know what to do with that. And it doesn't matter if you've known Darby a month or that she's the one who proposed. The fact remains, you're getting *married.*"

"There are things I need to explain later, okay? But for right now, can you please just forget her?"

"No." She wrenched her arm out of his grip. "Of course not. And it's not a good look that you can."

"Trust me when I tell you, Darby's okay with us talking. She understands." He was sending her an urgent message, and she was too riled up to receive it. "The only thing that matters right now is us, Elz." He jerked her closer to him. "You and me."

"Nothing makes sense to me, and I'm tired. I'm tired, and I want to go to the hotel and…and…process things. Okay? Just let me go."

"I can't do that. I can't let you go."

"We live in the same town. At some point, I'm sure we'll meet for coffee."

"I don't want coffee with you," he roared. He closed his eyes and let out a calming breath, but he didn't loosen his hold. "I've made a mess of things, and I'm trying very hard to fix them. I won't stop until I do."

Her hands closed around his wrists. His skin was hot, his muscles hard. "You can't fix this. Too much time has passed."

"Does it feel like that to you? Because it sure doesn't to me. Not at all. Swear to God, it feels like us. Like it always was. We are meant to be together."

"Really? Because in all this time, we never bothered to make our way back to each other. You left me to make money. And even after you reached your goal, you still made more movies. I mean, seriously, let's stop talking about fantasy and get to the bottom line. You made movies for *thirty years*, Trevor."

"I *was* the franchise. We had a massive cast and crew. We supported an entire town that grew and thrived. If I walked away, it would've all shut down."

"So, you carried the weight of that on your shoulders?" A memory flickered at the edges of her mind.

"It *was* on my shoulders. You probably didn't notice, but I only had a few scenes in the fifth movie. That's because I quit. The film flopped, the franchise was going to end, and that meant the cast and crew would be out of work. The townspeople would lose their livelihoods. They begged me to come back. Pleaded with me."

And then, the memory flared to life. "The list."

"What?"

"Nothing." Right before walking out the door, he'd shown her the list they'd put together in the diner. He'd said it was his motivation. He carried the weight of the world on his shoulders.

He always had.

"I know I sound full of myself. I know it sounds ridiculous, but the fact remained, they would've ended the franchise if I'd left."

"It doesn't sound ridiculous at all." He just didn't know how charming and open and friendly and appealing he was.

Of course he didn't. Because his parents were stingy with praise. With love. He wasn't allowed to be handsome or smart or anything frivolous. He had to be dutiful. His only value was helping. Fixing. Working.

She was beginning to understand him so much better. "What made you finally pull the plug?"

"My son. I saw the way he stepped up to take care of two little girls he didn't father, and I knew he was a better man than I could ever be. Of course, I couldn't just quit, so I suggested they do a next generation. I agreed to do small bits in the next two films, but other than that, I'm free."

So, this is why he's marrying a woman he met after knowing her for a month. "So, your parents dictated the first half of your life, and the filmmakers dictated the second?"

"Yeah, exactly. And that's done. The rest of my time on this earth is going to be about me doing what I want."

"Which is marrying Darby." She threw it out like an accusation.

"No. *No.*"

"Dammit, Trevor. Are you marrying her or not?"

"I got engaged two days ago."

"There you go again. Skirting around the truth. You want to clear the air on what happened in our past, but I can't do that when you're hiding something about your future."

"I understand that. I do." He lowered his gaze to the floor, one hand rubbing his jaw. Then, it swung back up, and he looked right into her eyes. "But for tonight, I'm asking you a favor. Can we just be two friends from Riverton who happened to meet in Iceland? I want to talk to you, catch up."

"I honestly don't know if I can do that."

Cupping her elbows, he bent his knees so she was eye level. "But will you try? Please? I have an Elzy-shaped hole in my heart, and I need to heal it. I need this. Don't you?"

Of course she did.

She wasn't even going to pretend otherwise.

The gastropub was packed and buzzing with conversation. A Christmas tree in the corner twinkled with multi-colored lights, and the servers wore red aprons and Santa hats.

They'd ordered six tasting dishes to share, and they'd been talking so much, they'd hardly eaten.

Jess reached for her wine glass and sipped the crisp Chardonnay. "You know what I can't figure out?"

"What?" He dipped the focaccia into the smoked bell pepper tartare.

"You hated reading in high school. How did you memorize whole scripts?"

"I didn't need to. Oh, come on. You know I didn't act. I shouted as I led soldiers into battle. I yelled a lot. You know what was required of me."

"You don't give yourself enough credit." It dawned on her that his success was the antithesis of his family's values. Because it put him in the spotlight. It enriched him—and only him. "Come on, I saw you angry, wounded, sad… You did a beautiful job. You even cried when your wife died."

"When all five of them died." He gave a wry smile. "We really needed new writers. They kept pulling the same emotional strings in every script."

"Well, it worked." She sliced into her hanger steak. "You know what I think?"

"I'd love to know what you think."

"You were raised by martyrs. So, of course, you never found your passion. You weren't allowed to do anything so self-indulgent."

"Oh, I found it all right. I just didn't keep it."

Me.

He means me.

And the more he said it, the easier it was to believe. "Because you were taught your needs came second to those who relied on you." When the full revelation hit, she sat back in her seat. "When you left me, you thought you had no choice but to take care of my family and your parents."

"Right. I told you that."

"No." She shook her head. "What I mean is, you weren't allowed to have the kind of happiness we had together. It made you feel like you were doing something wrong. You were supposed to put off personal happiness until everyone else in your life was settled. You parents raised you to believe your needs came last."

"I… Yes. You're right."

She'd skirted around it before, but she'd never seen it so clearly. "Trevor, your dad had money in the bank. He could've moved to Florida and fished for the rest of his life. Instead, he died alone in a tractor eating the same ham sandwich he'd eaten every day of his life for fifty years."

Trevor stopped chewing. He reached for his water glass.

"And you just told me you stayed in a career you never even wanted because you 'owed' it to the cast, crew, and townspeople." She reached across and squeezed his hand. "Your parents were wrong. You get to be happy. You get to be fulfilled." She drew in a breath before saying the one thing that might just kill her. But he needed to hear it. "And if Darby's your happiness, you have to grab it with all your might."

Frustration flashed in his eyes, and he pushed his plate away. "I think you're right." He shot her a look. "About my *parents*. I don't think I realized what a chokehold they had on me."

"Well, they're the ones who taught you how the world works. But they were wrong." The clarity gave her some peace. *It wasn't about me. It was the way he was programmed.*

"Your dad would be the guy on the plane who saves his wife and son and the people in the seats in front of him and next to him and behind him but dies because he never put on his own mask."

"He'd think he died a hero. But really, he died on his principles."

"Which didn't exactly keep him warm at night."

"No." Lifting his water glass, he motioned for the server. "My father was not a happy man."

"Remember that picture from the paper?" It was the Fourth of July, and everyone lined up on Federal Boulevard to watch the parade. As usual, a photograph hit the front page of the *Riverton Ranger*. Of course, his parents didn't waste time on frivolous events like that, so they hadn't attended.

"Oh yeah. Nothing sums up my dad better than that."

And then, one day, Trevor and Jessica were wrapping presents for a treasure hunt, using newspapers, and they spotted his dad in the shot. Everyone was smiling—parents standing behind strollers, grandparents waving flags, children eating ice cream cones—having a great time. And there was Mr. Montgomery, doing a chore in town, scowling, squinting, and looking miserable.

"I never wanted to be him." His eyes held deep sadness.

"Well, you're not. You went out and had an exciting, different life. It was nothing like his."

"You're looking at it from the outside. I'm talking about in here." He pressed a hand to his chest. "My life's been about duty and obligation." Flattening his palms on the table, he leaned forward. "I got it all wrong, but I hope you understand why. I didn't see a way out. I didn't see a way to get you that ranch in Calamity unless I took a big chance."

"Well, guess what, Trevor?" Her tone turned defiant. "I got it all on my own."

As they neared her hotel, the briny scent of the sea grew stronger. In the harbor, moonlight rocked on the water, and the masts and stays rose tall off sailboats. The hulking bodies of cruise ships lent a sense of foreboding.

It had been a good night. She not only understood him better, but they'd had fun together.

Which brought them to a scary place—were they looking for closure or opening the door to something more? And what if they didn't want the same thing?

When she got to her room, she'd call Amber. Try to unravel this messy heap of feelings.

"What's with all the shoes in the window?" He gestured to a store as they walked past.

She was glad for the reprieve. She needed to get out of her own head. "It's a cute tradition here. Each of the thirteen nights before Christmas, one of the Yule lads comes down from his cave in the mountains to bring little gifts to kids who leave shoes in their windows."

"That's right. I heard about that. And if they're bad, they might get a rotten potato."

"Ew." She laughed. "I didn't know about that part."

"I'll skip the potato, but I like the idea of my grandkids running downstairs to check the shoes and finding a little treat. I might do that."

"Grandkids." She was finding it easier to accept his family now. "It's hard to believe we're that old."

"Hey, I had Cole young. *Very* young. You have no idea how confusing it is to look in the mirror and see my dad's face when I feel the same now as I did in my twenties."

"Either you're completely clueless, or you're fishing for a compliment." She nudged him. "Because you look nothing like him." Mr. Montgomery lived his life outdoors in brutal sun and cold. He had leather skin and a solemn expression. "And I'm pretty sure last year's *Rolling Stone* article said you were more handsome at the end of the franchise than you were at the beginning. 'And that's saying something.'"

He grinned, but she could tell from the way he tipped his chin down that he was uncomfortable with the subject. "I was thinking the same about you."

"Well, I dye my hair." She self-consciously touched it. "I don't know how much gray I have."

"Now, who's fishing? Elz, you're gorgeous. Everywhere we go, heads turn."

"Yeah, that happens when you hang out with a movie star."

"Ha. Nope. They don't recognize me without my kilt."

Ahead of them, a large group gathered on the sidewalk. Coupled with the music pouring out of the building, she realized it was a club. They continued walking until they heard the familiar beat of "Whoomp! (There it is)."

Reflexively, they looked at each other and burst out laughing. Of course, it was a popular and recognizable party song, so it wasn't like it was some huge coincidence. But this was *their* song. They used to dance like fools every time it came on the radio. They'd roll down the windows in Trevor's truck and thrash around in their seats.

Sensory memories flooded in—the elation of being with him, her hair whipping around her face, arms pumping, hips twisting. She'd been totally uninhibited with him. She hadn't held back a single part of her.

Back then, she thought she'd had so many problems. She was filled with angst. Only now, looking back, could she see how wonderful their childhood had been.

Because they'd had each other.

He was the best first love she could've asked for. He'd been there for her when her mom died—and all the years after—when grief would rise up out of nowhere and flatten her like a bowling pin. He was there for her highs and lows, and he was the man determined to make her dreams come true.

And yes, he'd gone about it the wrong way, but maybe it was time to let go of the pain he hadn't meant to cause. "Trevor—" But when she looked over, he wasn't there.

She turned around to find him grooving to their song, and the sight of her ex-boyfriend— and current movie star —jumping and spinning, dropping low and popping up, first one arm then the other swooping, had warmth spreading through her. Because he wasn't the entitled celebrity she'd created in her mind. He was still the boy she'd once loved so completely.

A small crowd had gathered to watch him, and he caught her hand, tugging her close. Their gazes locked, and a well of emotion threatened to break free.

"Wait, is that—?" a woman began.

But before she could finish her sentence, Trevor wrapped

an arm around Jess's waist and swept her into the club. They left their bags and jackets at the coat check and then moved onto the dance floor.

It was dark, loud, and packed. Bodies were crammed together on the dance floor, going wild with the familiar song, while on stage, a band tuned their instruments.

But Jess was still humming, head spinning. Watching him dance to their song, feeling the heat of his body... *This isn't good for me.*

It's not going to end well.

The song cut off abruptly, and a man spoke into the microphone. "Welcome to the Whiskey Bar, ladies and gents. Tonight, we have a special treat for you. In from London, let's give a big welcome to One Bad Decision."

As the room erupted in applause, Trevor led her deeper into the crowd. When they settled, facing the stage, he stood behind her. They didn't touch, but he was close enough for her to know he was there. It felt...protective.

The band launched into their set. People started dancing, and servers pushed through, their trays held high. But she barely registered the music. Because after an evening together, something had shifted between her and Trevor. The change was undeniable.

A wall was torn down, defenses laid to rest.

Space had opened.

God, all these years, she'd carried a whole bushel of anger and pain, dragged it from one home to another. It weighed her down and left her struggling for breath.

She'd known about the deprivation and neglect of his childhood. Of course she had. She'd not only witnessed it, but she'd tried to compensate for it.

But she'd been an outsider looking in.

For him, it was a belief system wired into his very being. At the time, he couldn't have made any other choice.

He wanted to be with her more than anything, but he couldn't have her until he made sure everyone else was happy and settled.

Yeah, she got it now. She did.

He took a step closer, his hands lightly cupping her hips. "You want a drink?"

His deep, sexy voice in her ear sent a flash of heat across her body. With her defenses down, she was all soft and gooey inside. She wanted him to wrap his big, strong arms around her. She wanted to bury her face in his chest. She wanted… God, she wanted so much with him.

All she could do was shake her head.

The melody picked up, and more people swarmed the dance floor. The crowd pressed closer, forcing her to take a step back. She wound up flush against Trevor's hard, hot body.

A yearning crawled up from the depths and swamped her. She needed to be closer, but at the same time, she couldn't have that. Because…

Darby.

Remembering his fiancée doused her with cold water. "We should go." Her voice got lost under the crushing noise, but she didn't care. He'd either follow or he wouldn't. But she was going to the hotel. She'd gotten what she wanted, and spending more time with him was just going to hurt.

Aiming for the coat check, she threaded through the crowd, grabbed her belongings, and pushed through the doors. The abrupt shift from hot to cold shocked her body and cleared her mind.

"Hey." He caught up with her. "Are you all right?"

"I'm fine. I have a busy day tomorrow." Her hotel was just across the boulevard, situated snugly against the harbor. She started for it.

"Elzy, wait. Talk to me. You're angry. What did I do?"

Not only was he right, but he hadn't done anything wrong. "Nothing. I promise. It's just time for me to go to bed. I'm here for work, remember?" She couldn't take one more minute with him. His scent, his extreme masculinity, his *desire* for her—it was all too much for her system to take. But she knew him. Knew his persistence, so she stopped and faced him. "We're good. I forgive you. I really do. But that's where it ends. I forgive you, and now, we carry on."

He let her get several feet away before he shouted, "After everything I said, you think I'm going back to a life sentence without you? I don't fucking think so."

She whirled around to him. "You're getting married, Trevor." On the brink of losing control, she spoke in a harsh whisper. "So, just stop it. Stop pretending there's a future when you've got a fiancée whose father might be in the hospital. You haven't even checked in with her."

"Because he's not hurt. I told you that. She only said it to buy me time with you."

"What?" Okay, now, she was totally confused. "Why would your future wife want us together?"

He stalked over to her and got right up in her face. "I'm not talking about her. I'm talking about us."

"There is no us." *Dammit.* He had to stop this. It was too much. He was too much. His energy surrounded her, engulfed her. "Get that through your thick head. There's no us anymore, and there never will be."

"Bullshit." He hauled her up against him and planted his mouth over hers.

My God. Instantly, she melted into the soft, wet, heat of his mouth. He clutched her to him, his hands digging into the flesh of her ass. And suddenly, she lost all sense of time and place.

She was heading to class, and Trevor was pulling her into a dark corner, pressing her against the wall, and kissing her until she was a hot mess of lust.

Their sweaty bodies were tangled in the back of her Pontiac. The frantic thrusting, the desperate need for friction. His breath at her ear. *I love you. I love you so much. I have to have you.*

That night in LA, when he'd come home from his shift at the diner and tried to be quiet so he wouldn't wake her. She'd thrown off the covers, run down the hallway, and leaped into his arms. His big hands cradled her bottom, as he walked her to the couch, bent her over the arm, and thrust into her.

Right then, she needed to touch him, shove her hands under his shirt and feel his skin. His hunger stoked her need, woke up the feral part she thought she'd outgrown. But she hadn't at all. Because it was him. Only him. And she was desperate to get closer, to reclaim all that had been lost…

No. She could never go back to a world where she trusted her heart to him.

She shoved him away.

With a wild-eyed look, he stared at her. "Elzy, what…? Is it because you think I'm engaged?"

What did that mean? *Because you* think *I'm engaged?* Was he, or wasn't he?

Her lips were still wet from their kiss. Her body tingled, and the pulse between her legs throbbed. The draw was so intense she had to get away from him. "No. It's because *I* am."

He reared back. "You're *what*?" He glanced down at her ring finger.

"I don't wear it when I travel. But I'm…I have a fiancé."

Shock turned him rigid.

"That's right, Trevor. I'm getting married."

Chapter Eleven

Even this late at night, the hotel was busy. People waited their turn to take pictures in front of a massive Christmas tree. Laughter and conversation came from a crowded bar, and groups gathered around a central fireplace.

And Trevor sat in a chair, still reeling.

She's getting married.

All this time, he thought the obstacle was Darby.

But no. Elzy's engaged.

She loves another man.

No wonder she had no interest in talking to him.

After she dropped the bomb, she stalked off to the hotel. He'd followed from a distance, his legs stiff. He'd watched her move briskly across the lobby to the elevator bay.

And then, he'd had to sit down. Around him, people chatted and laughed. Everyone was in the holiday spirit, dressed up and drinking cocktails.

And Elzy was getting married.

His phone vibrated, and he pulled it out of his pocket.

Darby: How's it going? Are you still with her?

He didn't want to talk, but she deserved an answer.

Trevor: You still with your dad? How is he?

Darby: Haha. We're back at the hotel. Did it work?

Trevor: Yes.

Darby: Good. Does that mean you're still with her? ARE YOU IN HER HOTEL ROOM RIGHT NOW?

Trevor: No.

And then, he typed the words just so they'd sink in.

Trevor: She's engaged.

The phone rang, and he answered immediately.

"You're kidding me, right?" Darby asked in total disbelief. "She's getting married?"

"Yeah." A server approached with a smile, saw his expression, and quickly diverted to a group of people seated around a low table.

"Are you okay?" Darby asked. "You don't sound good."

"I'm processing." Which was impossible with this current of anxiety running through him.

Does this mean I've lost her for good?

He reached into the bag of gifts at his feet and rummaged around until his hand closed around the ring box. When he cracked it open, he got a jolt to his nervous system.

Because it was made for her. It was perfect.

But would she ever wear it?

And what had her fiancé gotten her? Something plain, traditional, dull?

No. No. No.

If she could kiss him the way she had, then she had to be settling for that guy. He knew it in his bones.

"Okay, well," Darby said. "What does this mean?"

"I kissed her." At the memory, his body came back to life. Sensation pricked under his skin, and heat churned out from his core.

"Did she kiss you back? I assume this was before you found out she's engaged."

Hell yeah, she kissed me. He could still taste the desire on her tongue and feel the press of her body. Her tits were bigger, her hair smelled different, but the hunger—the passion…

It's still there.

Everything that mattered between them was still there. He knew it from the spark in their conversation and the way she lit up at his touch.

It's still fucking there.

"Trev? Are you okay?"

He got up. "Yeah. I am."

"Are you heading back now? You can wake me up if you want to talk."

He headed across the lobby. "I'm getting a room. If she's staying here, then I'm staying too."

"You just said she's engaged."

"Exactly. She's not married yet. The ball's still in play."
For the first time in his life, *his* happiness was a priority.
Because he knew without a doubt, she felt the same way.
And she wasn't going to marry anyone but him.

Jess tossed the makeup wipe in the bin. "If I had any doubts about Joel, it ended with that kiss."

It was so hot, so fiery, she'd melted into him. For those magical seconds, time stopped. Nothing separated them—not mind, body, or soul.

"Well, I mean, I'm glad. I'd hate for you to settle." Amber's voice sounded rough from sleep.

She'd called her sister in the dead of night to talk. She hadn't even hesitated. *And you know what?* It was such a relief to be a sister—not a mom.

And that was the thing. She was so tired of carrying the weight of the world. Being a mom to her siblings, running a household for her dad, building a business so her family would be secure.

She knew she could rely on herself. Had proven it countless times. But…boy, being sheltered in Trevor's arms had made her feel protected. Safe. She knew, without a doubt, if she'd stayed with him, he'd be in this bed with her.

And that could not happen.

Because she didn't know him anymore. Sure, the chemistry was still there. But who wouldn't be attracted to that man?

They'd had a good talk, and she'd learned a lot—but only the parts related to why he'd left her. Other than that, they'd lived a whole life apart. It was ridiculous to think those thirty years didn't matter.

I've changed, I know that. He has too. They couldn't just pick up where they'd left off.

Which was why she'd made a beeline for the elevators. "What is it about him though?" She poured lotion onto her palm.

"What do you mean?" Amber asked through a yawn.

"I've dated plenty of men. I got serious with a few. I was going to *marry* Joel. But the way I feel about Trevor... I've never felt it for anyone else."

"Oh, well. It's probably easy to slip into the skin of an old relationship."

"Right?" *There you go.* "That's it exactly." It was nothing more than that.

"Oh, I didn't mean—"

"You nailed it. That explains why I'm so comfortable with him. It's like our teenage selves are talking to each other. But we're not kids anymore. A whole lot of life has happened since then. We're different people now."

"What? No, that's not what I meant."

"Well, what did you mean?" She tapped the speaker button on her phone, so she could rub the lotion onto her face.

"That the essence of you both is still there. That's why it's so easy to slip right back into it. It happens with me and Jenna. Even though she moved away when I was a senior in high school, and we only get to talk a couple times a year, we still pick up right where we left off. There's a real comfort to being around old friends."

"Hey, I'm trying not to fall for him here, and you're not helping."

Her sister laughed. "You know, you can tell yourself anything you want, but the truth is in your feelings. How does it feel to be around Trevor?"

"It feels annoying, thanks for asking." Because it was just as big and powerful as when they were kids. "And the worst part is, it makes me see how different I am around Joel."

"Different how?"

"I don't know. I guess I'm just not completely myself with him. I never fully relax. I don't let go."

"Hon, I don't think I've ever seen you let go. You're the boss, the mother, the owner… As long as I've known you, you've been in badass mode. And I'm guessing that started after Mom died."

She couldn't deny the truth of that. "A therapist once told me when a parent dies, there's a terrifying sense of helplessness. Who will feed you? Who will buy your clothes? Who's going to protect you from those scary noises when you're lying in bed alone in the dark? I wasn't comfortable with that feeling, so I took control."

"I can vouch for that." Amber sounded like she was proud of her sister.

Which meant she didn't get it. "He said I was the most tenacious person he'd ever met." She paused. "And it wasn't a compliment. It was no way to live, and I'd burn myself out. He said it was okay for me to let go. That I was fine. I was safe. And I didn't need to hold on so tightly."

"Yeah, I can see that. What'd he say about Trevor?"

"He said losing a parent leaves you with a 'breathtaking

loneliness.' And that eight-year-old me understood she was alone now." She flicked off the bathroom light and headed for the bed. "And you know what? That's exactly how I felt when Trevor left me in that motel room." After she'd curled up in the fetal position and bawled her eyes out, she'd walked out of that motel with a clear sense of, *Well, I guess I'm on my own now.*

She'd gone right back to the chapel and asked them to tear up the marriage license. Then, she'd driven back to Riverton, alternating between gut-wrenching bouts of crying and stern talks to herself about focusing on the future, on her family.

Had it been some kind of self-fulfilling prophecy? If Trevor viewed the world through the lens of his parents' beliefs, maybe she'd seen it through the eyes of a little girl who'd lost her mom.

"And you *were* on your own," Amber said. "It's true. That's our fault."

"Hey, there's no blame here. You were five when Mom died."

"Okay, but Dad let you raise us. He was relieved when you came home and took over. And I was so freaked out about my pregnancy that I handed everything over to you— including Bri. You were more of a mom to her in that first year than I was."

"Because you were sixteen. You were a child."

"Hon, you were twenty, and you stepped into the role without a hint of resentment. Which means I never had to experience any of the loneliness you just described because I had you. But who did you have?"

The question stirred up an ache deep inside. "For a long time, I had Trevor. Which was why it devastated me when he left. But at the same time, maybe I was expecting it. I mean, if my own mom abandoned me, wouldn't everyone else do it too? Obviously, it wasn't rational."

"But it's how a kid would internalize it. Well, look. You're an adult now. You can see the world through a different lens."

A sharp spike of hope set her heart racing. "If you think that future includes Trevor, you're forgetting he's engaged to another woman."

"I wasn't talking about him. I'm talking about you. We were kids when we lost Mom, but you're a woman now, and you have a choice to make. You can guard your heart from the possibility that someone you love will leave you, or you can be brave and go for it. Come on, Jess. Don't you think it's time to let yourself love again?"

"Is that line from a Hallmark movie? Because I think I've heard it before."

"I don't know if it is, but it should be. That was good. I should write a romance novel. *Oh*. Even better, why don't you live one? Go all second chance with your first love."

"Maybe I will." But she didn't think so. She wouldn't share his personal life with her sister, but Trevor was hardwired to make his happiness the very last priority.

It'd be easy to get back together with him. It'd be passionate and exciting and all those good things. But they were different people now. After a few days, they'd realize the only thing holding them together was memories.

"Not everyone leaves, Jess. You know how I know that?

Because as soon as we get off the phone, I'm going to spoon with my husband who's loved me since I was a twenty-one-year-old single mom, who stood by me through post-partum, who turned to me for help when his business failed and loved me even harder when I went through perimenopause early. So, I really, truly, hope you let go of your fears because, for me, personally, I'm not entirely sure what else in life is worth living for but love. Now, I'm going back to sleep. If you need me, I'm here." Her sister disconnected.

Unnerved, Jess slid under the covers. Everything Amber said resonated, leaving Jess scared. Because, really, how did you change the way you looked at the world? Her fears ran deep. They were woven into the very fiber of her being. How did she extract them?

In any event, there was one thing she had to do. Not even considering the time, she scrolled through her recent calls and found Joel halfway down the page. Yeah, it had been that long since they'd spoken. *That's just sad.* She hit his number.

It rang a few times before it connected, but instead of his voice, she heard laughter and conversation as he fumbled the phone. "Hello? Jess? Are you there?"

"Yeah, I'm here. I'm sorry to bother you."

"No, no. It's fine. What's wrong? Are you okay? Hang on. Let me go somewhere quiet."

"Joel, slow down. I'm fine. Don't worry."

The noises faded. "Okay, I'm in my room. How's it going? Everything good?"

"It's been interesting." He didn't even know she was in Iceland. "How are things going with your family? We haven't talked at all since you left." Saying it out loud to her fiancé highlighted how messed up it was.

"They're bad. My daughter's a wreck. Her jerk of a husband's had a girlfriend for six months—that we know of —and yet, he's still blowing up Ashley's phone because she dared to move out."

"She must be devastated."

"We're not letting her be. We've engaged a top lawyer, and we're putting her to work changing passwords, printing out bank statements, that kind of thing. Now is not the time for her to fall apart."

"Well, it sounds like you and your ex have a good handle on this." She hesitated to offer advice, given he'd made it clear it wasn't her family. But then again, they were close enough to consider marriage. Why not speak her mind? "I just hope someone's there for her emotionally."

He laughed. "My ex and I aren't really built that way, but yeah, I hear you. She's got friends going all the way back to grade school, so she's got plenty of people to talk to. What about you? All set for the gala?"

"Yes, everything's on track. But I'm actually not at the resort. I'm in Iceland."

"What do you mean? *Iceland?*"

"After you left, I remembered a consulting offer I'd gotten, and since I'd arranged to take the time off anyway… I went ahead and took it."

"That's crazy. I've always wanted to go there."

"It's a surreal place, that's for sure. But there's something we need to talk about." Maybe she could save this relationship after all. She'd held back so much of herself. Maybe if they talked through their problems, they'd get to something deeper. "It makes me sad that you had no idea where I was."

"Well, you didn't tell me."

"Right, but don't you think it's odd that we haven't talked to each other since you left?"

"I told you how crazy it's been here. We had to find an attorney, call the banks—"

"Joel. We're engaged. And you cut me out of your Christmas plans to take care of your daughter. If we're going to be married, shouldn't I be part of that family?"

"I can see how you'd feel that way." His tone was level, composed.

Just like a lawyer. "Yeah, it hurt. And to be honest, that's the real reason I took this job."

"I wasn't blowing you off. I just don't think it's the best time to introduce you to them."

She gave him a moment, hoping he'd hear what he said.

"I mean, you'll be my family too," he said a little too quickly. "But right now, my daughter needs me."

"Well, of course. But it's Christmas, and you dumped me like I was some woman you're seeing, and I guess this time apart has made me think about things, and something doesn't feel right with us."

"Jess, come on. If something like this happened to your sisters, you wouldn't even hesitate to drop me. Your family's always come first. You've made that clear from the beginning."

Her heart sank. He was right about that. "Let me ask you something, okay?"

"Of course. Anything."

"Why do you want to marry me? What about me makes you want to spend your life with me?"

He gave an uncomfortable laugh. "My ex asked the same question."

She got that he was living under his ex-wife's roof and dealing with a serious family matter, but she didn't like that they were having intimate conversations. *About me.* Yeah, something was definitely wrong. She hadn't seen it because she'd been so preoccupied with the resort. "And what did you tell her?"

"That I'd never met a woman more intelligent. Someone who challenges me intellectually."

"Your ex is an attorney."

"True. But you're caring too, and she's very much like me—all business. The way you look after your sisters, nieces, and nephews, the way you hold your family together… I admire that. My ex never cared about creating family traditions. She has eighty-hour weeks, and she wants to relax over a holiday—not decorate, cook, and wrap. Thanksgiving and Christmas meals were—and still are—catered. But you, you push through your exhaustion because you care so much about your family's experience. Even in your twenties, you put in the extra effort to make sure your sisters came downstairs to see presents under the tree. In the middle of launching a resort, you're helping plan your niece's wedding."

Those reasons were not as flattering as he might think. None of them had to do with a sizzling connection, a bond, or anything romantic at all. But also, he'd pointed out something important. She did a great job juggling all the balls—except for one. Him. She hadn't prioritized him at all.

That's so sad.

I was going to marry this man.

And it really drove home what Amber said. She could guard her heart, or she could be brave.

Let's do that.

Let's be brave.

"I love you, Jess. I really do. I don't know if I'm giving you the right words. I'm not a man who's in touch with my feelings. But I know you make my life better."

"How do you want to make my life better?"

"I want to travel with you, see the world. All the things I didn't get to do because I was working toward becoming a partner and then opening my own firm. I was raising kids and trying to be the kind of husband my ex wanted. You don't have any expectations for me. You let me be whoever I am. You don't nag me all the time."

"Oh, I'm pretty sure if we spent more time together, the nagging would kick in."

He laughed. "I think we can cut to the chase. You're breaking up with me. Is there anything I can do to change your mind? I'd hate to lose you."

He'd hate to lose me?

Wow. What kind of person settled for such a lackluster relationship? *A coward.* "Since you left, neither of us has bothered to check in with each other. That's pretty telling, don't you think?"

"Will you do me a favor?" he asked. "Will you hold off your decision until we see each other again?"

No. Because she was seeing clearly now. "Coming to Iceland, taking a break from my real life, has given me the space to see our connection isn't strong enough. It's not your fault. It's not mine. It's two people who are not excited enough about each other." And maybe it wasn't fair because she'd never again be a sixteen-year-old girl racing around the countryside with a beautiful boy who adored her. Maybe no other relationship could compare to a first love, but unfortunately, she'd just spent an entire evening with hers, and she knew she could never settle for bland feelings again.

Not after that kiss.

"I'm sorry, Joel."

"I blew it. I'm sorry for cutting you out. I'm sorry for making you feel like you weren't important to me."

"Again, it's not your fault. We just didn't work."

After she got off the phone, she rolled onto her side. Strangely, she didn't feel sad.

She felt relieved.

This sense of lightness, of possibility, made her feel hopeful.

As she shut off the lamp, she remembered she'd silenced her phone during dinner. *Oops.* She'd better take a quick look at her messages.

She hoped Joel didn't try to press his case. As an attorney, he could argue his point of view for days. He liked to win. But there was no arguing his way back into a relationship where she wasn't someone's first choice.

Been there, done that.

As she scrolled through the texts and emails, only one name caught her attention.

Trevor.

Trevor: You've got to come out here. You won't believe this.

Trevor: Elz, seriously. Come outside.

What did he want? They weren't going to figure anything out tonight. She should just ignore him, go to sleep.

Yeah, right. Like that's going to happen.

Trevor: If I knew what floor you were on, I'd throw rocks at your window. GET DOWN HERE.

Trevor: Look out the window.

He made everything fun and exciting. Throwing off the covers, she hurried across the room and pulled back the black-out curtains to see the most surreal sight. A green ribbon of light danced in the sky.

Jessica: Is that the northern lights?

Trevor: Yes. You better be on your way down here.

Jessica: Coming.

She slid her feet back into worn shearling slippers, grabbed her key card, and hurried out the door. The thrill of it should've been a warning. It was her childhood all over again. Pebbles at her window, a note slipped into her hand before fifth period, his tires spitting out gravel as he jerked the steering wheel to take her on a spur-of-the-moment adventure.

But she didn't care. Anticipation pumped through her, fueling her steps, until she burst outside into the freezing cold night. People lined the wharf, heads tipped back, and even while she knew to look up at the sky, her gaze traveled from one silhouette to the next until it landed expertly on his.

Turned out, nothing was more familiar than his shape, size, and mannerisms.

Of course, he found her too. And the joy lighting his features outrivaled the spectacle in the sky. Standing a head and shoulders taller than anyone else around him, he waved her over.

Excitement burst in her chest, sparks raining down inside her, and she broke into a run. When she reached him, he clutched her shoulders and took in her features as if he had so much to say but couldn't find the words.

Only when someone said, "I can't believe it. I've waited a lifetime to see this," did she jolt back to the moment and pay attention.

Emerald-green ribbons of light rippled and swirled against the midnight sky. "Unbelievable."

Trevor stood close, their bodies brushing against each other. She could feel the restraint in his clenched muscles, as though fighting against his need to wrap an arm around her waist.

It had always been like this, this compulsion to touch. In church, on hikes, at the rodeo, he had a hand on her, their thighs pressed together. Always.

It was so hard to stay in the moment, impossible to keep from crashing through the barrier of time and landing on the seat of his truck where his hands would grip her ass, moving her on him, her back hitting the steering wheel, her knee pressed to the door.

"Fuck. Fuck. Fuck. *Elzy, my Elzy."*

Or when he'd come over for dinner, and she'd prop her feet on his knees under the table, his hand wrapping around her ankle. *Possession. Connection.*

Need. Yearning.

Love.

So much love.

People around them gasped, oohed, and aahed. And Jess forced herself to enjoy this once-in-a-lifetime display of lights. After a minute, everyone grew so mesmerized, they stopped talking. The only sounds were the halyards clanking and water lapping against the dock.

When Trevor reached for her hand, she gazed up at him. The love and relief in his eyes both thrilled and warmed her.

And in that moment, she felt a shift. The weight pressing down on her chest lifted. The bindings around her heart broke free.

In their place, something new rushed in.

Forgiveness.

As they stood there, gazes locked, she could remember what they'd meant to each other. He'd been a great boyfriend—the best. She sincerely believed what they'd had was real.

And he was so young when he'd left her. So inexperienced.

Most importantly, he'd done what he believed was best for them.

I forgive you.

She didn't know what it meant for them. Maybe nothing more than smiling when they drove past each other in Calamity. Or when she saw him through a restaurant window, she'd wave.

Oh, come on. Who are you kidding?

She didn't think she'd ever get to a place where she could be pals with this man.

It was all or nothing, and she'd gotten the *closure* she needed.

Anything more would just be torture.

She was done.

Chapter Twelve

TREVOR ANSWERED DARBY'S FACETIME CALL ON HIS WAY back to his room.

"You won't believe this." She had her eye mask hitched up her forehead and her face clean of makeup.

"What?" He shouldn't have answered. He was still reeling from the way Elzy looked at him on the pier, and he couldn't give his friend the attention she deserved.

The way the moonlight made Elzy's skin glow, the affection in her eyes... She'd looked so very beautiful. He'd walked her to the elevator bay, willing her to invite him to her room, but the doors parted, she'd walked inside, and that was that. She left.

"Emil and I were texting. And then, out of nowhere, he just stopped. So, I get ready for bed...I get *in* bed...and then, he texts me, 'Let me in.'"

He pulled out his key card and pushed the door open. "He came to the hotel?"

"Yep. We just spent an hour talking."

"Was it good?"

"Honestly, he came in hot." She chuckled. "He was pissed that, even after he explained his situation, I never tried to get back with him. I just moved on. I told him why. That neither of us could compromise. That long distance to Iceland would never have worked, but that just got him even more pissed off."

"Because you didn't care enough to try. In his mind, if you'd stayed together, you might've found a way to be together."

"That's exactly what he said."

That was how he'd felt about Elzy. She'd cut him off and never let him back in. He'd been pissed, hurt, and missing her for thirty damn years. "So, how'd it end?"

"We kissed."

"Oh." Propping his phone up against a pillow, he sat in a chair to untie his boots. "I wasn't expecting that."

"I know. Neither was I. But he's such a quiet, strong man, so when he blows up, it's just really…explosive."

"He hides his feelings, leaving you questioning whether he has them. And then, when he proves them, your ego gets the hit it needs."

"Wait. Are you saying I only want him because I never know where I stand with him?" she asked.

"I don't know. You tell me. Do you still like him? Do you like *talking* to him? Or is it just attraction?"

"I like being with him. I think he's a really good man." She paused. "And I can't keep my hands off him."

"So, why did he leave?"

"I don't know. He said, 'I'm taking you to breakfast. Be ready at seven.' And then, he left. God, he's so hot."

"Sounds like there's hope for you guys."

He couldn't get Elzy's expression out of his mind. The longing mixed with confusion. Resistance. She clearly wanted to be with him, but she didn't trust him.

And as much as he understood it, he wanted a second chance to prove himself.

"Maybe. I'll see him at breakfast." Darby fell onto her back, flopping her arms dramatically. "And maybe this time, I'll be open to compromise."

"Sounds good." He stood up and unbuckled his pants. While his body was on this call with Darby, his spirit was on the pier, watching the aurora borealis beside Elzy. She hadn't grabbed a coat before coming downstairs, so she was freezing. She'd tipped her head, that long, thick hair spilling down her back, and took in the light show.

He'd wrapped an arm around her, and when she'd huddled up against him, he'd taken it as a green light to step behind her and encircle her in his arms. He could've stood like that forever.

Anything was better than going back to his room. Without her.

Now that he'd found her, he couldn't stand being apart.

"Well, I should let you go." She sat up. "Wait a minute. What's all that stuff you bought?"

He glanced at the heavy bags on the floor. "I got some souvenirs for the grandkids." Well, the majority was for Elzy, but she didn't need to know that. Now, he had to figure out how to get it to her. She didn't need all this extra shit in her suitcase. He'd ask the concierge to ship it. "I'm going to shower."

"Okay. So, I'll see you here tomorrow for the wine tasting?"

I'll be wherever Elzy is. "I assume that's the plan. I'll text her in the morning."

"She's dodgy, that one. If she can find another way to get back here, I wouldn't put it past her to do it."

"Then, I'll sleep outside her door. She'll have to step over me to get away."

Darby laughed. "She doesn't know how lucky she is to have you. See you tomorrow." She disconnected.

After turning on the shower, he stripped off the rest of his clothes. Closing his eyes, he let the hot water sink into his cold skin.

Images flashed in his mind. Elzy's delight when she looked at the puffin mugs. Later at dinner, the way her eyelids had fluttered shut when she'd tasted the cinnamon whipped cream on her apple tart.

And the heat in her eyes when she'd leaned in to kiss him. Holy shit, that had turned him on. He'd wanted to drag her into the club's bathroom and fuck her senseless.

He had to win her back. Had to. The ache, the need, the drive…it was out of control.

Fuck.

He slammed the faucet shut and got out of the stall.

He wasn't joking about sleeping outside her door. He'd do it.

Because Darby was right. Elzy would absolutely sneak away. Maybe she was doing it right now. Talking to the concierge about hiring a driver. Renting a car.

Fuck. He had to get to her. Stay close. He couldn't let her go.

Please, Elzy, forgive me.

Put me out of my fucking misery.

You think I haven't learned my lesson? For Christ's sake, I spent thirty years without you. I will never hurt you again.

But he couldn't sleep outside her door. Right? No, of course not. He had to wait till morning. He'd text her.

Fuck that. She's leaving the day after tomorrow. He pulled his phone out of his jeans pocket and called her.

Droplets of water sluiced off his skin and puddled around his feet. Snatching a towel, he rubbed it over his body. With shaking hands, he watched the screen. She wasn't picking up.

Maybe she'd gone to sleep.

The front desk wouldn't give him her room number—and he'd sue the crap out of them if they did—so all he could do was wait till the morning.

The call ended.

Shit. Fuck. What could he do?

Nothing. *If she doesn't want to see you, there's nothing you can do.*

A moment later, she texted.

Elzy: What's up?

Trevor: Can we talk?

Elzy: About what? I'm about to go to sleep.

Sleep was the furthest thing from his mind. He'd had her in his arms again. He'd gotten to kiss the mouth that had brought him indescribable pleasure. Having her so close but still out of reach was driving him out of his mind.

She'd felt the electricity between them too. He knew she

did. Those sounds she'd made, the way she'd pressed up against him, trying to get closer. Yeah, she'd felt it, too.

> Trevor: I miss you.

Three dots danced across the screen. Then, stopped. Danced again, then stopped.

She thinks I'm engaged. Of course she's not going to talk to me.

He had a choice to make. He could keep up the ruse to stay in Iceland with her. Or…

Or he could get real with her.

Because he was done fucking around.

> Trevor: Darby and I aren't engaged.

His phone rang, and he answered immediately.

Before he could speak, she said, "What are you talking about? When did you break up?"

"I knew I wouldn't marry her the moment I laid eyes on you. I told her I couldn't do it."

"You ended your engagement because you ran into me in Iceland? What kind of love is that?"

"It was never about love. Not for either of us. It was two people who settled for companionship. But that ended the moment I saw you. My God, Elzy, I will never settle for anything less than what we had."

"Trevor, we're not…we're just talking. There's nothing here."

"Bullshit. It's all still here. All of it. And even if you don't want to give me another chance—"

"Another chance? Do you hear yourself?"

"To be honest, my heart's banging like a drum, so I can't hear much of anything." He stuttered out a laugh, but just this…talking to her…having her on the other end of the line…helped. "Can I come to your room?"

"No, you can't come to my room." Her voice rose to near hysteria. "What good will that do?"

"You know exactly what it'll do. And I know you feel it too, or I wouldn't be asking you to cheat on your fiancé. I saw it in your eyes, and I felt it in your kiss. You don't want him how a woman wants the man she's marrying."

She went quiet. Was she considering it?

And then, she said, quietly, "I'm not engaged anymore. I broke up with him."

"When?" he demanded.

"Tonight. As soon as I got back to the room."

Holy shit. Fuck, yes. "Because of me?"

"Of course, it's not because of you. How big is your ego?"

"It's not about my ego. Elzy, come on. It's us. We can have us again. Don't you want this?"

She let out a huff of breath. "I don't know what I want. God, you just…You make my head spin. Look, I don't want to hurt you, but I don't think we're on the same page. Chemistry isn't connected to trust, so it doesn't mean anything."

Elation jacked him up. Gave him wings. "It means everything." Because she didn't say no. And because chemistry was enough for now. It would bond them together long enough for him to earn her trust.

And he would.

He would absolutely earn her trust.

"Trevor, I don't know what you want from me."

"I want your forgiveness. I think I saw it in your eyes tonight. Am I wrong?"

"No, you're not wrong. I do forgive you. And I even forgive myself for the way I handled things. But that's all we needed to do. Forgive ourselves. Maybe—"

"There's not an ounce of maybe in my body. Elzy, let me come up and see you. *Please.*"

"I think we should just sleep on it. See how we feel in the morning."

"Fuck that. We've lost enough time, and I'm done waiting. I'm done living my life without you." He knew he was coming on too strong, but she needed to hear it. "From the moment I walked away from you, I've been lost. No matter how much success I've had or how many people I've met along the way, without you I'm just so fucking alone. Do you understand me? I am wandering this earth alone."

"Yes, I understand you."

"Elzy, I need you to take me back. I made a terrible mistake, I fucked up, but please *let me come home.*"

In the silence following his plea, blood roared in his ears, and his heart pounded.

Had he come on too strong? Had he lost his chance with her?

Even through the fear blazing through him, his gut told him he'd done the right thing. He'd laid his heart in her hands.

From this point on, it was up to her.

Come on, Elz.

Take me back.

But still, nothing but silence. Incredibly, it gave him hope because she hadn't said no. She hadn't told him to fuck off.

So, he waited.

Until, finally, she spoke. "Room twenty-two-twelve."

What have you done?

Elzy hurried into the bathroom, but she didn't know why. She didn't have time to shower. Shave. Put on makeup.

Why would I put on makeup?

She turned back around, wondering if she should clean up the room. After tossing her boots into the closet, she stuffed her scarf and hat into a drawer.

This is ridiculous. You're not having a dinner party.

Just calm down.

She looked down at her flannel pajamas and ratty old slippers. She didn't know why she'd taken them into the city with her. She hadn't planned on spending the night. Habit, maybe? She was so used to peeling off her work clothes and getting comfortable that she'd just shoved them into her giant tote.

But really, when had she become so frumpy?

Am *I frumpy?* She glanced at the mirror over the dresser. *I don't feel frumpy.*

How could anyone feel dull when Trevor Montgomery touched her like she was the sexiest woman in the entire world? And that was it, wasn't it? Trevor saw *her.* Not her oversized pajamas. Not what car she drove or how many decorative pillows she had on her couch. He didn't notice her lipstick. He just wanted *her.*

He wanted to consume her. All of her.

No wonder she'd never loved anyone else. No one wanted her the way he did.

But is this real? Or is he just carried away in the moment?

They were different people now. She was so afraid of diving in, only to discover they had nothing more in common than a shared childhood in Riverton.

First love was so powerful.

But it was too late. Because a knock on the door was accompanied by a commanding, deeply masculine voice. "Elzy?"

Her body jolted as if she'd heard a car backfiring.

"Elz?"

Oh, dammit. She stared at the door. War raged inside her mind. As badly as she wanted him, she was also scared to death.

No, that's not true. This isn't fear.

It's excitement.

And that was terrifying. Because they'd have sex, and then, what would happen when she woke up in the morning? She couldn't go back to that Vegas motel room and watch him walk away. She couldn't be devastated all over again.

No, no. You were blindsided. That's why it hurt so much.

This time, you know what's going to happen. You're going to have one night of passion. And then, you'll be free of him. For good.

"Elzy, dammit. Open up."

Could she though? It was easier said than done.

Because the moment she let him in, she'd be in for it. There'd be no holding him back. *No holding* me *back.*

She was starved for him. Desperate.

And that was all she really needed to know. For just one night, she needed to be loved by him.

She flipped the security lock, lowered the handle, and then…

He burst into the room, crowded her against the wall, tipped her chin with his big hand, and kissed her.

This man wasted no time licking into her mouth and claiming her.

And it was just so overwhelming. It was pure relief to let go, to submit to desire—

To stop being in control of everything.

His hands cupped her face, as his tongue coaxed hers into play, and his muscular body caged her in against the wall. His dizzying kisses short-circuited her mind and blew out her grid, and when he shoved a thigh between her legs, the friction ignited her desire.

She scraped her fingernails across his scalp and hitched a leg up to his hip. She needed to feel him everywhere. He knew that. Of course he did. No one read her like this man. He dragged his hands down her body, over her breasts, around her rib cage, until he clutched her ass and lifted her.

As he carried her to the bed, he never pulled his mouth away, never let up his wordless plea to forgive him, want him, love him. He held her tightly as he put a knee on the mattress and walked her up to the pillows.

He set her down like a treasure, like a feast, and then, pulled back to take her in.

The adoration in his eyes sank deep, restoring her,

healing her. At the same time, it kicked up a pulse between her legs that demanded relief. She held her arms out for him, and he grabbed her hands, kissing each palm in turn.

"I've imagined this moment every night for thirty years," he said. "And I can't believe I'm living it. I can't believe I found you again and that you want me as much as I want you."

Of course I do. The longing never went away. I just got really good at masking it. But she swallowed the words. She could tell herself it was because she needed his body on top of hers, that she needed his touch, but deep down, she knew why.

Because they weren't on the same page, and she needed to tell him the truth. "We're not back together. I need you to understand that."

A flash of pain ravaged his features, and he went very still.

"This is just one night. I need to know you're okay with that." When he didn't answer, her body rioted. It was crying out to be touched by him, but she couldn't hurt him. "Trevor, I think you broke us."

"I *know*. But will you give me a chance to heal us?"

"I don't think we can be fixed." Emotion choked her. Heat flamed up her neck. "I'm sorry, Trevor. I'm sorry for shutting you out. I'm sorry..." And then, out of nowhere, she was crying. "*I* broke us too." She remembered dropping to a crouch behind the counter when he entered the feedstore. Pressing herself behind the dumpster. She could still feel the cold metal and smell the rotting garbage. "You came back for me, but I was so stupid. I wish so badly things had turned out differently."

"Sweetheart…" He kissed her tears. "Baby." He kissed each cheek, the tip of her nose, her chin. "We were young." His thumb swiped a tear. "But we're here now. Don't you see? We found our way back to each other. Elzy, baby, we get a second chance to make it right. Let's do that, okay? Let's make it right."

A surge of happiness, gratitude, and affection came rushing in, and all she could do was nod. He kissed her gently this time, his hand cupping her neck in a light but possessive grip. Heat flared, and she arched her back.

"My Elzy." His mouth made a slow path down her neck. "My beautiful, sexy, wild Calamity Jane."

"I'm not that girl anymore."

"I think, with me, maybe you can be."

And that was when she decided to find out. Because when things broke, they healed stronger. And really, what other choice did she have?

She knew their chemistry was more than lust. It was more than the residual feelings of a first love.

She might've changed, grown, *matured,* but in the heart of her, she *was* the same girl. She'd just swaddled herself in layers of armor to protect herself from getting hurt again. And she hadn't. But guess what? She hadn't loved again either. She hadn't experienced any highs, other than the birth of a niece or nephew, the achievement of scoring an impressive consulting job, or winning a permit from the town.

Those were all good, but they weren't soul-satisfying.

And maybe being with Trevor would heal her. Make her whole again.

As he pressed a trail of kisses along her collarbone, she

unbuttoned her flannel top. He spread it open, unwrapping his gift, his warm hands gliding up her stomach and gently covering her breasts. "Take off your granny pants."

Laughing, she lifted her hips and slid them down. "They're cute. My entire family has them. We wear them on Christmas Day."

"If we were together, you wouldn't wear anything on Christmas Day. Or any other day. I'd keep you naked." His hands caressed her body, and he kissed a fiery trail down her torso until he reached the cove between her legs. His broad shoulders spread her wider, his hands slid under her bottom, and he raised her to his mouth.

And then, his tongue seared a path through her folds. Pleasure spread hot and electric through her body, and she released a sigh of pure contentment.

He reached for her breasts—because he knew how sensitive her nipples were, he *remembered*, and he'd always, always put her first. As delicious tension spiked, she cupped his head, pulling him closer, her hands fisting in his hair.

He devoured her, and she loved it.

Her legs wrapped around his waist, her hips rocked, and desire streamed hot and urgent until she was crying out. Drenched in pleasure, she closed her eyes and planted her feet on either side of him. Her bottom lifted off the mattress, her neck arched, and she wasn't sure how much more tension she could take. It was too good, the bliss so potent, so wild, it pushed her beyond anything she'd ever experienced.

This passionate, lusty man never let up. His tongue circled her clit, his fingers pinched her nipple, while his other hand gripped her ass. All of it coalesced into an explosion that shot her right out of her body and sent her soaring into a universe glittering with stars and drenched in euphoria.

One climax after another kept her floating, spinning, and deliriously joyful.

She came down slowly, her ass landing softly on the bed. Trevor kissed each inner thigh, then reared over her, grinning proudly.

"Settle down, Casanova," she teased. But with her soft and unguarded, tenderness washed over her. And she cupped his cheek. "We were so good together."

"We *are* still good together. There will never be anyone else. Tell me you understand that. It's you and me, Elz. I don't know how the world works. I don't understand the metaphysics of how we're connected or why. I only know you're part of me. The best part." He kissed her with a passion that left her mindless. His hand skimmed down her neck and caressed her breast. The rasp of his palm over her nipple had her squirming, a new tension building.

He shifted back and covered her breast with his hot, wet mouth. When his tongue flicked over her sensitive peak, her hips pitched up hard.

Rising over her again, he said, "I don't have a condom." He watched her intently, questioningly.

Delirious with need, she found it hard to think. She only knew the problem wasn't on her end. "I'm on the pill."

His features tightened with anticipation. "I use protection. Every time. Since Cole…"

She nodded. She got it. He didn't want another surprise baby.

"You're good?" he asked. "I can—"

"I'm so good I can hardly stand it." She grasped his cock and brought him to her.

"Thank fuck." He watched as he eased inside her. His eyelids fluttered closed, and he shuddered. "You feel so good."

He filled her so completely she went mindless with lust. The friction aroused every cell, making them vibrate with pleasure.

Slowly, he pulled out and then thrust back in. "You feel this, Elz? Nothing like it in the whole world."

"I feel it." She ran her fingers over the strained muscles in his arms. "Don't hold back. Give me all of you, Trevor. Give me everything I've missed."

Her request unleashed him. He slammed in hard and didn't waste a moment before giving her exactly what she wanted. "You're so fucking tight. So hot."

With each thrust, his hips punched, and he drove her up the mattress. His lust for her was thrilling, empowering.

"Hold on to the headboard." Beads of perspiration formed over his lip and dotted his hairline. "You make me feral. *Fuck.*"

Her skin was on fire, and his powerful thrusts made her burn. Her palms flattened on the cool wood, her ankles latched around his hips, and she lost herself completely in Trevor Montgomery's passion for her.

And then, he tucked his face into her neck, driving into her. *Slam.* "I'm going to come." *Slam. Slam.* "I'm gonna come so fucking hard." He thrust harder, faster, in short, tight punches. His features flushed a deep red, the tendons in his neck corded, and then, he shouted, "Elzy."

In a frenzy of need, he pumped, hips twisting as if trying

to embed himself as deeply as possible, and when, finally, he slowed, he lowered himself on top of her, shifting to her side. He pressed kisses all over her face, his hand scraping her hair off her damp forehead. "My Elzy. I promise to make it good for you, but right now, I have to sleep." He wrapped an arm across her and snugged her up to him as tightly as possible. "Haven't slept since I saw you walk into that dining room. God, you're beautiful." His eyes closed and his voice slurred with exhaustion. "Promise this isn't a dream?"

"Oh, it's very real."

"You won't leave me, right?" he asked.

Before she could answer, he let go, his muscles relaxed, and he succumbed to sleep.

Which was for the best.

Because her answer would upset him.

Yes, their connection still sizzled and crackled. Yes, the emotions were all there.

And, yes, she believed he meant everything he said.

But she wasn't ready to give him what he wanted.

Not after two days together.

And maybe not ever.

But that wasn't the point. Tonight was about forgiveness—for both of them.

Seeing him again, grappling with their issues, had freed her.

It showed her she didn't want to be alone anymore. But she also didn't want to settle for companionship. What she had with Joel wasn't enough.

If nothing else, the last two days had shown her that.

So, this is good. Her hand settled on top of his where it clung to her hip.

Yes, it's all good. When I go back home, I'll be healthier. More open to a true relationship.

And Trevor…

Anxiety blasted through her at the idea of losing him again.

Well, she wouldn't think about a future that might never happen.

All she had was this moment.

Chapter Thirteen

Trevor woke up happy.

No, it was better than that. He was content.

With a grin on his face, he stretched. Before opening his eyes, he breathed in her scent, and it sent him right back into her arms, her mouth, her body. The press of his face into her neck, the sting of her fists in his hair.

She's back.

She's mine.

Gratitude got a hard grip on him, and he made a silent vow to never take her for granted. To always listen, pay attention. To talk to her before making decisions.

Opening his eyes, he rolled onto his side, ready to kiss her shoulder.

But her side of the bed was empty. It startled him, but it was okay. Air thick with steam reassured him she was showering. She had a busy day planned.

He'd give her some space, stay under the covers a little longer. The first thing he'd do when he got home was put his house on the market. What memories did it hold for him, other than his failure as a father and the painful loneliness of living in a home with nannies?

Besides, they'd need a place of their own.

Robbers Roost.

Yeah. Second on the list was to start looking for ranches.

They'd tour properties together, and he just knew her mind would start spinning out design and renovation ideas. He smiled when he pictured those slate-blue kitchen cabinets she'd always wanted. Had her tastes changed?

He couldn't wait for the day both their families came together for the holidays. His childhood had been so damn sad, so quiet, that he looked forward to Christmases, birthdays, and Easter egg hunts with lots of laughter, cookies baking, and children racing around.

Me and Elzy.

Wild Billy and Calamity Jane.

Forever.

Damn, how many times had they made love last night? Arousal kept awakening him, and he'd found his hands roaming her body, his face burrowing into her neck. When he'd grabbed hold of her breast and squeezed, she'd moaned so sexily, he'd had to slide inside her hot, slick heat.

His cock went stiff at the memory. He was insatiable for her.

"Elz?" He threw back the covers, but when she didn't answer, he tensed.

Because he remembered.

We're not back together. I need you to understand that.

This is just one night. I need to know you're okay with that.

No, I'm not fucking okay with that. He stalked to the

bathroom. The faint dampness and scent of perfumed soap and lotion lingered, but it was empty.

When he saw she'd taken her tote bags, fear exploded in his chest. He grabbed his slacks and dug into the pockets until he found his phone.

Trevor: Hey, where are you?

Elzy: Waiting to talk to the concierge. I need to rent a car and get directions.

Trevor: I have a car. And GPS. I can get us back to the hotel.

Elzy: I'm not going to the hotel. I'm going north.

This is bullshit. He called her.

"Hey." She sounded pleasant and professional.

"*Hey?*" After the night they spent together, that was all he got? "Were you planning on taking off without me?"

She didn't answer right away. "No."

"You took everything with you."

"Okay, yes, I'm leaving. You know I've got a tight schedule—that's now become even tighter thanks to a storm. But if you want to have breakfast before I leave, that's fine."

He scraped a hand through his hair. "Breakfast? You think I want fucking breakfast with you? Elzy, I want forever. I want you for the rest of my life and all the way across eternity."

"I told you last night—"

"I know what you told me. But that was before I looked into your eyes and saw your actual feelings. And now, you're telling me it meant nothing? Because it rocked my fucking world, Elz."

"Trevor, I'm sorry, but I have to go. It's my turn with the concierge. I'll talk to you later."

She disconnected.

Oh, hell no.

Look, he took full accountability for her reluctance. He wasn't foolish enough to think she could trust him again so easily. Which was fine. He'd be patient. He'd give her all the time she needed to learn he'd changed and wouldn't make the same mistake again.

What he wouldn't give her was space.

Nope. None of that shit.

In yesterday's pants and dress shirt and carrying the bags of gifts, Trevor strode out of the elevator to find thirteen costumed men dressed as Yule lads in the lobby.

Wearing fake white beards and wool beanies, they carried burlap sacks of candy canes. Playing up their roles as tricksters, they yanked hats off kids, spun women around as if they were on the dance floor, and broke into random summersaults and cartwheels.

Despite the chaos, he found Elzy immediately. She stood by the fireplace watching him approach. With her chin tipped, a mask of professionalism in place, he could practically hear her internal thoughts: *I told you last night was closure. Nothing more.*

Yeah, fuck that. The moment he reached her, he dropped his bags, wound an arm around her waist, and jerked her up against him. He kissed her right there in the lobby, a deep, slow, exploration of the only mouth he would ever taste again.

When she was well and truly soft and pliant in his arms, he said, "Hungry?"

Pink stained her cheeks, and he'd kissed the lipstick off her mouth. "I could eat." As he grinned at her shaky voice, she reached into her purse and pulled out a sleek, black tube.

When she moved to apply the red lipstick, he said, "Unless you want to run out of that shit, don't bother."

She tossed it back into her purse, but he didn't miss the smile she was fighting. "There's a restaurant I'd like to try," she said. "My car should be here by then."

"Sounds like we have options. We either un-rent it, or we drive your rental, and I leave Chris's car here. Up to you." *Either way, I'm going with you.*

And before he could come up with a single reason to convince this competent, independent, professional, badass woman why she needed his help *or* his company, she said, "I can't un-rent the car, but if you want to drive, then I'll be able to get some work done."

"Sounds like a plan. Well, let's not burn any more daylight." Of course, that expression didn't apply to Iceland in winter. At this early hour, it was still dark outside. He grabbed her bags and headed for the concierge. "Can you hang on to these for about an hour?"

"You got it." The man wrote out a ticket and handed it over.

"Thanks, man."

"Oh, wait. Just one second." She dug into one of her bags and pulled out a blue beanie with a puffin emblem. "Here." She handed it to him.

"Thanks." For the last twelve hours, he'd forgotten all about kilts and selfie sticks. Forgot about the last thirty years of his life in motion pictures. But he was glad for the disguise. He didn't want anyone to interrupt his time with her.

As he headed into the revolving door, she held back, as if waiting for the second enclosure, but he grabbed her hand and hauled her into his. "I don't like that you ran from me," he said quietly in their private, glassed space. "But if you really want me to back off, I will. You call the shots. But just so there's no doubt, I want this. Us." Before she could answer, they spilled out onto the frosty pavement. "Damn, it's cold."

"That's because the storm's moving in faster than they expected." She glanced up at the cloud cover. "Which is why I've changed my plans."

"Changed them how?"

"I can't miss my niece's wedding tomorrow, so I moved up my flight. I'll spend an hour or so with Piers and then head right back to the city."

She could keep trying to convince herself they were nothing but high school flames getting high on the fumes of first love, but the tremble in her hands and heat in her eyes said otherwise.

That's why she's running. Because last night proved the passion, the love, still burned bright. Until she told him to fuck off, he was not giving up.

"It's hard to get used to this kind of darkness at seven in the morning."

"Right?" She laughed.

They joined a crowd gathered at the crosswalk. "So, what about the wine tasting? Are you skipping it?"

She cut him a look. "Since there's no wedding, Chris can choose his own sommelier. I'm not needed for that."

"Yeah, I'm sorry for misleading you." Not a good start to earning her trust.

"Misleading, huh? Is that what we're calling it?"

They headed across the street. "The moment I told you the truth, you would've sent me packing. I wouldn't have had any reason to go to the tastings, and I couldn't risk it. I couldn't miss out on this time with you. And, if you noticed, I didn't pretend to be engaged. I wasn't playing a role. I just didn't announce that we'd called it off."

"Whatever."

Now was not the time to defend bad behavior. He brought their joined hands to his mouth and kissed the back of hers. "Nothing's 'whatever' with us. I deceived you, and I'm sorry. It won't happen again."

He had one day left with her. One day to convince her to give him a second chance. He couldn't afford any missteps.

"That's it right there." She pointed to a restaurant with glowing yellow windows. The wreath hanging on the restaurant door was made of books and lit by four electric candles. "The concierge recommended it. You haven't eaten yet, have you?"

"Are you serious?" he asked. "I barely had time to shower."

"Good. I'm starving." She stopped to read the menu. "This looks great. What do you think?" When she looked up at him, she seemed surprised to find him standing so close.

Get used to it. "Why did you run?"

"I didn't *run*." The light from the restaurant illuminated the cloud of vapor coming out of her mouth when she spoke. "I think you forget I'm here to work. Chris isn't paying me to lounge around in bed with my ex-boyfriend."

He held her gaze because there was nothing to say. They both knew she was lying.

She let out a frustrated breath. "Fine. I ran."

"Why?"

"Because we're not on the same page and now is not the time to have that conversation."

He sure as hell had his work cut out for him. But they had to get on the road, and the aroma of coffee was so strong, his stomach grumbled. "Let's grab a table." He held the door open, his hand pressing lightly against her lower back as he followed her into the bright, festive café. "Wait. This is a bookstore."

"It's both."

The place was mobbed. "What's going on here?"

"Apparently, in Iceland, everyone reads a book on Christmas Eve. How great is that? I might have to make it a thing with my own family."

He wasn't much of a reader, but an image hit of the two of them in his sitting room, a fire blazing, curled up on the loveseat as they drank hot tea and read. The only sound would be the pops and crackles from the fire. "That's a tradition I can get behind."

As long as I'm with you.

"They also open their presents on Christmas Eve."

"What does that leave for Christmas Day?"

She shrugged. "That's when they visit family and have

parties. I learned all about it from the concierge. Which proves my point about how important their role is in a resort."

She was doing it again. Wearing the "consultant" mask. "Let's look for books after we eat."

"I won't be here tomorrow night, remember?" she asked. "I'm leaving tonight."

"Okay, but we're starting that tradition for ourselves, right? After you're done celebrating with your family, you can read." *And I'll do the same wherever I am.*

He had several open invitations to spend holidays with good friends. His producer, Darby… But the only place he wanted to be was with his son and grandkids.

He'd call Cole and ask him how best to be in their lives. Time was too precious. He didn't want to miss a moment with the people he loved. He'd done enough of that.

After they settled into their booth by the window, they placed their orders and waited for their coffees.

Her phone buzzed, and she read the screen. "I told Piers we'd have to skip whale watching, but he said it was canceled anyhow."

"The whales are probably hanging out in their underwater caves, reading books and sipping hot cider."

She laughed. "Oh, I don't know about that. He says the orcas are pretty active, so I'm bummed to miss out on that. But the point is to get a sense of his personality, you know? How he handles pressure, how good he is at communicating. I can only get that from spending time with him."

"Got it. Well, I'm just the driver, so whatever you need me to do, I'm down."

"As long as we head back by noon, I'll have plenty of time to get to the airport."

The clock was ticking, and he wasn't going to babble about travel plans anymore. "You said we're not on the same page, and that's something we have to talk about. If you tell me you don't feel the same way I do, and you want me to leave you alone, I'll do that. It will suck, but I'll respect your wishes. But if there's any hope for us, then I'm not giving up."

She sighed in resignation. "Trevor, I'm not the same woman you left alone in that motel room. That woman was free to run wild with you. That woman loved and trusted with her whole heart. That woman… She's gone. This woman sitting here with you today is different. You might not like her."

Okay, wow. He hadn't expected that answer. "I've met a lot of people in my life, and the truth is, I haven't clicked with many of them. I just haven't. I don't know why. I can't explain it, but with you, even after all this time, it's real, and it's powerful. And I don't want to live without it." He started to reach across the table for her hand, but he stopped himself. *She doesn't want it.* "Do you feel anything even close to what I do?"

"Yes, of course I do. I think last night answered that."

"But?"

"When we were twenty, you didn't know what you wanted to do with your life. You didn't want to farm. You weren't interested in law or medicine. And now, you're in the same position. Your career is over, and you don't know what you want to do next. And I know you. You crave meaning. I don't want to throw myself into this with you, only for you to walk away the moment you find your calling."

Fuck it. He reached for her hand. "Sweetheart, *you're* my calling. I wasn't allowed to think or even act on it, but it's always been my truth. And I don't care how it sounds. I don't care what anyone thinks. The only thing I've ever wanted is to be with you. I want us to buy a ranch in Calamity. I want us to—"

"Here you go." The server set their plates down in front of them.

"This looks great." Elzy beamed a smile. "Thank you."

"Can I get you anything else?" the server asked.

"No, this is perfect." Elzy stirred the granola and fresh berries into her yogurt. "Mm. Good." She dabbed her mouth with a napkin. "Did you ever try directing or producing?"

"Nah." *Really?* She was going to ignore his confession? He'd never admitted that to anyone before. After spreading cream cheese on his dense, dark rye bread, he topped it with smoked salmon and pickled onions. "I've been offered lots of jobs over the years. My agent liked to talk about 'stretching' my acting skills. But I'm not interested in crying or delivering some emotional performance. The role of James Mackintosh was perfect for me because all I had to do was run onto the battlefield and—"

"Make love to beautiful co-stars. Over thirteen films, you had children and wives die, you've had sex with countless women—"

"None of it was real. You know that, right?"

"Of course. I'm just saying, I think you're a better actor than you realized."

"Elzy." He broke into a slow grin. "Does that mean you watched my movies?"

With a sniff, she flicked invisible crumbs away from her bowl. "Who hasn't?"

"Did you go by yourself?" he asked.

"Sometimes."

He leaned across the table. "Did you touch yourself?"

She balled up her napkin and tossed it at him. "You're disgusting."

With a smug smile, he went back to eating. "I notice you didn't answer the question."

"No, Trevor. I didn't *pleasure myself* in a movie theater."

He tipped his head to the side. "So, you waited till you got home?"

"No. I hated you, remember?"

He handed her the napkin. "Sometimes, hate sex is the best. Do you remember when you were so mad at me you skipped school—"

"And you hot-wired Jimmy Labrosky's truck and drove to my house?"

He laughed. "I could see you running around locking doors and windows—"

"And yet you still got in." Grinning, she rolled her eyes. "Who climbs onto a roof?"

"The guy whose girlfriend accuses him unjustly of fucking around with another girl."

"Uh, you were screwing around. I saw it with my own eyes."

"You saw a man who didn't want to be at a party. I went upstairs to be left alone."

"It was a bedroom. And you went upstairs because you

were having a tantrum. You wanted to leave, and I wanted to stay."

"Between the farm, school, and the football team, I didn't have enough time alone with you."

"So, you decided to spend what time you did have with Precious Grace Olson?"

Even though it was the most ridiculous conversation in the world—rehashing something that happened when they were seventeen—he still loved it. Because she was smiling, and the shared history was stitching them back together.

"Since you need a refresher, I'll remind you I was in there alone before she came in."

"Right, and then you wound up cuddling in bed."

"That's not how you found us, and you know it. She was freaking out because Bill Oberlansky threw up on her shoes. She rinsed her legs off in the bathtub, and I got her a towel. I was only talking to her because she was crying. Period. I did nothing wrong, and you know that because you 'saw it with your own eyes.'"

"And you're telling me if you'd walked into a bedroom during a party and found me canoodling with Bill Oberlansky, you wouldn't have been upset?"

"I would've knocked him out cold."

"Okay, see?" She sounded triumphant. "You should not be alone in a bedroom with another girl."

"Especially one as pretty as Precious Grace Olson?"

"Okay, now, you're just winding me up. She was not that pretty."

"She was the Wind River Queen two years in a row."

"Well, then, you should've dated her." She had that fire in her eyes that got him all stirred up.

"I never wanted her. I only ever wanted you. And did you forget that she smelled like Bill Oberlansky's puke that night? There was no canoodling, I can promise you."

"Well, that's true. Okay, you win. But you still broke the attic window and chased me around my house in the middle of the school day."

"The window was already broken. I just finished it off." Which was why he'd wanted to earn enough money, so their families didn't have to live like that anymore. "And it was hardly a chase."

"Gee, sorry if I couldn't outrun a six-three man with zero body fat."

"Or maybe you wanted me to catch you so you could run your hands all over this zero-body fat chest of mine. Hey, Elz." He started to unbutton his shirt. "Remember that six-pack you used to lick?"

She burst out laughing.

But the smile faded when a woman approached their table. She leaned over and said, "I know this is so bad, and I should leave you alone, but come on. You're Trevor Montgomery. I've loved you longer than I've loved my husband. I know you're not wearing your kilt, but can I get just one little selfie? I promise not to make a scene or draw attention to you." She squeezed into the small booth beside him and handed her phone to Elzy. "Will you please take one?"

He hated the interruption, hated the way a fan turned Elzy into an outsider. This woman had popped the bubble of intimacy, and he didn't like it. But the only alternative to taking the selfie would be to put Elzy in the picture, and if the media found it, they'd track her down and station themselves outside her house. So, he smiled, and the woman thanked him and quietly slipped away.

"I'm sorry."

"Don't be." She seemed okay with it. "You're a movie star. I'm sure it happens all the time."

"It rarely happens in Calamity." How did he get them back on track?

"But this is a good opportunity to get the inside scoop." She leaned across the table and whispered, "Commando or boxers?"

"Sweetheart, the whole world wants the answer to that. You think I'm giving it up that easily?"

She laughed.

"Well, there you go. Looks like I just bought myself more time with you." He motioned to get the server's attention. It was time to hit the road where he could be alone with her.

Chapter Fourteen

WHILE TREVOR DROVE, JESSICA PRETENDED TO BE engrossed in something on her laptop screen.

But she wasn't seeing words or colors or pendant hanging lights.

She was back in the café.

You're my calling.

Of all the things he'd said over the past two days, that was the one that hit home.

I don't care how it sounds. I don't care what anyone thinks. The only thing I've ever wanted is to be with you.

He'd changed the landscape when he'd said it with such plain-spoken, raw honesty.

It rocked her world. Because if she believed him—and she did—it meant… Well, it meant they'd have a future.

If she wanted one.

Every minute spent with him hacked away at her walls. That distance she kept talking about? Every story they told, every memory they shared, erased it.

And that scared the crap out of her.

Because now what would keep her heart safe? What was to stop her from falling in love with him all over again?

Even worse, she knew she'd never fallen *out* of love.

If you had, you'd have felt indifference. You'd have stopped thinking about him.

Instead, she'd carried fury, loathing, anguish… Yep, all the passionate emotions.

She glanced out the window. Over the last hour, they'd driven along the shoreline, through tunnels, and across miles of farmland.

She'd managed to get some work done, of course. Even though they had more time to plan now, Chris knew he wanted to hire the Westman Island chef, so she'd sent him an email and added his wife to the list of pastry chefs to interview. She'd talked to a dozen Pullman family members who were as friendly as Chris and Darby. All were ready to get to work.

A text came in.

> Chris: Sommelier's a no. She's unwilling to leave her job in Reykjavik to come out to "the middle of nowhere." She said she'd "wait and see if the place turns into something" before she'll consider it.

"Crap." Her voice cracked the silence.

> Jessica: There are plenty of sommeliers in the world. We'll find someone even better.

> Chris: I like your attitude.

> Jessica: But now that there's no wedding, we're in no rush.

> Chris: True. You mad about that? I promise I didn't know. My sister didn't tell me until we got in the car to see my poor father who'd fallen down a set of imaginary stairs.

> Jessica: Not at all. I've hit everything on my to-do list. It's all good.

> Chris: Let me know how it goes with Piers.

> Jessica: Will do.

She set her phone in the cup holder.

"Everything okay?" Trevor's deep voice hit her core in the most delicious way.

Had she always been this affected by it? She didn't remember, but she liked uncovering new aspects to their relationship. "The sommelier doesn't want to work out in the sticks."

"You said she's the only one in the country, so it's not unexpected, right?"

She nodded. "We'll find someone."

Snow flurries hit the windshield, and he flicked on the wipers. "Look at that. It's already started." His fingers tightened on the steering wheel. "How many resorts of your own have you opened?"

"Sweetwater's my third—and last."

"Why last?"

"Working with unreliable vendors and contractors, irrational people, living out of a suitcase…it's just a lot, and I'm ready to slow down."

"What will that look like for you?" he asked. "How will you spend your time?"

"Well, I'm still going to be involved. I love it. It's truly the best thing I've ever done. But I never want to live in a hotel again, so I'd like to buy a place of my own. Nothing big. But…peaceful."

"In Calamity, right?"

"Well, I dragged my entire family out there, so I'd better stay." She laughed.

He had a wistful expression. "That was always the difference between us. You understood that spending time with your family was what kept them together. I thought it was giving them financial security."

"But you know now, and that's what matters. You have the rest of your life to give your son what you failed to give him the first half of his life."

He reached for her hand and just as he squeezed it, the car jerked. "Shit." Eyes on the road, he turned into the slide. He wasn't going too fast, so he easily corrected. "Ice patch."

The sky was darkening, and flurries turned to a steady snowfall.

"Maybe we should pull over." On one side of the highway, a scrubby field led down to a slate-gray ocean. The other side was mountainous. There wasn't a house in sight.

"Yeah, it's not safe to drive."

"Let me text Piers and see if there's a hotel or restaurant up ahead. Maybe get a coffee."

"Sounds good."

Jessica: Hey, the storm's coming in faster than we expected. The roads are icy, so we think it's best to get off the road. GPS says we're thirty-two minutes away from you.

Piers: Good idea.

Jessica: Is there anything out here? Hotel, restaurant, gas station?

Piers: Unfortunately, you won't see civilization for another twenty minutes. Have you passed an orange lighthouse?

"Did we see an orange lighthouse?" she asked Trevor. "No, but I wasn't paying attention."

Jessica: We didn't notice one.

Piers: You would've seen it. Okay, listen. The highway's going to make a slow curve around to the left. You'll see the lighthouse at the end of the promontory.

Jessica: Got it. Will look out for it.

Piers: It's closed for the winter, but I know the family that owns it. Let me call them, and they'll open it for you.

Jessica: It's so close to Christmas. I don't want to bother anyone.

Piers: They won't want you on the highway during a snowstorm. Plus, it's a hotel in the summer, so it's set up for guests. Stay the night if you need to.

> Jessica: Oh, no. I have a—

But she didn't bother sending it. What could he do about it? "I'm going to miss my flight."

"It's possible. But we should be able to get you out first thing in the morning."

"Tomorrow's Christmas Eve. Everything might be booked."

"Elzy?"

She glanced at him.

"I'll get you on a flight the moment the runways are cleared."

She smiled. "The perks of being a movie star?"

"Yep."

"No wonder you wouldn't change anything."

"Hey, now. I said I wouldn't change anything because of Cole. Not because I can afford to charter a jet."

"What about getting a reservation in a fancy restaurant that's booked a year in advance?"

He hunched a shoulder. "Eh. I don't call that one in very often."

"But you probably get the presidential suite in every hotel you book?"

"Now, that's a nice perk. Yes, I'm beginning to see your point."

She laughed. "And you probably get backstage passes to all your favorite bands. And they'd probably open Disneyland just for you and your granddaughters."

"Probably. But I haven't pulled shit like that."

"Oh, come on. Not once have the words, 'Do you know who I am?' come out of your mouth?"

He gave her a chiding look. "Not one time."

"Well, that's because you don't need to. You have this magical energy field around you. When you walk by, doors open and flowers bloom. Little fairies follow you, sprinkling their pixie dust all over the land."

"Yeah." He laughed. "That glitter gets fucking everywhere."

"You have to admit you lead a charmed life. While the rest of us have bad hair days and clogged toilets, you're untouched by it all."

"Is that right? You think there's a plumber living in a wing of my mansion? An entire staff of handymen playing cards and smoking cigars waiting around until I need them to fix the broken garbage disposal?" His good mood was flagging.

"Don't you?"

"You know how I grew up. I can change a flat, fix a plow, birth a calf, and duct tape a pair of Converse All-Stars."

"Ooh, I love a handy man."

"Handy or handsy?" he asked.

"Now that depends on whose hands."

"Fair point."

"Did you do your own stunts?" she asked.

"Absolutely. That was the fun part."

"So, you're telling me, you actually landed in a pile of manure?"

He grinned. "Exactly how many times did you watch each of my films? Did you take notes?"

"Well, let's be honest. Some moments were more memorable than others."

"Like me landing in a heap of pig shit?" he asked.

"That was particularly satisfying. So was the time that woman slapped you. You cheating son of a bitch."

"That shit stung." He touched a hand to his cheek. "But —and I hate to break it to you—*Titanic* was filmed in a pool. And nothing on the table in banquet scenes is actual food. It's created by an artist. Sex is simulated and supervised by an intimacy coordinator. Oh, and whiskey is actually iced tea."

"Wait just a minute. In a pool? So, it wasn't actually freezing, and Kate and Leonardo weren't in the middle of the ocean? My God. How else can you shatter my illusions and take all the fun away from movies?"

"The food in the great hall of my films was cast in resin. And for close-ups, they invent weird concoctions to make it look real. Like an ice cream sundae might be mashed potatoes covered in motor oil."

"Well, thank you, Trevor. Thank you for sucking all the magic out of it." She reached for the car door handle. "I think we're done here."

"Hey, you asked. But that's my point. You can keep insisting my life's nothing but roses and sunshine, but it just isn't true. My reality isn't what it looks like on social media. No one's is."

"You're right. And I'm sorry I keep doing that."

"I get it. You want to hold on to your idea of me. But I'm not the inexperienced guy who left and never looked back. I'm someone who once loved every single part of you, who never wanted to hurt you—never wanted to live without you. I just fucked up, Elz. I fucked up, and I'm trying to make it right. I'm trying to get us back."

"I'm not sure it's possible."

"Well, then, prepare yourself. Because I'll die trying."

How could she not smile at a statement like that? She whacked him on the arm. "You haven't changed one bit."

"Which means?"

"You're a passionate man who goes after what he wants."

"Nothing wrong with that, right? But the important piece is whether he *gets* what he wants."

"It sure looks like it," she muttered. Because she genuinely liked this man. And the more time she spent with him, the harder it was to deny their crackling connection. It was his touch, sure, but it was also the energy in their conversation. She didn't have that with anyone else.

He was right. His insistence on clearing up the misunderstandings and offering a true picture of his life and his experiences was breaking down her defenses. Affection was pouring in through every crack and hole.

"One of the extras used to hang out in my trailer, and we'd talk about everything under the sun. He talked about the multiverse and how we're living countless lives at the same time. And it gave me comfort that somewhere, on some mystical plane, I was living my life with you. Most nights before I fell asleep, I dreamed about it." He shook his head. "I figured it was probably bullshit, but that didn't stop me from wanting to get there. How the fuck do I get to that plane of existence where we're together?"

Tears burned the backs of her eyes, and a painful knot formed in her throat. "What did it look like? Our life together."

"We had a ranch in Calamity."

Of course we did. "Robbers Roost."

"We took long hikes. I built us a tree swing."

"You better put a cushion on it. They're not as comfortable as they look."

"You think I want my girl to have a sore ass? Of course, I did." He smiled.

My girl. She liked that. It made her feel all warm and soft inside.

Something struck her. From the moment he walked out of that motel room, she'd gone hard. All that bad-bitch energy she applied to tackling a newborn and building a career had kept her locked in it.

But it was Trevor who allowed her to be soft. And that was really nice.

"I pictured us cooking together," he continued. "Laughing a lot. Spending our nights in front of a roaring fire."

"Reading or talking?"

"Talking. Making out."

"Seriously, that's what we're doing?" she asked. "We're 'making out'?"

"Hey, I was giving you the romantic version. You want the truth? Fine. We were fucking. There was a lot of fucking going on in my dreams."

She laughed. "Were we poor?"

"You know, I didn't really go there. I was mostly thinking of where to hide a rubber spider. My favorite is in your slipper, so you'd feel something with your toes."

"Jerk. Did I retaliate?"

"Oh, hell yeah. It's become a thing. We've done it for years. I got more creative about it. You..." He grimaced. "Not so much."

Her laughter filled the car. "Do we have kids?"

"Yeah. Lots of them."

The ache in her heart had her smile fading. "I'll bet you're a great dad."

"The best. You want to know why?"

She nodded.

"Because you taught me how to be there for them. How to listen. You taught me what they need most is me, my time. I learned from your example to give them what I needed from my parents but never got."

Tears spilled a hot trail down her cheeks. Her heart could barely stand the life they'd missed out on. She would've loved it.

"There it is," he said.

They'd reached the curve in the road, and a bright orange lighthouse rose tall in the mist. She texted Piers.

> Jessica: We see it.

> Piers: Great. Door's unlocked. Clean towels on the counter. He's already got a fire going.

> Jessica: Amazing! How do we pay him?

> Piers: He's not looking for payment. It's just one night.

> Jessica: Thank you so much! We appreciate this more than you know!

> Piers: Will I see you tomorrow?

She glanced at Trevor, believing he'd do anything to get her home to her family for Christmas Eve.

Jessica: I don't think so. Let's talk in January, and then, I'll come back in the spring.

Piers: Sounds good. Merry Christmas!

Jessica: Merry Christmas!

The driveway had not been plowed, so it was impossible to see where they were going. Trevor white-knuckled the wheel, concentrating on getting them as close to the lighthouse as possible.

"I wonder where the family lives." She unbuckled as soon as he cut the engine. "I haven't seen any sign of life out here."

"Go on inside. I'll grab our bags."

That morning after breakfast, they'd bought a few essentials like underwear and toiletries, so they were set for the basics. And Trevor got a parka and gloves—thank goodness for that.

Too bad they hadn't thought to buy some food. She clutched the neckline of her coat and dashed up the steps. Icy wind whipped her face.

She held the door open, waiting for Trevor, who had his arms loaded with bags. He rushed inside, and she slammed the brutal wind out behind him.

"Damn." He stomped his shoes on the welcome mat.

Part of her still lingered in the multiverse world he'd created for them, so she didn't respond. She couldn't. It was too sweet, too perfect.

But also, unbearably sad to think of all they'd missed out on.

"Look at this place," he said.

The bottom floor of the lighthouse had a welcome desk, a few chairs, and a coffee and tea station. Empty, of course. But she found a note on the counter.

> *Welcome to the Rán Lighthouse!*
>
> *We're very happy to host you. Please make yourself at home. I've set out fresh towels, sheets, and extra blankets in the Bird's Eye Room at the very top—that's for our most special guests—and I've left some toiletries in the bathroom. We turned on utilities, so you should already have hot water.*
>
> *When you leave, please text Piers to let us know.*
>
> *Merry Christmas!*

"That's so nice of them." As she reached for some of the bags, she heard tires crunching over ice. "Who could that be?"

Trevor set his load down to answer the knock at the door. A woman with a wool hat and puffy, bright orange coat stood there with several insulated bags. "Welcome. I brought you some food."

"That's so nice of you." Jessica hurried over. "You didn't have to do that."

Three children came in behind her, arms full of goodies. "It's nearly Christmas, and you're stranded. We wanted to."

"Thank you." Trevor relieved the kids of their offerings. "This is very kind of you."

"You're welcome," the woman said. "This should tide

you over, but if you need anything else, just let me know. I've taped my phone number to the red bag. Now, don't try to clean up when you leave. Treat it like any hotel room you'd stay in. Okay, we'll be off. Be safe."

"I don't even know how to thank you for your generosity." Jessica walked them to the door. "By the way, what does Rán mean?"

"It's the Norse goddess of water." The woman headed out, and the kids followed her.

"She lures sailors into her watery depths," the oldest child's voice got snatched away by the wind.

"And she catches them in her net," another called.

"Rán means robber," the littlest said.

Jess waved goodbye and then closed the door behind them. She turned back to Trevor. "Of course it does."

"What could be more fitting for a couple of outlaws from Wyoming?" Even as he tried for levity, he was watching her carefully.

Because this man could read her like a book, and he had to sense her sadness. But what was the point in dwelling on all they'd lost? They had this moment. And who knew what the future might bring? She reached for the insulated totes. "Can you believe they did all this? I wonder what they brought us."

"Let's go find out." Trevor loaded up.

"I mean, if we had to get stuck in a snowstorm, this is the way to go, am I right?" There. She sounded normal. Fun.

"You got that right." He led the way to the elevator.

They loaded everything and then settled in for the ride to the top. They were alone in a little box filled with the scents of roasted meat and warm bread. "That world I described of us?"

See, he did know her. She nodded.

"We can have it."

"Oh, well, I'm not going to have nine children with you."

"What about grandkids? Grand nieces and nephews? Cousins, aunts, uncles, in-laws. We can have the big family we always wanted. It'll just look a little different."

She smiled because his endless optimism and his absolute confidence in their future made her unabashedly happy.

And now, she was completely alone with him in a lighthouse on the southern coast of Iceland.

Whatever will we do to pass the time?

Chapter Fifteen

"You have *got* to see this," she called.

Trevor hauled the last couple of bags from the elevator and joined her in the top-floor suite.

"Isn't this incredible?" she asked.

He knew she meant the three-hundred-sixty-degree windows, the fluffy white comforter, and the rustic wood furniture, but he was captivated by her.

The way she smiled so unreservedly undid him. Because it meant she was no longer encumbered by anger and resentment.

It meant she truly forgave him.

And that threw the door open to the possibility she'd take him back.

"What do you think?" She gestured around the circular room.

He was distracted by a fierce need to reach for her, kiss her senseless, and tumble her onto the bed, but she wanted an answer, so he paid attention to his surroundings.

Maybe he'd expected a nautical theme for an

oceanfront guesthouse because he was surprised to find a treehouse. A fabricated tree took up one corner of the room, and plate glass windows let in the night sky. The snow covering the skylight muffled sound and created a cozy sense of well-being in the middle of a raging storm. "It's nice."

"Wait, look inside." She showed him the knot holes in the tree, all of them glowing with a buttery light.

Each held a different scene in a fairy's life. "That's cool. My grandkids would get a kick out of this." In one, a fae with translucent wings wore an apron and held a rolling pin, flour dusted on her cheeks. In another, a family sat at a table sharing a big meal. A dog had a whole turkey in his mouth, and the dad chased him.

"Here." The moment she relieved him of some of the bags, she got busy setting up a picnic on the café table. "Wow, she thought of everything." She held up napkin-wrapped cutlery. "She even wrote little notes telling us what each dish is. This is smoked lamb." She pulled more cartons out. "Peas, cabbage, and this is flatbread." Unwrapping it, she showed him the lattice-work design of the round, thin bread. "It's so pretty."

Overcome with happiness, he could only nod. To be alone in this tiny space, to have her relaxed and warm and… sweet… It was almost more happiness than he could bear.

She continued pulling out food. "Pickled herring. Ginger cookies. And look. Christmas ale. I hope she gave us a bottle opener." She rooted around the depths of an insulated bag. "Got it. I should seriously hire this woman. An hour ago, she found out we were stranded, and she pulled all this together. She's amazing."

He realized he was just standing there, watching her, and that kicked him into gear. He set their purchases on the bed.

"You ready to eat?" she asked.

"Sure." He joined her at the table.

"I'm going to have a little of everything." She bit into the flatbread. "Mm. This is great. Oh, look, there's a note. It says, 'This is leaf bread. It's an Icelandic Christmas tradition.' Here." She handed him a piece. "Try it."

He took a bite but barely tasted anything. Wind battered the windows and whisked the snow this way and that, and even though they were insulated and safe, the storm kept up a threatening roar outside the walls of their tower.

"Are you okay? You're being awfully quiet." She set down her fork. "Look at me so focused on myself and my plans, I didn't even think about yours. Are you supposed to be with Darby and her family tomorrow night?"

"No, I'm good. I have nowhere to be. I'd planned on spending Christmas with my son, but the kids are sick. In fact, that's what prompted my engagement."

"I'm not connecting the dots."

"Eh." He waved a hand. "Long story."

She sat back in her chair and folded her hands across her stomach. "You won't believe this, but I've got absolutely nowhere to be for the foreseeable future."

He laughed. "True, true. Okay, well, I told you I retired so I could be a better father and grandfather, but it's not going as well as I'd hoped."

"Why? What's wrong?"

"I don't know. Let's just say I'm not sure of my place in the family."

"You're the grandfather. That pretty much makes you the Big Kahuna. The top dog."

"Yeah, I don't think it works like that. They've got four little girls, and it's pure chaos at their house. I thought if I jumped right in—you know, babysat, changed diapers, made dinner—I'd become part of the family. But I'm not. I'm a guest who gets in the way." He laughed like it was a joke.

But she nodded as if understanding where he was coming from. "You don't know how well I can relate. I'm on the outside too. They're immediate family, and I'm… not. Don't get me wrong. I know they love me and want me around. It's just that I'm the aunt, the sister—I'm not the core family." She took a sip of beer. "Does your son not trust you yet?"

"I don't think it's him. Cole's a great kid. Totally open and forgiving. I think it's more about his wife."

"How so?"

He hesitated. Did he really want to talk about this? He wasn't going to look good.

"You know, you say you want to get back with me, but that's never going to happen if you filter out what you tell me." She watched him carefully. "If you're not an open book, if you're picking and choosing which stories to share, then I'm never going to fully trust you. I'm not stupid. You know that, right? I can tell when you're not being transparent."

"I don't think you're stupid at all. I think I'm going to make *myself* look like an ass by telling you what my daughter-in-law said about me. It's embarrassing."

"Oh, goodie." She rubbed her hands together. "Trevor

Montgomery's not perfect. Give me all the details. Let's go. Did you fart at the dinner table? Did you steal cake out of the hands of a baby? That's it, right? You shoved that cake in your mouth while all four teary-eyed little girls sat there and watched?"

"Thank you for creating a safe space for me to share my vulnerabilities."

She cracked up, flinging a piece of bread at him. "Oh, just say it. I'm sure it's not as bad as you think."

"Fine. But first, get that evil gleam out of your eyes."

She blinked furiously several times. "Is it gone?"

"You're enjoying this too much." He held up his hands in surrender. "But, fine. A few months ago, I heard my daughter-in-law say she couldn't handle one more person in the house." He was surprised at the hurt it still delivered. "I'd just cleaned the kitchen after dinner, helped with bath time, and read stories to the older two. I felt good, you know? Like I was contributing. So, to find out I was an imposition. It…" His mind blanked as he searched for a word that wouldn't make him sound pathetic. But then, she wanted the truth, so he gave it. "It hurt. So, I've backed off. It sucks, but I'm giving them their space. It's a big adjustment, going from two to four kids, so I get it. Anyway, at the airport, when I was heading back to Calamity for Christmas, I got a text from my son telling me the kids were all sick."

"And you took that as code for 'Don't come. We want to spend Christmas by ourselves, as a family?'"

His gaze cut to her. *How did you know that?*

"It's no surprise you'd hear it that way." She smiled.

"Your parents were martyrs. They made you feel like an imposition your entire life."

"I don't know if it was that bad." But even as he said it, he knew Elzy was right.

"Oh, come on. They paid the farmhands—which was the right thing to do—but at the expense of their own health and well-being. They lived and died by their principles."

He couldn't argue about that.

"Remember, I worked in the feedstore, so I heard all the gossip. And you were a big topic of conversation."

"Me? Why?"

"Because you were this happy, confident boy who'd show up to school in jeans that didn't fit. The soles of your shoes flapped. And they were all upset because there wasn't a damn thing they could do to help."

"Did anyone talk to my parents?"

"Oh yeah. For sure. The church ladies spent a lot of time trying to convince them of the damage they were doing to you."

"I wouldn't call it *damage*." Although maybe it was time to stop defending their actions and see his parents for who they really were. *Maybe that's how the healing begins.*

"Really? You were a growing boy, and they fed you nothing but tomatoes and bread for an entire summer. And when the community wanted to help, your parents wouldn't let them. In fact, if you had new shoes, it would mean they were vain and self-focused. You were living proof that they were 'good' people."

"You never told me this."

"That's because I'm only putting it together right now.

But even as a kid, I can remember how it felt when I came over. Your dad was either outside working or in his office. When your mom asked if she could fix me a plate, she had this pained expression like she was dreading my answer."

"What do you mean?"

"Her eyes begged me to say no. They were both exhausted and didn't want to be bothered with anything outside of the farm, their chores, and the basics of life. My point is, I felt like just being in their house was an imposition."

Something shifted inside him, a clearing that enabled him to see his past from a new perspective.

Yeah. Me, too.

"And I can't even imagine what it was like for you," she continued. "When they didn't go to your football games, you got the message you didn't matter. When they fed you tomatoes and bread, what else did you hear but you weren't important? Forget that they didn't read to you or buy you toys. Trevor, they didn't meet your basic needs by feeding and clothing you." She grew impassioned. "They neglected you. There's just no other way to say it."

"I think you're right, but it was confusing. Because they painted a different picture." It was like glancing into a mirror as you walked past, only to see a different image than what you expected. "They believed they were doing the righteous thing. Like you said, godly."

His parents were hardworking people. They were honest, moral people.

They worked the land.

They went to church.

Did they smile much? No. There was no joking around in their house.

They never set down their hoes to come to his graduation.

But that was normal for farmers. Or so he'd been led to believe.

He just hadn't seen it as neglect.

"You know, I don't think I understood until just now that taking the job in Scotland was how you showed your love."

His fork clattered on the table. "Are you serious? I said it at the time. I said, 'I have to do this for us.'"

"I know, I know. But remember, I had an entirely different perspective."

"Jesus, Elz. You knew how bad it was. My mom wouldn't buy her medication because they had to pay the farmhands first."

"I know. I just had a different understanding of love. How to show it."

"I can't tell you how many nights I'd wake up and check for the light under my door. It meant my dad was at the kitchen table again with his books and his pencil, trying to figure out what to do with the pennies in his bank account. In a good year, he had to pay off debt. He could never get ahead. Do you understand what I'm saying? My parents were never going to get ahead. They were going to stay in that cycle until they died."

"I knew it wasn't a great childhood, but I don't think I understood how bad it was for you."

"Of course you didn't. Because I was *happy* when I was

with you. I was fucking miserable when I was at home. And scared."

"Scared?"

He shrugged. "The loneliness, the quiet… It wasn't a good feeling."

"That's probably why our bond was so strong. Because I was lost and scared without my mom, and you were lost and scared in a house with parents who ignored you."

Bullshit. "Our bond was strong because you're in here, Elzy." He smacked his chest. "You know it because you feel it too. You're just scared to trust it. And that's on me. I did that, but I will spend the rest of my life proving myself. I know what it's like to live without you, and I'll never make that mistake again."

He saw the exact moment it happened. The softening in her eyes, the ease in her shoulders. She'd let down her guard.

And he was going to swoop the fuck in. "You want to know why I never dated anyone seriously? Because I never stopped waiting for you. I knew I'd find you again. I had to. Nothing else made sense. Have you ever lost anything so important you can't stop looking? You toss the whole house, search the car… You just can't let it go? It turns into this frantic feeling of loss?"

"Yes. I know exactly what that feels like."

"That's what I've lived with for thirty years."

"I know." She sounded resigned, like she hated to admit that she did too.

"But we did it, Elz." His chair scraped back, and he stood up. "We made it back to each other." He came closer, crouching at her side. "Tell me you feel this too." He placed her hand over his thundering heart. "It's not just me?"

"Yes, of course I do. How could I not?" She let it rest there for a moment before pulling it away. "But it's different for me. I had to mourn you. I had to learn to live without you. I had to let go."

"But we don't have to do that anymore."

"You were the boy who couldn't be in the same room without touching me. When my mom died, you rode your bike to my house and sat with me. You were eight, Trevor. And how many times did I walk into my classroom and find a flower on my desk? A bag of M&M's under my pillow? Remember when I was sick and missed a whole week of school? Trevor, you brought me popsicles the first day, a sketchbook and markers the second day, three DVDs the day after that... I mean, I went from that kind of absolute adoration to"—she snapped her fingers—"nothing. Just like that, you were gone. Can you imagine what that felt like?"

"No. I can't."

"So, what I'm saying is you left me. You spent the last thirty years regretting it. I spent it healing. I'm healed now, Trevor."

Anguish threatened to grab hold and yank him under, but his determination wouldn't let it. "That's why it'll work between us now. We're both healed."

She didn't look too sure about that.

And that was fair. He still carried guilt where she and Cole were concerned. "Okay, fine. I'm not as far along as you are. But I'm working on it. Can I get credit for that?"

"Sure. Now, sit down and finish eating."

"I'm still the guy who can't be in the same room and not touch you," he grumbled, but he did as she asked.

"Yeah, well, that's one of the things I've missed the most."

"Being touched?" It made him curious about her fiancé. What kind of relationship did they have?

"No. It's more…" She waved her fork as she tried to find the words. "You know what I learned about being a mom?" Her eyes went wide. "Not that I'm a mom. I'm not. But being the oldest sister and aunt, I feel like I make the magic, but I don't get to experience it. It's hard to explain."

"For the record, you're a mom. Maybe not biologically, but in every other sense of the word."

"Yeah, probably. But I just mean I'm the one who hosts the birthday parties and fills the stockings. I cook the big holiday meals."

"Your sisters never host?"

"Not really. Well, the year I had surgery, Kelly hosted—"

"Whoa, hang on. What kind of surgery?"

"Oh, it was just a cyst. It wasn't a big deal. I'm just saying I've been a lot of things in my life. I've worn a lot of hats, but I haven't been the main character in a relationship since the day you left."

He couldn't eat. Could barely keep himself seated. His need for this woman overwhelmed him. "You realize, in a parallel universe, we're eating this dinner in bed, right?"

She stilled.

"You're sitting on my lap, and I'm feeding you these potatoes because you like them more than I do, and you're thinking you shouldn't eat carbs, especially ones with salt and butter, and I'm telling you that your body is perfect, and I love your curves, and I like watching your ass jiggle while I fuck you from behind."

"Well, that's completely inappropriate." Her features flushed, and she licked her bottom lip. "Go on."

He picked his chair up and moved it right next to hers, placing his hands on her thighs. "You kiss me because you like knowing you can be completely yourself around me. You can chew with your mouth open and laugh so hard your face gets weird-looking—"

"What do you mean by 'weird-looking'?"

But he ignored her. "And you know I'll see a woman who loves food and has a gusto for life that makes me want to get closer, to soak up all that passion and break through whatever membrane keeps our bodies and souls separated."

She scraped her fingernails from his temples to the back of his head. "No one's ever loved me the way you do."

"That's because we're made for each other. In this life and every life, it's always going to be Elzy and me. Wild Bill and Calamity Jane. Do you believe me?"

She searched his eyes, color surging into her cheeks. Confidence took hold. "Yes. I think I do."

"Thank fuck." He lowered his head onto her shoulder and held her as close as he could with two armrests in the way.

Her hands fisted in his hair. "Trevor?" she whispered.

"Yeah?" Need rode so high, he couldn't look at her. Because if he saw even a hint of consent, he'd…

"I don't want it to be a parallel life. I want it to be us. Now."

Intention surged through him. He got up so fast the dishes rattled. Sliding his hands under her ass, he lifted her and carried her to the bed. Dumping her onto the mattress, he grinned at the way she laughed, so free and unencumbered. The humor faded as he gazed into the eyes he'd missed desperately. "You want to be with me?"

Biting her bottom lip, she squirmed beneath him and nodded.

"I don't mean fucking. I'm asking you if you're going to give us a second chance." He held her gaze, letting her know how serious he was. Life or death, he had everything riding on her answer.

But she didn't even hesitate. "Yes, Trevor." She pulled him down on top of her sweet, sexy body. "But you have to promise you won't hurt me again."

"Elzy, I finally have you back. I won't do anything to hurt us. You're mine." He kissed her cheek. "Mine." And then, her other cheek. "Mine." He kissed the tip of her nose. "I will dedicate my life to making you happy. I'll treasure you and listen to you, love you and support you." He couldn't wait another moment to claim her mouth.

Once he fell into the soft, slick heat, desire yanked him under. A slow, delicious churn of arousal sent his nerves thrumming. He loved the way she responded to him, matching his need, his hunger.

Lowering his hips, he wedged his cock between her legs. Her scent, her hands in his hair, the press of her plump breasts against his chest, enflamed him. Sitting up, he peeled off her wool socks. Kissing the soles of her feet, he smoothed his hands up her thighs until he reached the waistband of her pants. After unbuttoning and unzipping them, he peeled them off her body, then went back for the scrap of hot pink lace that stretched across her hips. The damp patch on the gusset of her panties stirred him up, and he yanked them off, burying his face between her legs and licking the wet length of her.

She gasped, her ass rising off the mattress, and grabbed the back of his head to keep him close. He wasn't going anywhere. He wanted her moans and the restless shift of her hips. And he fucking loved that gush of slickness when he licked just the right spot.

As his tongue flicked and circled the little nub, she rocked against his mouth, her fingers curling in his hair. Her sounds grew more frantic, and he loved it. Loved the way she let go and surrendered to pleasure.

He wanted this—her—*them*. Wanted it more than anything, and he couldn't believe he had her back.

She reared up, tearing off her sweater and unclasping her bra. Pulling him up by his shoulders, she kissed him desperately, wildly. "I almost walked away from this. I almost let fear keep me from us."

"I would never have given up. You have to know that. I'll spend the rest of my life winning you back."

"Get naked. I want all of you."

She didn't need to ask twice. With hungry eyes, she watched as he jumped off the bed and tossed aside his clothes. "I hate every second we lost."

"It's gone." Or so he hoped. "It's over."

The moment he tossed his black boxer briefs aside, she reached for his hips and pulled him to her. Her warm hand fastened around his cock, and she licked around the head.

Sensation tore through him, and he squeezed his eyes shut. That hot tongue worked him all over, getting him wet, driving him wild, and then, when she sucked him into her mouth, it flicked and explored him from tip to base. *Oh yeah. Fuck yeah.* His hands clamped the back of her head, and his hips rocked. It took every ounce of restraint to control himself.

Pleasure spun through him, winding him up, and he needed more, harder. She must've sensed it because she grabbed his ass and pulled him hard up against her, taking his cock deep into her throat. He pumped, frantic now, but his climax was just out of reach. And he knew why.

He needed all of her, their bodies pressed together, her pussy clamped around him like a slick, wet fist. So, he pulled out, tipped her back onto the mattress, and straddled her. Cupping her breasts, he pushed them together and lowered his face into her cleavage.

Her feminine scent connected with his core. Lust spiked so hard it almost hurt. He sucked a nipple into his mouth and pinched the other while his cock rocked over her stomach.

"Need you," she gasped. "Now."

Stretching out over her, he lined up at her wet opening and sank into her tight, hot channel. "You feel so good." When her legs wrapped around his hips and her hands clutched his ass, he drove into her. He loved the way she met his thrusts, loved the sexy sounds she made every time he slammed home.

But he was going to come too soon, so he pulled out and flipped her over. Hiking up her hips, he slammed back inside. The jiggle of her ass, the bounce of her tits, made him lose his mind. He reached for her, filling his palms with her breasts, holding them lightly enough to feel them shake.

When he pinched her nipples, a rush of desire spilled all

over his cock, and he kept one hand on her breast while the other sought her clit.

And then, he drove into her again and again. He lost himself completely in sensation, desire, need. And when her head tipped back, when she cried out, when her hips swiveled and twisted as if she were trying to get him inside her as deeply as possible, he lost control.

He came in fiery waves, one climax following another. Stars exploded behind his eyelids, and he soared through a state of pure elation.

Elzy, Elzy, Elzy.

She's back.

We're together.

The revelation triggered another wave of orgasms, and his brain short-circuited. He practically blacked out.

Finally, when he settled down, he fell onto his side, dragging her limp body up against him. "Swear to God, Elzy. Nothing will ever come between us again."

Chapter Sixteen

THE SECOND TIME THEY MADE LOVE, IT WAS SLOWER, more erotic. He'd kept her on the edge for so long she'd threatened to get herself off. But he'd just batted away her hand and took his sweet time.

As he'd rocked into her at a torturously delicious pace, he'd kissed the curve of her neck. "I missed this part the most." He'd feathered his fingers down to her collarbone and licked the dip. "Or maybe it's this one." Then, he'd cupped her breasts. "Mm. No. Definitely these."

And when she'd bucked her hips to get him to focus on the action below the waist, he'd said, "You're not rushing me. This mouth has already mapped every square inch of your body, and now, it's going to revisit all its favorite places, so just sit back and enjoy the ride."

When he'd finally focused his attention between her legs, he'd picked up the pace and delivered an orgasm so cataclysmic, she'd nearly blacked out.

Now, she snuggled up against him, and she'd never been more perfectly relaxed and satisfied.

When he brushed his fingers down her arm, one of his tattoos caught her attention. She grabbed his wrist. "Wait, what is this?" It was gold and black, designed to look like it was sparkling. "I've never seen one like it."

"That's a trinity knot. It's three separate entities that are interconnected."

"And what are the entities?"

"Our past." He traced the path with a finger. "Our present. And our future."

She gazed up at him, taking in the five o'clock shadow, his thick hair tangled from her hands, and affection rushed her so hard her heart fluttered out of control. "What inspired it? Just life in general?"

"I was thinking about you." He sat up, bunching the pillows behind him. "All of them are for you." On his chest, he pointed to a compass. "'You're my best friend, my lover, my peace, my motivation, my inspiration, my North Star, and the love of my life.'"

"Your wedding vows." She couldn't believe it. "You remember what you said?"

"I remember everything." He rolled to show her the ink on his back. "That's Wild Bill and Calamity Jane."

A wild west man and woman rode horses side by side through mountainous terrain.

Her fingers traced the outline on his warm skin. "You did not."

He grinned. "I did."

"Your entire body is dedicated to us." She was stunned at how wrong she'd gotten it. Everything she'd made up these past thirty years came from her fear, hurt, and anger. Not reality.

"What else would I ink on myself permanently but you? You're the love of my life."

"Well, that's just sad." And yet, she was grinning so wide, she probably looked weird.

"It was pretty fucking sad. Why do you think I want you back so badly? I can't look like a fool pining for a woman who doesn't want me. I have a reputation to uphold." He sniffed. "Sexiest man a-fuckin'-live."

She burst out laughing. "So glad I could be of service."

"We should get some sleep." He reared over her, toppling her onto her back and kissing her neck. "I'll be waking you up for more servicing all night long."

A bright light woke him up, and his eyes blinked open. It took a moment to place himself in the lighthouse, but the woman draped over him gave him a deep sense of well-being.

Oh, man, it was good. So fucking good.

He loved her. Loved her with every fiber of his being.

Over the years, people had suggested he'd idealized his first love, used it as a shield to protect himself from getting hurt again. But he'd never cared what they thought. He wouldn't say this to anyone, but the ink on his body was more than a love letter to Elzy.

It was an expression of his soul.

His phone flashed again. Maybe something was wrong with the girls? Careful not to wake Elz, he slid his legs off the bed and headed into the bathroom.

But no, nothing was wrong. Cole just sent a few pictures

of the girls. They were pretty damn cute all snuggled up together on the couch in matching Christmas pajamas, eyes riveted on what he assumed was the TV screen. Behind them, stockings lined the mantel.

He missed them. Wished he could be there. There was nothing like watching kids whisper with such innocence and sincerity into Santa's ear. Nothing like their intense concentration as they decorated sugar cookies, wanting to get the sprinkles in just the right pattern. He—

Wait a minute. Something was off with the stockings. He counted them. *One, two, three, four, five, six…*

Seven?

Did I get that right? There's a seventh stocking? He tried to enlarge the photo, but the image was too grainy to read the name. Awareness shook him wide awake.

Was that why they didn't want him around? Because someone else was staying with them for Christmas? Could be her mom. Sure, that made sense.

There was only one way to find out. He hit the Call button.

But instead of his son, Hailey answered. "Hey, movie star."

He chuckled. "How's it going? How're the girls?"

"They're better. But you know, it's just the flu. It's not that big of a deal."

He supposed he didn't need more confirmation than that. If she wasn't put out by the girls being sick, then she simply hadn't wanted one more person in the house.

Okay, that's fair. Seven people's a lot.

You had to make up the guest room, set out an extra plate. One more mouth to feed, one more person to clean up after.

But it had all worked out because the push had driven him to Iceland. Right into the arms of Elzy.

And there could be no better outcome. "Okay, well, I just wanted to check in. Is Cole around?"

"He ran out to the store. The girls want whipped cream in their cocoa."

"As they should."

But she didn't laugh. "They kept waiting for you to bring it. You promised them a sleigh ride with hot chocolate, but…"

But what? Why wasn't she finishing the sentence? "We'll definitely do that when I get home. You just let me know when it's okay to come visit."

"Trevor, can I say something to you?"

"Of course."

"You really hurt him. I just need you to know that."

"Hurt who?" What was she talking about? "My *son*?"

"I mean, you retired to spend time with him, and then, you blow him off for Christmas? You have to remember, he didn't get the big family holiday with siblings, aunts, uncles, grandparents… It means a lot to him."

"Hang on. He told me the girls were sick."

"They are, but kids are sick all the time. It's not that big a deal. It's not like we're quarantined over here."

He supposed it was time to have that conversation. "Hailey, I didn't change my flight on a whim. I wanted to be with you guys, but Cole texted—"

"I know what he wrote because he showed me. We analyzed it together because he couldn't figure out why you'd use it as an excuse to take off like that. You didn't even ask if we needed anything—which we don't. We're fine. It was just the abruptness of it, you know? He tells you the kids are sick, and boom, you're off to Iceland with your girlfriend."

Ah, hell. "That couldn't be further from the truth, but I can see how you thought that. Hailey, I know I've been underfoot—"

"Underfoot? What does that mean?"

Just say it. Bring it out in the open. "A couple of months ago, I was reading books to the kids before bed, and when I came out of Evvie's room, I heard you and Cole arguing. You said you just couldn't take one more person in your house. And I understand. You've got four kids. It's a lot. But I thought I was helping, and—"

"You are. Trevor, that is not—oh, my God—I can't believe you heard that."

"It's okay. Honestly, I get it."

"No, you don't. You know what my childhood was like. You know my mom's a 'free spirit.' Well, around September, she got a job making costumes for a singer here in town, and she wanted to live with us for a few months. I mean, I love her, but when she comes, she doesn't clean up after herself. She leaves her dirty clothes on the floor, and she doesn't put her dishes in the dishwasher. She's—"

"A fifth child." He couldn't believe he'd gotten it so wrong. "I'm sorry. I thought you meant me." At least now, thanks to Elzy, he could see why. It was a knee-jerk reaction to being an imposition in his childhood home.

"Not at all. It's not like we view you as a visitor or a guest. You're part of us. The kids love you, Trevor. *We* love you."

"Yeah, I guess I should've asked you about it."

"I wish you had. Is it too late? Can you come home for Christmas?"

She couldn't know what that simple concept meant to him. *Home for Christmas.* Something he'd longed for. Sure, his dad always cut down a tree, but they'd never done more than hang a few ornaments. No one got around to stringing the lights. They had eggs and bacon for breakfast, and then, his parents went back to work.

"Those animals can't feed themselves."

But he had a whole new life now, and he could make it whatever he wanted it to be. "I'm heading home in the morning. I'll be there."

"Oh, thank God."

"Hey, Hailey. Can I ask you something?"

"Of course."

"In the picture Cole sent me… Do I see seven stockings?"

She clicked her tongue to the roof of her mouth. "Yes. Because there are *seven* of us. And if you're not here to open your presents, we're going to have four very disappointed little girls."

It seemed impossible for one man to have this many blessings. It filled him to the brim. "Can I ask you a favor?"

"You bet. What's up?"

"Can you make an eighth one?"

"You mean for Darby?"

"No. I mean for Jessica Elsworth. She's going to be part of the family too."

He'd make sure of it.

Even though her phone told her it was morning, it was disorienting because the sky was as dark as night. The only light in the room came from the fairy windows.

And wrapped in Trevor's arms, Jessica knew there was no place she'd rather be.

Stretching, she smiled at her sore muscles. "You gave me quite the workout."

He yawned big and loud. "Right? You fucked me into a coma. I still can't feel my legs."

"Aw. You're such a romantic." She said it with a laugh and pretended to pull away.

But he tightened his hold and bit her shoulder. "I mean, if you think flowers say more than my cock and mouth and hands—"

"I don't." Her fingers gripped his arm. "Nothing will ever be more romantic than the way you want me."

He went quiet, the only movement his thumb stroking her inner wrist. "From the moment I saw you out that truck window, I've never seen or wanted anyone else. Do you understand what I'm saying? There is no one else for me."

"I do." He'd been so open and transparent with her. So vulnerable. While she'd withheld everything. And while it was scary to let herself go, he deserved it. "It's the same for me."

"Yeah?"

She kissed him on the mouth. "Yes, yes, yes." Then, she reached for her phone. "Now, I have a wedding to get to. You think the airport's open?"

"I'm less worried about the airport than the roads. We're in the middle of nowhere."

"True." Anxiety got a hold of her. "I can't miss the wedding. I just can't."

"You won't. That's a guarantee."

She opened a text from her sister.

> Amber: Bri doesn't want to risk you not being at her wedding. She'd rather reschedule.

"What? No, she can't do that."

"What's going on?" He pulled his arm away, freeing her.

She wanted it back. She wanted his strength and his confidence and his love. "My niece is talking about rescheduling."

"No." Sitting up, he swung his legs off the bed. "Tell them you'll be there."

"It's not like I can make any promises. We have no control over transportation."

He gave her a steady look but didn't say a word as he pulled out his phone and stood at the window.

Okay, she'd trust him to work that golden boy magic.

> Jessica: Tell her that's not necessary. The storm's over. I'll be there in time.

She knew her sister would be sleeping, but she sent one more text.

> Jessica: Do not cancel the wedding!

But even as she wrote it, she was riddled with doubt. It didn't seem possible.

"Yeah, then let's do it that way," Trevor said in a deep,

sleep-roughened voice. "How long will it take?" He crossed an arm over his chest. "Perfect. Thank you. We'll be ready." He turned to her. "We're good."

"What does that mean? It's about a two-hour drive to the airport. The flight's seven and a half hours—"

"Sweetheart." He cupped her elbows. "We'll make it."

"How?"

"There's a helicopter on its way to us right now. It'll take us to the airstrip, and we'll be shuttled right to the jet. You'll make it back in time. No problem."

"Are you serious?"

"Absolutely."

She set her phone down and wound her arms around his neck. "You got me a helicopter?"

His grin grew wider.

"You're such a show-off." *But you know what?* She appreciated his help so much.

"Can you think of another way to get us home in time for the wedding?"

"No, sir. I cannot."

"Good." He smacked her bottom. "I'm going to get in the shower." He pulled out a new pair of boxers and headed into the bathroom. When he glanced over his shoulder to find her staring at his tight, round ass, he said, "You've got a little"—he flicked a finger at the corner of his mouth— "drool right there."

She smiled, drunk with love. But instead of joining him right away, she stood there for a moment, letting it sink in.

Two pillows smushed from use.

Sheets pulled out from their tuck under the mattress.

Two pairs of pants on the floor.

A partner to problem-solve with.

A plus one.

Holy shit.

We're back.

She and Trevor were together again. *It's real.* And it struck her. That deep-rooted sense of loneliness that lived inside her—even when she was surrounded by the people she loved—was gone. She was whole again.

Was she scared? *Sure. Of course.* But time would fully heal her. Every minute of every day, they would prove themselves to each other.

And just knowing that was such a huge relief.

Okay, let's get going. She needed to make sure the wedding wasn't postponed, so she grabbed her phone and left a voice message for her sister.

It was then she noticed a message from someone she didn't recognize.

> Hey, this is Uncle Charlie. Jackson's dad's brother. I sat across from you at the rehearsal dinner. I tried to talk to you, but you were busy.

She remembered the groom's elderly uncle, but she didn't recall him trying to get her attention. She'd been in hostess mode, meeting Jackson's extended family and taking care of her own.

> Forgive an old coot for poking his nose where it doesn't belong, but—

Okay, he was cute. She settled in to read the rest of his message.

I heard some talk during the rehearsal. Some jokes were made about two women walking the bride down the aisle. I just thought you should know in case you wanted to back out.

Back out? What does he mean? A rustle of anxiety had her skimming the rest of his text to get to this point.

We all want the same thing, right? We want everyone's focus on the bride and groom—and not distracted by silly thoughts from the one or two knuckleheads in the room.

A sickening churn in her stomach had her moving to the window. She wouldn't do anything to ruin her niece's wedding. Of course, she didn't want anyone distracted. But what would they be thinking? What was wrong with her walking Bri down the aisle?

It's up to you, of course. But I wanted to bring it up in case you didn't want to draw negative attention.

What? Her first impulse was to reach out to her sister, but the wedding was that night, and she didn't want to stir up drama.

Jessica: Hi, Charlie. I'm sorry we didn't get a chance to talk, but I'll be sure to spend time with you at the wedding. I hope you know it wasn't my idea to walk with her. It was Bri's, and I'm honored to fulfill her wishes.

Oh, hey. Thank you for getting back to me. Like I said, I'm an old man sticking his nose in where it doesn't belong. I just know if it were me, I'd want to know if what I thought was an honor, someone else considered a pity gesture.

A chill crept into her heart. *Pity gesture?* The very idea shoved her from that warm, special place of being embraced by family out into the freezing cold.

Is it true?

When Bri asked, she'd been so touched, so *honored.* In the beginning, she'd been every bit as much of a mother to Bri as Amber had been because her sister was in school and working at the store.

Jess had given the job to her sister, so she'd have work experience to put on her résumé. She'd never minded putting her own life on hold. Someone had to take care of Bri. Her niece was an innocent baby. She needed to be loved and cared for.

Just the way my mom loved and cared for me.

Nothing was more important than that. Not that she remembered, but everyone in town loved to tell stories of how her mom worked with her babies in a sling wrapped around her chest. She took her children everywhere and never used a stroller.

Jess had wanted the same thing for Bri. So, when her niece asked her to walk her down the aisle—her mom on one side, her aunt on the other—Jessica had felt validated. Acknowledged. *Included.*

But now…she questioned everything.

Don't get me wrong.

I'm not embarrassed to be single and childless.

She just didn't want anyone to look at her with pity. She glanced outside, watching plates of ice undulate on the surface of the ocean. She couldn't believe how hurt she was. She didn't think it was true—she was very close to her niece. Well, all her sisters' kids.

She wished she could ask someone, but she couldn't bring it up. Not on Bri's wedding day. Maybe she should talk to Amber, let her know her feelings wouldn't be hurt in the slightest if she wanted to walk Bri down the aisle by herself.

No, you can't do that. That would cause a scene. And what would her sister say? *Oh, thank God. I wondered why you'd said yes. I'm the mom here.*

No, Amber would never say anything like that.

Jess didn't know what to think.

But you know what? Even if I don't walk her down the aisle, I'm going to be with Trevor. Happiness flooded her.

From now on, she'd have the love of her life at her side. There was tremendous peace in that.

And suddenly, she had a whole different kind of hunger. Already naked, she hurried into the bathroom. Curls of steam floated out of the shower stall and covered the mirror. The moment she stepped inside, her breath caught in her throat.

Water streamed down his body, his big hands moving swiftly to spread the soap over his ripped, inked torso, between his muscular legs, along his semi-hard shaft. If she didn't get her hands all over him…

His eyelids popped open, almost as if he heard her dirty

thoughts. He smirked and grabbed his cock. "You want some of this?"

"Not anymore, I don't."

He laughed, reaching for her hand and tugging her under the stream of water. With her back to his slippery chest, he shared the scented lather with her, his hands mimicking on her body what he'd just done to himself.

Leaning back against him, she submitted to his touch. The hot water saturating her hair and coursing down her body, the sensual glide of his hands over her breasts, down her belly, and between her legs, melted her worries and ignited her desire. She reached up, clasping her fingers around the back of his neck.

He lowered his chin onto her shoulder. "You're the most beautiful woman in the world."

"I am when you touch me." Overcome with affection for this man, she turned in his arms and kissed him. My God, the gentle stroke of his tongue, the clutch of his hands on her ass, squeezing and hauling her up against him…it was everything she needed.

The relief was so profound, her knees buckled.

To have him back, to feel this wholeness, this completeness…it was just overwhelming.

Gratitude mixed with lust, and she kissed a path down the strong column of his neck, from one nipple to the other, and down his stomach. Kneeling, she wrapped both hands around his cock. Pleasure softened his features, and heat burned in his eyes.

When she took him into her mouth, he moaned, and she sucked him deeply, wanting to drive him out of his mind.

He shifted his legs farther apart and cupped the back of her head, guiding her to the rhythm he needed. "Look at you. Fuck yeah."

God, that raspy, sex-drenched voice turned her wild with need.

"Nothin' prettier than that pink mouth stretched wide over my cock. Can you take more? Come on, honey. Take all of me."

He'd never talked to her like that when they were twenty.

And she loved it. The pulse between her legs grew unbearable, and she had to touch herself.

"Yeah, I don't think so." Hauling her up, he brought her to her full height and spun her around. "This pussy's mine. I'm the one who gets you off. You understand?" She nodded, as he slapped her hands against the wall. "No one but me. Now, brace." He pitched her hips back and slid his hot, hard cock through her folds, a slow thrust that teased her clit and made her tremble with need.

As he pulled back and drove inside, he caressed her breasts, his palm sliding across one nipple, to the other, and back again. The dual friction—between her legs and her sensitive peaks—wound her up so fast, she cried out. Her hips rammed back against him, and she ground herself on his cock.

"Yeah. Fuck yeah." His fingers slid into her wet heat and found her pleasure center. As his thrusts grew shorter, tighter, and more frantic, as he lost his rhythm, he rubbed circles around her.

When her body exploded with bliss, she plastered herself against the warm tiles and pushed her ass out. "*Trevor.*"

With his big hands on her hips, he drove into her with a ferocity that wound her up all over again. And when he came, his shout filled the shower stall. The steam, the heat, the absolute euphoria gave her an involuntary shudder.

He collapsed over her, wrapping his arms around her waist and holding her tightly. His breath gusted in her ear, and his fingers dug into her flesh. "I love you, Elz. I love you so much."

She wanted to say it back. She did. But resistance blocked her.

Look, it's okay not to say it back yet. So much had happened in a few short days. She'd ended her engagement, found Trevor—got involved in planning his wedding—got closure, found out she was an embarrassment to her niece, and wound up in bed with the man who'd once destroyed her.

You don't have to rush saying something so important.

But she didn't want to hurt him either, so she turned in his arms and kissed him, slow and sexy. "Thank you for taking care of this, Trevor. You don't know what a relief it is not to manage every single aspect of my life."

"Of course." He looked shaken.

Had she hurt him by not saying it back? Should she at least address it? Somehow, that seemed even worse. "You're coming with me, right? Or do you need to stay and talk to Darby?"

"I'm coming with you." Determination set his shoulders back. "I'm never going to leave your side again."

Relief swept through her. "Okay. Good. I hope you've got a tux."

He broke into a slow grin. "Yeah, I think I can scrounge one up."

The roar of the engine made it impossible to talk, so Jess took in the spectacular view from the helicopter. The Ring Road was sandwiched between mountains and ocean, but with clear skies, she had an aerial view of the rivulets in the snowy glacier.

Trevor had a tight clasp on her hand, his chin on her shoulder as they shared the view.

It was so familiar, so dear. So…heartwarming to have him back. She loved his insatiable need to touch her, be close. Now that the initial shock had worn off, she was ready to tell him she loved him. But not when she'd have to shout, and he'd say, "*What? What did you say?*"

"*I SAID I LOVE YOU.*"

She smiled. No, she'd wait for a better time.

As soon as they landed, they discovered a commercial flight taking off in less than an hour. Could they make it? They'd try.

They raced inside the airport only to find a line at the check-in kiosks. So, they waited, holding hands and stealing kisses.

"Everything all right?" he asked.

"Of course. Why?"

"You keep checking your phone."

She was, wasn't she? "I don't want to miss the flight."

"And if we do, we'll take a jet."

She nodded. "Right. Okay. I'm not used to that."

He smoothed a finger across her forehead. "Come on, sweetheart. What's on your mind?"

She hadn't even realized she was upset. But he did. "I haven't heard back from Amber, and I want to make sure they don't cancel the wedding."

They moved forward, sharing a station.

"Okay, but you keep looking at that text exchange." He pointed to the screen of her phone.

"Is there anything you don't notice?" She smiled at him.

"When it comes to you, no. What's going on?"

"I'm sure it's nothing. It's probably only in my head."

Finished checking in, they hurried to the security line. "Well, let me into your head. Maybe I can offer some perspective."

Good point. "Bri asked me to walk her down the aisle with her mom."

"That's nice. Not her dad?"

"So, her Dad's not in the picture at all. During college, he tried, but then, he moved for work, got married… Over time, he just stopped reaching out."

"And the stepdad?"

"They're very close, and she has roles for him too, just not this one. She wanted the honor of 'giving her away' to go to the people who were there for her from the beginning. Anyhow, I was very touched to be included, but this morning, I got a text from the groom's uncle. He said people were talking about my role at the rehearsal." She had a hard time even saying the words out loud. "I mean, I don't even know this guy, and he's telling me everyone thinks it's a 'pity gesture.'"

He gave a thoughtful nod. "You know the groom well, right?"

She nodded.

"You think his family would appoint this guy as the ambassador of wedding etiquette?"

She smiled. "No, I don't."

"So, then, he's just a guy stirring shit up. But you know, it sounds like your niece has been very intentional about her wedding. There's meaning in the date and the roles she assigned. So, I can't see a reason to offer her aunt a pity gesture when you'd be happy just to sit in the front row and watch the ceremony."

Her worries faded, and she squeezed his hand. "You're absolutely right." She loved him so much she could barely contain it all.

"No one knows the relationships like you do, so don't give this guy's opinion any power over you."

"You're right about that."

"Besides, I'll bet you were in the delivery room with Amber. You probably watched Bri take her first step. You were there from the beginning, so I'd bet she loves you like a mother."

"How do you know all that?"

"Weren't you?"

She laughed. He was making her feel so much better.

"I'll bet you even took her to her first day of kindergarten."

As they got in line, she nodded. "Amber didn't want to be pregnant, but she sure stepped up when the baby was born. She worked her butt off to finish high school and get job experience. She turned out to be a great mom."

"I'm not surprised. She had you as a role model."

She got up on her toes to kiss him on the mouth. "My champion."

"I know your heart. And I wouldn't listen to a word that troll says."

Fortunately, the line wasn't too long because their flight was about to start boarding. *I'm going to make it home in time.* "You're right. I know you are. But the thing is, I don't want to draw attention away from the bride and groom. I don't want people wondering why I'm walking her down the aisle instead of thinking how beautiful Bri looks." Which pretty much decided it for her. She'd take her seat and give Amber the honor.

Just as she set her toiletry bag in the bin, Trevor's phone buzzed. His brow furrowed when he saw who was calling. "Hey, Lisa. What's up?" He listened for a moment, features tensing. "Well, I'm sorry, but I can't do that." Whoever was talking spoke so sternly that he held up his finger to Jessica and gestured for the person behind him to take his place. "Hang on. I filmed my scenes. I met my contractual obligations. It's not my problem if their budget runs out on the thirty-first. I'm not giving up *my* holiday because of their screwup. You understand?"

Good for him. He's taking a stand. She stepped out of line, too, while he handled the situation.

"Oh, hey, Joe." He mouthed, "*My lawyer*" to her and then crossed an arm over his chest and listened.

She checked her phone. *Shoot.* They'd miss their flight if they didn't go right now. Not even for Trevor Montgomery would a plane keep its doors open.

With each second that passed, he grew angrier. "If the

franchise is ruined, it's not on me. I did my part, and now, it's done. I'm done."

An uneasy feeling slid through her. They knew him. Knew just how to push his buttons.

She could hear his lawyer's exercised voice talking a mile a minute and watched as Trevor grew more agitated. His jaw clamped shut, and he angled his body away from her. "Then, I guess I'll have to do it."

And that was the moment she knew why she hadn't told him she loved him.

Because at the back of her mind, a question hovered. Sure, he loved her. No question, he wanted her.

But had he changed the fundamental part that had driven him out of the motel room thirty years ago? When it came down to it, he wasn't built to put her first.

Because he'd never put his own happiness first. The lesson from his parents was too deeply and firmly entrenched.

Fuck it. She wasn't missing her niece's wedding over this man's issues. She put her belongings on the conveyor belt, passed through security, and race-walked to her gate.

She didn't bother looking back.

These days, she only looked forward.

Chapter Seventeen

Oh, God, it hurt. It hurt so badly.

Screw closure. No, seriously, it would've been better to never see him again than to relive her elopement day.

She knew he was a product of his upbringing. She'd come to terms with the fact that his happiness came last. What did she think would happen?

No, really, what did you think would happen?

Which line shouldn't she have crossed? Was it that first kiss? No, the northern lights. She should've ignored his texts. If she'd stayed in her hotel room that night, they wouldn't have made love, and she wouldn't have believed they had a chance.

She wished she hadn't let him touch her, kiss her, devour her. It wasn't fair to have something so good ripped away.

Twice.

But she wasn't going to wallow. She'd done enough of that thirty years ago. She was going to be present for her niece's wedding.

She sat alone in the first pew of her resort's cozy chapel.

She'd built it to give her guests a quiet, reverent space and to host the occasional wedding. Moonlight slanted through the stained-glass windows and dozens of white votive candles flickered on the altar. At the end of each row, a spray of gardenias offered a romantic scent.

She hadn't told Amber or Bri about the change in plans. To do so would require turning on her phone. And sorry, but she didn't want to see Trevor's pleas or excuses or anything he'd say to justify his choices.

There's nothing new there.

Contractually, he was obligated to reshoot scenes from his movie. Sure, she got it. But he could've put his foot down. He could've told them they were being unreasonable.

He could've put us first. But he just wasn't wired that way. *Forget him.*

She'd made the right choice in sitting this one out. They wouldn't have to address it or try to make her feel better. She knew she was important to them. She knew they loved her.

She just wasn't the mother. She was the aunt.

Trust me, I get it.

Even more importantly, she didn't want any other thought in the guests' minds than, *The bride's absolutely radiant.*

The wedding planner, Stella Cavanaugh—one of the first business owners Jessica had contacted in the hopes of booking weddings and honeymoons in her resort—hustled down the aisle toward her. "Hey, hon. We're about ready to get started."

Jess had expected this. She'd prepared her response. "You know, this is a special moment between a mother and a daughter." She kept her demeanor pleasant. "It's a once-in-a-lifetime kind of thing, so I'm going to let them have their time together."

Stella let out a breath and sat down beside her. "Uncle Charlie got to you, huh?"

Jess was horrified that the old man had discussed it publicly.

The wedding planner picked up her embarrassment because she set a hand on Jess's arm. "He brought it up at the rehearsal, and I promise you, everyone thought he was being ridiculous. I'm guessing, since he got no traction, he reached out to you privately?"

"He did, and that's exactly why I'm going to step back. He's planted a seed in people's minds, and I don't want anything to ruin Bri's day. Let's just keep it traditional."

"Bri put a lot of thought into every aspect of this wedding. You know what I mean? She planned it out carefully. If she wanted traditional, that's what she'd have done."

Fair point. "I hear you, but let's not make it a big deal. Let her mom walk her down the aisle, and let me sit here and watch. Okay?"

Stella gave a reluctant nod. Then, she squeezed Jess's arm and got up. "All right, then. It's go-time."

A few moments later, the seats filled up around her. Excitement shimmered in the air. Jess tried with all her might to stay just above the pain level. But she couldn't do it. She just couldn't. Sorrow rushed in, bowling over everything in its path.

She'd long ago accepted living a solo life. She loved her family—loved her *role* in her family. Nothing made her happier than seeing her sisters, nieces, and nephews live their best lives.

And I'm living mine.

If she hadn't had two and a half days with Trevor Montgomery, she'd be fine.

But she'd had that time with him. She'd basked in his adoration. Her body sang at his touch.

With her whole heart, she believed he loved her.

He just couldn't undo the programming he'd learned as a child.

And that was nothing she could fix.

But one thing was true. She could say it to herself, even if she couldn't tell him.

I love him.

I love him with everything I am.

And maybe one day, he'd get his shit together.

See that? There was still hope.

A murmur rippled through the congregation. Clothing swished as people turned in their seats, and people started whispering.

"Brianna, would you stop?" Kelly asked in a harsh whisper. "No one's supposed to see you yet."

Jess turned around in her seat. Her niece hustled down the aisle in all her bridal regalia. She thrust her bouquet at her other aunt and stared at Jessica wild-eyed. "Did I not plan every detail of this damn wedding?"

"You did." Jess glanced around to find everyone staring at them.

"More importantly, how is this a 'once-in-a-lifetime' moment if you're not in it?"

"Bri, the point was to not cause a scene." Her eyes widened as if to say, *Like you're doing right now.*

"I invited seventy-three people. They are the only people in the world who matter to me. They get me. Do you think they don't understand what you mean to me?"

Oh. Jess jerked upright. Tears stung the backs of her eyes, and pride infused her.

"She has a point, *Mom*," Kelly said.

"Shut up." Jess burst out laughing. "I'm not your mom. And again, I was trying to not make a scene."

"Well…big fail," Bri said. "Now, can you please get your ass up and walk me down the aisle? You might not have given birth to me, but you're every bit as much my momma as my mom."

"You're being ridiculous." Jess didn't even try to hide her smile as she got up and made her way to the vestibule. The entire congregation broke out in applause. "Oh, stop." But she was laughing.

"I can't believe you did that," Bri said to Jessica as she snatched the bouquet out of Kelly's hands. "I *love* you."

Jessica pulled her niece into her arms. "I love you too. I only ever want what's best for you."

"And I *told* you what's best for me." Bri clung to her. "Now, are we ready? I want to fast-forward to my Coco's Chocolates' cake. I'm going to drop my face in it."

"No kidding," Amber said. "It's all I can think about."

But Jess was holding tightly to the woman who was truly a daughter to her. "I love you, sweet pea. And I'm so proud of the woman you've become."

Bri pulled away, eyes glazed with tears. "You know my first memory? It was dark. I was cold. I heard scary noises.

And I remember I didn't say a single word. I didn't cry. I didn't call out. You want to know why?"

"Why?" Jess blinked back tears.

"Because I knew you'd come. It wasn't a hope or a wish. It was the absolute knowledge that my Yessy would come get me. And you know what? You did. You came right into my room and picked me up. You held me in your arms, and I knew I was safe. The only thing I remember is the certainty that you'd be there for me. That you'd never leave my side. And you haven't. You're my other momma, and you're walking me down the aisle."

Jess swallowed against the painful knot in her throat. "Okay, then. Let's do it. Let's get you married."

As they turned toward the chapel, Stella spoke quietly into her microphone. A moment later, the musicians began playing Brian Crain's "Butterfly Waltz," and the three women hooked arms and started walking down the aisle. All the congregants stood, their familiar faces beaming joy, and Jess smiled and nodded at everyone.

This is my family. My people. My community.

A quick thought about Trevor stabbed her heart, but no. She wouldn't let herself go there right now. Not on this beautiful, happy day.

That was for later tonight. When she was alone in bed, feet hurting from dancing, eyes red from crying after sending Bri and her husband off on their honeymoon, she'd let herself feel the loss. She'd remind herself the past few days were good, that she'd gotten the closure she'd needed. That he was a good man....

He just couldn't be her man.

Up ahead, the groom dipped his chin, discreetly wiping

away a stray tear, but there was no hiding his overwhelm at seeing the love of his life walking toward him.

As they reached the altar, Bri hugged both Jess and Amber, handed her bouquet to her mom, and then stepped into her groom's arms. They clung to each other for several long moments as the two women took their seats.

Jess clasped her sister's hand, and when they looked at each other, it was with a shared understanding. Bri had been through a lot in her life, and to know she'd found true love brought a profound sense of joy.

And if there was a hint of sorrow attached for Jess, it was only because she'd experienced a glimpse of bliss with her first love.

Just as the couple pulled apart to face the officiant, a murmur rippled across the chapel. A charged energy had everyone shifting in their seats for a second time.

"Is that Trevor Montgomery?" someone whispered.

Jess's heart thundered. Her hands went clammy. Her pulse fluttered wildly in her throat.

"What's he doing here?" someone asked.

"Oh, my God," the person behind her shouted.

Is he really here?

Did Trevor come to the wedding?

She didn't even turn around. She couldn't face the disappointment of it not being him.

"I thought you said he had to go to Scotland?" Amber whispered in a tone of disbelief.

She couldn't speak. Couldn't even nod. With her breath trapped in her lungs, she went lightheaded.

Finally, she glanced over her shoulder.

That gorgeous, tall, muscular man striding down the

aisle had his gaze fixed on her, intention so clear in his eyes, he might've been a predator. And, oh boy, would this hunter catch his prey. There wasn't a shred of doubt in him.

He came right up to her, forced himself onto a tightly packed pew, and reached for her hand. "I apologize for being late," he said to the officiant. "Please, go on."

The groom gawked, and the bride gave a comical thumbs-up gesture to Jess.

Jess was so flustered she could only flick her hands. *Go. Carry on.* She didn't want the attention on them.

But at the same time…

Oh, my God. He's here. He came.

When all the attention returned to the ceremony, she whispered, "Aren't you supposed to be in Scotland?"

"What did I tell you?" But he didn't even give her a moment to answer. "I said I'm never going to leave your side again. I'm going to be here no matter what—which you would've found out if you'd waited for the next sentence to come out of my mouth."

"You said they had until the end of the year. That's a week away."

"That's right. I'm in breach of contract if I don't reshoot scenes by then, but it doesn't stipulate *where* they film."

"What're you saying? Are you making the entire cast and crew come to *Calamity?*"

"Snowy terrain can be shot anywhere. Besides, you said your event hasn't sold out."

She wanted to burst out laughing, but she held it in. She wanted to straddle his lap and kiss him senseless. Instead, she gave him a prim answer. "It hasn't."

"Well, there you go. Now, it has. Two birds, one stone.

And with celebrities in attendance, you should get the publicity you need to put this place on the map."

She couldn't believe it. It was too much. It was amazing and beautiful and perfect. "You'll be thanked appropriately for this later." She brought their joined hands to her lap.

"We're good?" he asked.

She could only nod. They'd talk later.

Because in that moment, she had no words. She wanted to stay in this bubble of happiness forever.

She kissed his cheek, inhaling his masculine, clean scent, and rested her head on his shoulder.

And then, she whispered, "I love you."

He tipped her chin, forcing her to look into his eyes. "What was that?"

"I said I love you."

He shook his head, cupping an ear. "I'm sorry. I didn't get that."

She pressed her lips to his cheek in a lingering kiss. "I love you with all my heart."

Trevor didn't know much about living in the moment.

That ended when he'd lost Elzy. From then on, he'd held on to his past and thought only about stitching it to his future. He'd never let go of his drive to find her again.

And now that he had her, he wanted to leap over this wedding and the New Year's Eve gala and land in their ranch house, sitting close together on the couch, her wedding ring catching the light from a roaring fire.

But hey, he was on the dance floor of a swanky resort,

holding her in his arms as they swayed to a ballad from a country rock band. Life didn't get much better than this.

For the first time in years, he was content to live in the moment.

"You did an outstanding job with this place." He didn't want to shout over the music, so he spoke into her ear. Bonus: he got to brush against her soft cheek and breathe in her lovely scent.

"I'm proud of it."

He'd traveled a lot, stayed in some fine places, but the Sweetwater Spa and Resort was special. It was quiet, peaceful, and luxurious. And the service was top-notch. The staff seemed to anticipate the needs of each guest.

They'd turned the banquet room into a Christmas festival. Dinner tables circled the dance floor, and tiny white lights rained down from the ceiling.

"Looks like karma came for me, didn't it?" he asked.

She pulled away to look into his eyes. "What do you mean?"

"At the airport, it was my turn to watch you walk out of my life. My attorney tried to convince me everything was riding on this reshoot. He said they'd sue me for everything I'm worth if I didn't fly to Scotland before the end of the year. But I wasn't going to let anything come between us, so I—"

"You're not putting your savings at risk, are you?"

"It didn't come to that, but I sure as hell would have. Believe me, I've got my priorities straight. Besides, you know what I learned? Money comes and it goes. If I lost everything tomorrow, I could earn it all back."

"We'd do it together."

Which is what she'd said all along. "Exactly." He pressed a soft kiss to her mouth. "I don't care what we're doing or where I am. As long as I'm with you, I'm right where I want to be."

"Thank God for that. The idea of going another day without you…" She shook her head, a haunted look in her eyes. "I can't do it again. I just can't." Her fingers curled in his jacket, and she pressed closer.

He caressed her cheek with a thumb. "Never going to happen."

"I've never told this to anybody before, but…" She clutched his lapels now, gazing into his eyes with an earnestness, an urgency that had him wishing they were alone. "I never stopped thinking about you, *missing* you. Sometimes, I'd be on a job—walking along the beach or waiting for a meeting to start—or with my family—a birthday party, a graduation—and I would feel this…this hole in me. I thought it was loneliness, but that didn't explain why I always sensed your presence in that moment. I can't explain how the two were tied together."

"You don't have to. I know exactly what you mean. I felt it, too."

"You did?"

"Oh, yeah. That's why I knew you were inside me, part of me. It's why I was sure we'd find our way back to each other."

"It doesn't make sense, this connection. This bond. But it's real. Trevor Montgomery, you are my soulmate, and I love you with everything I am."

"*Yes.*" Warmth spread through him, and he wanted to

carry her out of this room and take her to his suite. He wanted her all to himself.

But of course, it was her niece's wedding, and they had to stay until the very end.

"I'm sorry I overreacted at the airport. But honestly, it was less about you than reading the pity gesture comment. I'm so used to being the third wheel, the best friend, the aunt…I'm the guest at everyone else's big life events. So, when I read it, it just…" She sighed. "It's an old wound."

"Yeah, well, fuck the rest of the world. You're my sun, and the only thing I've ever wanted to do is orbit around you. When you travel, I'll carry your suitcase. If you need to get up extra early for a meeting, I'll bring you coffee in bed." With a heart full of love, he smiled at her. "All I want is to be with you."

Finally, after they'd devoured the cake and sent the married couple off on their honeymoon, Trevor brought Elzy to his room.

"You know I have my own place here, right?" She seemed confused. "It's got a fridge and everything. Like, you know, my slippers and sweatpants."

He laughed but didn't want to give away too much. "We'll get those heels off, no worries there. Let me change out of my tux first."

"Good point."

Hand in hand, they walked down the hallway. The black textured wallpaper bordered with bronze scrollwork and the sconces with black lampshades lent an air of elegance. "This might be the fanciest hotel I've ever stayed in."

"That was the plan. I took my time with this one."

He opened the door to find the room service cart waiting in the foyer of his suite.

"What's this?" She lifted the silver dome. "Cookies?" In the carafe, she found hot chocolate. "Did you order this?"

He nodded, really damn pleased with the sparkle in her eyes.

"Did you know we deliver cookies and milk to every room with kids?" she asked.

"No, I didn't. But that's adorable."

"So, wait. You did this for *me*?"

She seemed so touched that he planted a kiss on her mouth. The roar of desire threatened to sweep him away, but he had a plan for tonight and touching her would have to wait.

She took a bite of a cookie. "Mm. They're still warm, and the chocolate chips are melted. Yummy."

He gasped. "Did you just eat Santa's cookie? Dammit, Elzy. Now, we're not getting any presents."

"Oh, believe me. I got the only present I've ever wanted."

"Which is…" He playfully touched his fingertips to his chest. "Me?"

She laughed. "Yes, you."

"Damn right." Taking her hand, he led her into the living room of his suite.

She came to a hard stop when she took in the Christmas tree and the string of white lights glinting off the silver, gold, and red decorations. "Did you do this?"

"It was a team effort. I chartered a jet, so I actually

landed before you, but I had to get things set up. You can thank your concierge for providing me with the supplies."

She noticed the presents surrounding the base of the tree. "What is all this?"

"I did some shopping in Iceland."

She glanced at him. "Oh. So, this is for your grandkids?"

"No, sweetheart. It's all for you." He picked up a gift, sloppily wrapped. "Sorry, it's messy. I had to dress and get to the chapel. That's why I was a little late."

"You think I care how it's wrapped? I can't believe you did this." She wrapped her arms around his neck. "You made the magic for *me*. Thank you."

"Sweetheart, you are the magic." He pulled away. "Now, come on. Let's change and open some presents."

"I don't have any clothes here."

"Huh. Let's see if we can find you something." He searched for the rectangular box. "Here. Open this while I get out of this suit." He started into the closet when she crooked a finger.

"Strip right here. I'll never get tired of looking at your body."

"Yeah, I get that a lot." He ducked when she threw her high heel at him. "Just open the present." He untied his dress shoes and kicked them off. Before joining her by the tree, he wheeled the room service table over. Beside the carafe of Coco's Hot Chocolate sat a crystal bowl of homemade marshmallows.

"You did all this for me. I can't believe it."

"Yeah, well, get used to it. This is your life now." He tipped his chin to the gift. "Go on."

She pulled off her other heel and gave him her back. "First, unzip me."

He did as she asked and then helped her peel it off her banging body.

In her bra and panties, she tore off the paper and pulled off the top of the box. "Are you serious?" She held up the flannel pajamas with a puffin design. "I wanted these so badly." Her smile lit up the room. "I had no idea you got them for me."

After unbuckling his belt, he hung his slacks on a hanger. "Yep. And next Christmas, we'll get onesies for everyone in our families."

She laughed as she stepped into the bottoms and pulled the top over her head. "These are so comfy."

His suitcase of clothes was still in Iceland and wouldn't be shipped until after the holidays, so he only had the pajama bottoms and Henley he'd bought that night in Reykjavik. He slipped those on before handing her another box. "This one next."

Her eyes lit up in pure delight when she saw the suede and shearling slippers. "You did not." He'd just sat down beside her, so when she lunged at him, she tackled him onto his back. "I can't believe this. Thank you so much."

"You're welcome."

"I don't have anything for you."

"You still don't get it. You're all I want. Elzy, with you, I have everything."

"It's perfect." Amber stood beside her in the dining room as they watched their guests enjoy a fabulous New Year's Eve dinner.

"It really is."

"I love you, Jess." Out of nowhere, her sister hugged her. "You're the best person I know."

Startled, she held her close. "Where did that come from?"

Amber pulled away, cheeks flushed with emotion. "Seeing you so happy with Trevor… It's just…I'm the reason you guys broke up, and it makes me feel so much better knowing you found your way back together."

"What? That's not true at all."

"And that's why I never brought it up. Because I knew you'd say that. But you would've gone to Scotland with him if I hadn't gotten pregnant, and as unfair as it was to you, I honestly don't know what I would've done if you hadn't come home. I didn't appreciate your sacrifice until Bri went to kindergarten, and I heard stories from other single moms. Up until then, I took you for granted. Of course, you'd watch my baby while I was in school. Of course, you'd give up your entire life to make sure I had the best future possible."

"I have no regrets about that. Not one. If I hadn't come home, we wouldn't be the strong family we are today."

"I agree, and that's why I love and admire you so much. You showed me through your actions what family meant. I learned my values and priorities from you." She teared up. "It could've turned out very differently for me. I'm just so damn lucky to have you as my sister."

A fierce sense of love came over her. "It couldn't have

turned out any other way. There was no other choice but for me to come home. But even if I hadn't, you'd have figured it out. That's the woman you are. Once you held Bri in your arms, you got it. You truly became a mom. You did it yourself."

"All right, ladies," Lars said as he approached. "I don't know why you're crying in the middle of the most expensive dinner some of our guests have ever had, but it's not a good look."

They both burst out laughing and fell into each other's arms. "I love you," Amber said.

"I love you more."

And then Lars grinned and shook his head. "Okay, now, you're really drawing attention to yourselves. Come on. It's time to get into our swimsuits."

The sisters pulled apart. "Hang on," Amber said. "I'm part owner of this place. I organize the events. I don't actually have to *do* the polar plunge, right?"

Trevor joined them. "Oh, hell yes." He wrapped his arms around Jess's waist and pulled her against his chest. "We lead by example."

"Cool. Are you going to wear a kilt?" Amber teased.

"Nope. I've met my obligations, and now, I'm a free man." Trevor reached for her hand and kissed her knuckles. "I'm retiring it."

The four of them headed out of the dining room. "You should send it to the Smithsonian," Lars said.

"Actually, he's opening a museum in Scotland," Jessica said. "The next-generation movies aren't getting the same interest as the original, and Trevor talked to some of the local business owners about keeping the town a tourist attraction."

At the juncture of hallways where they'd go off in different directions, Jess said, "See you in the hot tub."

"Or not—" Amber called in a singsong voice over her shoulder.

"What was that about?" Jess asked Trevor.

"We're not going to do the communal thing." He tugged her toward their suite. "We have other plans."

"Excuse me? I'm not missing the fireworks. The team I hired used to do them for the Magic Kingdom."

He chuckled. "You won't miss anything."

"Trevor Montgomery, are you going to spoil me even more?"

"You better get used to it. I have a lot to make up for."

She stopped him. Cupping his cheeks, she looked deeply into his eyes. "No, you don't. I don't need presents or special treats or…or trips. Listen to me when I say I only need you. *Us.*"

He pulled her closer. "Elz, I spent most of my life thinking something was wrong with me because I didn't have a passion for a job or a career—or even a hobby—when the whole time, I knew I did. I knew what it was, but it wasn't acceptable. Because my passion is you. And I'm finally happy because I'm doing exactly what I want. And that's being with you. So, are you going to let me spoil you for the rest of your life?"

"Well, I mean, if it makes you happy, then who am I to complain?" she teased.

. . .

They all held hands—the sisters, their husbands, Jess and Trevor—as they ran into the lake. Everyone was laughing and shrieking, but thanks to the hot springs, the temperature wasn't terrible.

It was actually refreshing, and it woke Jessica up after a heavy and delicious meal. She had goosebumps on her arms, and her toes sank into the muddy lake bottom, but she was perfectly and completely content.

She wanted to hold on to his moment forever. This resort was the jewel in her treasure box of life achievements, she had her family safe and happy around her…

And she had the love of her life, her soulmate.

Her Wild Bill.

Trevor came up behind her and enfolded her in his arms. "You all right?"

"I couldn't be better. I really couldn't."

He rubbed her arms. "Come on. Let's warm up." Leaving the others behind, they headed to the cabanas, where staff waited with warmed, oversized towels. He draped one around her shoulders and wrapped the other around his waist.

Instead of joining the others in the communal tubs, he led her dripping wet through the hallway to their suite.

"Where are we going?" She'd missed this sense of fun and adventure with him so much.

Their suite had a private deck with a spectacular view of the lake. Only, he'd transformed it with fairy lights and flickering candles. A bottle of champagne chilled in a silver bucket, and two flutes sat on a tray alongside chocolate-covered strawberries.

"When did you do this?" she asked since he'd been by her side all night.

"Before dinner."

"But we came back to the room to get into our swimsuits?"

"And housekeeping lit the candles and plugged in the lights after we left. Now, come on.

The fireworks are about to start."

While she settled into the hot, bubbling water, he poured the champagne. Once he sat down beside her, he lifted her onto his lap. She rested her head against his shoulder and watched as the first rocket launched. She'd gone over the show tirelessly with the designers, so she knew just what to expect. She'd seen the diagrams and the schematics.

But nothing could have prepared her for the dazzling display of color and glittering lights, the pop and bang, and the familiar whistle that accompanied the shower of sparks that burned out on the icy lake.

From the communal area, she could hear the oohs and aahs, and it made her so happy to provide this experience for her guests. "It's magnificent."

Trevor kissed her cheek. "*You* are."

The rough press of his lips let her know he was experiencing this same surge of emotion. This bond between them, this sense of…completeness made her at once giddy and at peace. She squeezed his forearms where they belted around her.

During the finale, one of his arms left her waist, but she was too mesmerized to see what he was doing. The moment it ended, with red-and-gold sparks still glittering in the sky, he lifted her hand and slid a sparkling diamond ring onto her finger. It was rose gold and came in three separate pieces. Altogether, it looked regal. Fit for a queen.

She jerked up. "This is stunning. Where did you get this?" This wasn't the kind of engagement ring sold at just any jeweler. It was too unique.

"I found it in Iceland. In that jewelry store."

She eyed him skeptically. "You bought me an engagement ring on our first night alone together in thirty years?"

"Yes. Is that weird?" He fought a grin.

She laughed. "Not at all. If I'd seen this, I would've bought it too. It's magnificent."

But he'd gone serious, his gaze intense. "I love you, Elz. I love everything about you. Will you marry me?"

"Again?"

He grinned. "This time, it's forever."

"In my heart, I honestly don't think I ever stopped being married to you, but, yes, Trevor, I'll marry you. Forever, this time."

Epilogue

"We probably should've planned this out better." Jessica snuggled against her husband in the back of the town car. She'd slept most of the flight, so at least she felt rested. Which was important because it was Christmas Eve, and they were hosting a party.

"We'll be fine." Her husband sounded his usual confident self.

"I'm not sure how you can say that when we've got twenty people coming over."

"The house is decorated. We just need to flip the switch on all those lights."

It was so much more than that. "I need to get the food set up."

"We ordered everything." With a loose grip on her arm, his thumb stroked soothingly. "It's all good."

"I still have to heat stuff up."

"And I'm here to help you."

"That's true." She calmed down a little. "Besides, I'm so

glad we got to celebrate our one-year anniversary in the same place we found each other again."

He tipped her chin to place a kiss on her mouth. "I celebrate us every day, but I'm glad the press was there to make a big deal out of what you've done to the resort."

"It was really good to see Darby and Emil." The couple couldn't keep their hands off each other. "They seem so happy together."

They'd just returned from the opening of Hotel Pullman. The place had turned out even better than she'd first envisioned.

As the driver turned into the driveway, she sat up to put in the code. While they waited for the heavy iron gate to open, she took in the black steel ranch sign.

ROBBERS ROOST

Their gazes crashed together, and smiles lit up their faces. "We did it. We got our ranch."

He kissed her. "And I got the girl."

She climbed onto his lap and clasped her hands behind his neck. "I only have one minute to say this before we get home and have to start getting ready, but Trevor Montgomery, you're the love of my life, the other half of my soul, and while I can be happy without you, I'm not complete. I love you, my sweet, dirty-mouthed outlaw." She kissed him, scraping her hands through his hair.

He started to tumble her onto the seat when the car lurched to a stop outside their home.

"Hm, the party can wait." She kept her mouth close to

his. "We have more important things to do. Things that involve licking. And sucking."

"That sounds good, but we might want to hold off till later."

"Since when don't you want some good lovin'?"

"When our children, grandchildren, sisters, brothers-in-law, nieces, and nephews are watching." He hit the button to lower her tinted window.

She whipped around to find her house lit up and the entire clan standing out front. It took her a moment to make sense of what she was seeing. They'd been gone a week, so she'd expected a dark house and a cold kitchen.

And what was *that*? "Is that a horse and carriage?"

"Yep."

"What in the world?" She gaped at the display of lights in the pine trees and a giant blow-up Santa on the front lawn. "You rented kiosks?"

"Yep. One for hot cocoa and the other for crepes."

She burst out laughing. "Look at you, making the magic for me." But before she could properly thank him, everyone descended on the car. Lars opened her door, and the moment she got out, her family surrounded her with hugs and kisses.

It was perfect. Everything she'd ever wanted. She reached for Trevor's hand, and amid all the love, chatter, and hugs, they shared a moment of understanding.

We did it.

We got here.

Two kids from a farm town made all their dreams come true.

In the great room of his ranch house, Trevor had two kids on his lap and both his and Elzy's combined families surrounding him. He couldn't have been happier.

A total of twenty-three stockings hung off the mantle, and a twelve-foot Douglas fir took up one corner of the large room. Strings of white lights shone off the pretty glass ornaments, and prettily wrapped presents were piled underneath.

His wife—*hang on, let me say it again: my wife, my beautiful bride*—and no, he'd never get tired of saying it—came out from the kitchen (with its slate-blue cabinets) carrying a giant cocoa board. It had everything from peppermint sticks and marshmallows to whipped cream and sprinkles to adorn mugs of cocoa (bought piping hot from Coco's Chocolates in town).

The kids scrambled off him to gather around the low table, and everyone got busy pouring, dunking, and drinking.

But one child was missing. Paisley, his pensive, watchful, smart granddaughter.

Even though she'd been with the Montgomery family for four years, she still held back just a little. Not in a way that others might notice. But enough that it caught the attention of her parents.

Quietly, he left the room. Maybe the chaos was too much for her. He'd see if she wanted to bake cookies with him. She'd like that.

In contemplating their custom home's design, Elzy wanted to include a ridiculous number of guest bedrooms so each of their grandkids, nephews, and nieces all had rooms of their own.

The quiet hallway was lined on one side with windows overlooking the Teton Range. Moonlight made the snow glitter. Man, he loved this house.

He found Paisley's door ajar, so he knocked lightly to let her know he was there.

She jolted, shoving something under her pillow.

Huh. What was that about? Ten seemed young for secrets. "Hey. How's it going? Mind if I hang out with you for a minute?"

She nodded, but her features darkened with guilt.

With his back against the bedframe, he sank to the floor. "Pretty noisy down there."

"It's all right." She crossed her legs on the bed. "I like it."

"Yeah? Grandma just set out a cocoa board." He grinned. "Know what that is?"

She nodded. "I helped her make it. She was going to use whole candy canes, but I told her to crush some of them."

"That's a good idea. Do you like mint with your chocolate?"

Her gaze darted to the pillow. "Not really. I like my chocolate to taste like chocolate."

"Pais, we're like two peas in a pod. I couldn't agree more." They sat in silence for a moment. "You got something on your mind?" He got up to sit beside her. "I saw you hide something under your pillow." He found the direct approach worked best with kids. Transparency made it easier for them to trust. "I don't want to get into your business, but if you want to talk about it, I'm here for you."

Her hesitation worried him. He'd like to get closer to

her, but he didn't know how. Of course, she'd lost both her parents when she was six, and that had to affect her sense of well-being and safety in the world.

The past year, he'd spent lots of time with his family. He'd gotten close to all four of his granddaughters, but where the other three threw themselves headfirst into relationships, Paisley didn't show much emotion.

Finally, though, she reached under the pillow and pulled out a framed photograph.

In his mind's eye, he saw the empty space in Cole and Hailey's picture-lined hallway.

So that's where it went.

She didn't hand it to him, so he waited patiently for her to speak.

"I remember some stuff."

A chill swept across his skin. After Cole and Hailey became guardians to Paisley and Evvie, they'd taken the girls back to their home to collect as many mementos as they could. Those framed photos in the hallway were meant to keep their parents alive in the girls' minds.

Where Evvie was only three when she'd lost them and didn't have many memories, Paisley was six, so she probably did.

"What do you remember?" he asked quietly.

"My dad sang to me while I was in the bathtub."

"Oh, yeah? What'd he sing?"

Gaze fixed on the comforter, she hunched a shoulder.

"What else do you remember?" he prodded.

"He made pancakes."

"Oh, you love those. You'd eat them every morning if you could."

"My dad made them for dinner. I remember because he played music and sang along to the songs. Me and Evvie danced in the kitchen."

"That's a great memory."

When she caught his gaze, her eyes were guarded. Where was she going with this?

"And your mom?" he asked.

Tears glistened, and she sniffed. "She sang to me too. But it was different. She'd hold me like this." She lifted both arms in a cradling gesture. "And she'd rock me and sing lullabies. Even when I was big."

"Did you like that?"

Tears spilled down her cheeks.

"Your mom and dad loved you so much. You must miss them."

Now, she was bawling. He wrapped his arms around her. Her body went hot and damp, and still, he held her. Let her cry it out for as long as she needed.

Maybe Cole and Hailey could talk about her parents more. Take her to the cemetery. She needed something. He just wasn't sure what.

But when she pulled away, she angrily swiped away tears. "I don't."

"You don't what, punkin?"

"I don't miss them. I don't remember them."

He wanted to get it right but wasn't sure what she meant. He lifted the photograph. "You remember your mom rocking you, but it's like looking at a picture? You remember that she sang, but you can't hear her voice or remember what her perfume smelled like?"

She nodded aggressively and started crying again.

"And you're sad because you forgot what their voices sound like?"

"No. I'm sad because I'm *mean*. Because it hurts their feelings that I forget them."

"Come here, punkin." She shifted over to him, and he cupped her chin. "Listen to me. There's not a mean bone in your body. You're a smart, creative, compassionate young woman, and I'm very proud of you."

She hiccupped, her little chest heaving.

"I want to explain something to you. There are a lot of ways to communicate with people. Do you know what I mean?"

Shaking her head, she lifted the hem of her shirt to dry her face.

"Okay, well, one way for me to communicate is to say, Paisley, I'm angry at you. Another way is, I can look at you like this." He made an angry expression. "What's another way?"

"You can ignore someone. That's what Mrs. Powell does. If you do something bad, and you don't apologize, she ignores you. Kayla Gentile was mad at me because she saw me eating an ice cream cone in town with Janelle and Delia, and now, she doesn't look at me when she walks past me in the hall."

"Wow, okay. That's definitely a way to say you're angry."

She nodded.

"And there's one more way to communicate." He lifted her hand and placed it over her heart. "Your parents aren't here anymore, so they can't hear your words, and they can't see your expressions. But they can feel you. The spirit of you. And if the spirit of you is about love, then that's what you're communicating to them. Does this make sense?"

"So, Mommy can't see me when I give my broccoli to Maximus?"

He burst out laughing. "She can't, but when you give Max your carrots, he poops them out, and we can tell that way. They also can't see when you take M&M's from Liza's cup."

Her cheeks flamed red. "You saw that?"

"Yeah, but it's okay. She didn't even notice. Next time you spill your candy though, just ask me for more, okay?"

"Okay. I'm sorry."

"Don't worry about it. So, no, your parents can't see that. But they *can* feel your love for them."

"They're not mad that I forget what they sound like?"

"They pick up the worry in your spirit, but no, they're not mad about anything. Close your eyes, keep your hand on your heart, and tell me what they're communicating to you right now?"

She went very still and did as he asked.

As he waited, curious what she would say, he caught movement out of the corner of his eye. Cole stood on the other side of the door, listening.

Paisley drew in a sharp breath. "They love me, and they miss me very much."

His heart twisted hard, bringing a sting of tears to his eyes. "Yeah." He had to clear his voice. "That makes sense."

When she opened her eyes, she held up the framed photograph. "Am I in trouble for taking it off the wall?"

"No, but you know you can ask your mom and dad for anything, right? They love you and want you to be happy."

"Oh, I know. But if I took a picture, then Evvy would take one too, and then Liza and Roxie will, and then my dad will put his foot down and make us all put them back."

Trevor smiled. "Well, how about we don't tell the others? We can leave this photo right here on your nightstand at my house. Does that work?"

She reared up on her knees and threw her arms around him. "I love you, Grandpa. You're my favorite."

Crushed with emotion, he held the little girl in his arms. Joy for the bond he'd made with her clashed with sorrow for the one he hadn't made with his son at this age. "I love you, Pais."

"Can I have that cocoa now?" She pulled away and jumped off the bed as if she hadn't ripped his heart wide open.

"You bet." He set up the photo on her nightstand and, together, they headed out of her room.

He expected to see Cole waiting there, but the hallway was empty. He hoped he hadn't overstepped by taking a precious moment meant for a father.

When they got back to the family room, he spotted his son watching Paisley race to the cocoa board. Cole came up to him. "Thanks, Dad." He clapped him on the shoulder. "Thanks for being there for her. What you said? That was pretty amazing. I'm not sure how I would've handled it."

He was too choked up to answer. Fortunately, at that moment, one of the kids knocked over her cocoa, and Cole bolted into action.

Warm hands reached around his waist, and Elzy got up on her toes and kissed his cheek. "We did good, Mr. Elsworth, don't you think?"

"We sure did, Mrs. Montgomery." He pulled her around and into his arms. "I have everything a man could ever want right here."

Thank you for reading WHEN YOU WERE MINE. Are you dying to know what happened to Darby and Emil? Scan the QR code to read their story.

What's up next in Calamity Falls? I've got a brand-new series for you about four rough-and-tumble brothers who grew up in a biker club and discover a shocking truth about their father—and the mother they never knew. You're going to love the first book in the series, CAN'T GET OVER YOU, about a kindergarten teacher who winds up nannying for her ex-boyfriend, a badass biker! Look for this Christmas love story coming October 2025. Available for preorder on all platforms. #secondchanceromance #nannyromance #singledadromance #runawaybride

And if you love swoony, holiday romances where couples find true love later in life, grab ALL I WANT FOR

CHRISTMAS IS YOU, the first book in the Mistletoe and Silver Foxes series.

Need more Calamity Falls, where the people are wild at heart?

The Bowie Brothers
KEEP ON LOVING YOU
WE BELONG TOGETHER
THE VERY THOUGHT OF YOU
JUST THE WAY YOU ARE

The Cavanaugh Sisters
IT WAS ALWAYS YOU
CAN'T HELP FALLING IN LOVE
COME AWAY WITH ME
WHOLE LOTTA LOVE
YOU'RE STILL THE ONE

The Renegades (Hockey)
THE DEEPER I FALL
LOVE ME LIKE YOU DO
TRULY, MADLY, DEEPLY
NEVER IN MY WILDEST DREAMS

Mistletoe and Silver Foxes
ALL I WANT FOR CHRISTMAS IS YOU
WHEN YOU WERE MINE

The Wild Wolff Village Serials
KISS ME SLOWLY
ANYWHERE WITH YOU
BABY I'M YOURS

Have you read the Rock Star Romance series? Come meet the sexy rockers of Blue Fire:

YOU REALLY GOT ME
I WANT YOU TO WANT ME
TAKE ME HOME TONIGHT
MORE THAN A FEELING

Grab a FREE copy of PLANES, TRAINS, AND HEAD OVER HEELS. And come hang out with me on Facebook, TikTok, Twitter, Instagram, Goodreads, and Pinterest or in my private reader group.

Ready to dive into the next Calamity Falls series? Here's an excerpt of CAN'T GET OVER YOU:

JUST BEFORE HEADING OUT OF THE DRESSING ROOM with her bridal party, Finlay Keller remembered the gift. "Oh, wait. Hang on a sec. I forgot one thing."

Her bridesmaids gave her an incredulous look, and Janey, her oldest and closest friend, said, "You walk down the aisle in five minutes."

"I know. I promise it won't take me longer than that." She just had to run to the car. Once her friends left, she dug her groom's present out of her tote bag. Her heart did a little jig.

He's going to love this.

Her fiancé's dad had passed away when he was a teenager, and Barry didn't have much to remember him by. The one thing he'd always wanted was his dad's watch. It went missing after the accident that took his life, and no one had been able to find it.

She'd gone through some boxes in his parents' attic and found the purchase order and the serial number, so she'd been able to track it down. She couldn't wait to give it to him.

Tucking it under her arm, she lifted the hem of her wedding gown and hurried out. As she made her way along the empty hallway, she heard the hum of conversation in the church and smelled the gorgeous pine and cinnamon from the candles for her winter wedding.

A frisson of happiness sped down her spine. She couldn't believe it.

All her dreams were coming true.

She and Barry were two peas in a pod. They wanted the same things out of life—the white picket fence, two kids, and a golden retriever—and a quiet, family-oriented life.

Hitting the lever of the side door, she stepped out into the frigid air of the Teton mountains. Good thing Barry had parked his BMW right there. She opened the trunk to find it stuffed with their luggage.

They'd spend their wedding night at the Sweetwater Spa and Resort, then leave for their honeymoon the next day.

She couldn't wait for her life with Barry to begin. *He's going to be a great dad.*

Right then, she got an unwanted flash of her childhood.

A boy with dark eyes. Messy hair, worn clothes, and secrets. So many secrets.

The boy she'd snuck out to spend stolen moments with because she couldn't get enough of him.

The boy she'd thought she'd marry.

If she had, her life would've been nothing like this. Not that she cared about the Louis Vuitton luggage or Barry's BMW. No, the point was that they hadn't wanted the same things.

Well, Jude hadn't wanted *her*. He'd loved his bike club lifestyle more.

So, really, it was a waste of time and energy to think about what might have been.

"Finlay?" The wedding planner leaned out of the doorway. "One minute to show-time."

She gave the woman a thumbs-up and set the gift at the back of the trunk.

But wait. Something crinkled. It was a present tucked away in the corner.

See how cute we are?

We both bought presents for each other.

Peas in a pod.

Except…the wrapping paper was colorful balloons. It looked like something for a child. She shouldn't do this, but curiosity got the better of her and she tugged the white envelope out from under the red bow. Fortunately, it wasn't sealed, so she glanced around and, finding herself alone, pulled out the card.

Dear Chloe,

I'm sorry I couldn't be there for your birthday, but I promise to make it up to you.

Love,
Daddy

Daddy?

Her heart thundered, and despite the freezing cold, perspiration popped out over her upper lip.

No, no. Don't freak out. There's an explanation.

But fear fractured her mind, and she couldn't think straight.

She forced a few deep breaths. *Okay, hold on.*

Maybe it wasn't Barry's. He could be holding it for his sister. His brother.

A friend.

Sure, one of his friends.

But none of them were dads.

Look at the handwriting.

It was definitely Barry's.

But he's not a father.

Is he cheating on me?

She thought about all the hunting and fishing trips he and his friends went on, but he always sent pictures and texts. He always came home with stories and stinky clothes.

What about an ex? He was only twenty-four. His only other serious relationship was with his college girlfriend, but they'd broken up three years ago. She lived in another state.

Well, what're you going to do?

Confront him? Marry him anyway?

Make a decision.

I'm not bailing on him because I found a present in his car. That's ridiculous.

Closing the trunk, she hurried back inside, determined to put the gift out of her mind.

I'll talk to him tonight.

As she approached the bridal party, the wedding planner spoke into her microphone, and the chamber trio launched into the processional.

Her best friend handed her the bouquet and mouthed, "Everything okay?"

Finlay nodded and tried for a smile. She stood in the vestibule, butterflies in her stomach and pinched toes from the fancy shoes her almost mother-in-law had gifted her. With each couple that made their way down the aisle, she grew more agitated. More anxious.

Until it was just her and her dad.

"You don't look good."

Finlay laughed. "Thanks, Dad."

"You know what I mean. You're beautiful, angel. But you don't look happy to walk down that aisle." He jingled the keys in his pants pocket. "Car's outside."

She wished so badly she hadn't seen that present. But now wasn't the time to talk to her dad about it. "I'm good, Dad. Promise."

"You sure?" Her big, burly dad took no crap. If she told him her concerns, he'd march right up to the altar and confront the groom.

She set her hand on his arm. "Positive."

And then, the wedding planner nudged them, and they stepped into the church. Amid a shush of fabric, the congregants rose to their feet.

But she didn't look at them. She was focused on her fiancé who stood on the dais watching her.

Are you lying to me?

Are you cheating?

Now that she'd had some time to think about it, she could say that, yes, Barry was acting differently. The other day, she'd looked out the window and found him in the parking lot of their apartment complex. He'd been upset.

She'd thought maybe the house had fallen through, but instead of coming inside, he'd gotten in his car and driven off.

When he'd finally come home, and she'd confronted him, he'd told her he'd gotten bad news about a work thing.

But see, he never said, "work thing." He told her every detail of his job as a wealth manager. She knew the lingo.

Still, she kept moving forward. She'd hear him out. He'd have a logical explanation—even if she couldn't think of one herself.

Except… That was his handwriting.

No doubt about it.

But it was confusing because Barry watched her approach, radiating pure happiness. He lowered his face into a hand and used two fingers to swipe away the tears.

He loves me.

He wants a life with me.

Her gut knew it.

So, what's going on?

A rustling sound caught her attention. She glanced over to see a mother struggling to keep her restless child seated.

As she slowly moved by, Finlay registered that the girl was trying to rip off her tights, while the mom fought to keep them on.

As a kindergarten teacher, she was used to kids acting out. In her classroom, if they wanted to take off their shoes or bulky coats, she let them. She'd learned to pick her battles.

Finally, they reached the altar. Her dad kissed her cheek and took his seat beside her mom. Finlay handed her bouquet to Janey. *It's time.*

Here we go.

The butterflies in her tummy turned to bats swooping. She pressed a hand to her stomach. But nothing felt right.

Everything was off.

The dress she'd loved and tried on a dozen times felt itchy. Her skin was damp. Hot. One of the bobby pins in her hair dug into her scalp just behind her ear.

"Good evening, everyone," the pastor began.

But as he continued on, Finlay could only hear a muffled murmur, as if the ceremony took place underwater. She was sweating now, and she thought she might throw up. But nobody suspected a thing. The pastor kept talking, the congregants laughed every now and then, and her groom kept wiping tears.

Finally, Barry turned to her and said his vows. As words poured out of his mouth, he slid a ring onto her finger.

Only when he said, "I thee wed," did the fog clear. Because it was her turn.

Unfortunately, her mind was preoccupied with balloons.

Love, Daddy.

Daddy.

Again, it was unquestionably Barry's handwriting. He hadn't written the card as a favor for a friend. He wasn't helping out a sibling.

No.

"And now, Finlay, you may say your vows," the pastor said.

Instead, she turned to the congregation. "Is there a Chloe here?"

Immediately, the little girl who'd won the battle over her tights stood on the pew and shouted, "I Cwowie."

Finlay's gaze shifted to the mother. She sucked in a harsh breath. "What's your ex doing at our wedding?" she asked Barry.

He jerked over. When he spotted the woman and her child, he let out a deep exhalation. His shoulders slumped.

"You invited your ex to our wedding?" she asked.

Instead of answering, his eyelids squeezed shut. His head tipped back. "Fuck," he whispered.

"Is Chloe your daughter?" she demanded.

His eyelids flew open. "Yes, but I can explain. It's not what you think."

"Yes?" Her dad shot out of his seat. "You have a *daughter*? What the *hell* are you talking about?" He made a beeline for the groom.

Barry's mom popped out of her seat as if she could intercept Finlay's barrel-chested dad. "No, no, no. My son doesn't have a child."

"Oh, yes, he does." With her child in her arms, the ex hurried down the aisle. "I'm sorry, Finlay, but you deserve to know the truth before you exchange vows."

But Finlay needed answers from her groom. "How long have you known?"

"I just found out. I swear."

Love, Daddy.

No, he did not just find out.

"When?" she insisted.

"I told him three months ago." The ex reached the altar and pushed through the throng of family and bridal party. "He said he wanted to be part of her life, so I moved here. We're not together. It's not like that. But he is her father. He took a DNA test."

Her dad went ballistic, Barry's mom demanded answers, and Janey looked ready to punch the groom in the face. Their guests were whispering, talking, and shifting in their seats. It was pure chaos.

Slowly, Finlay backed away from them. She made her way to the back of the sanctuary and down a short flight of stairs. She pushed through a door and found herself in the frigid cold once again.

Good thing she was numb. But as she looked around the parking lot, she realized she had nowhere to go. They'd only just closed on the house, and since they were going on their honeymoon, they'd scheduled the movers for when they came back. There wasn't a lick of furniture in it.

Their apartment—no, she wouldn't go there.

So then, what? *Where do I go?* If she went to her parents' house…

A roar of motorcycles invaded her thoughts.

Even though it'd been an entire decade since she'd last seen Jude, she still thought of him every time she heard that sound. She looked for those eyes inside every helmet.

But none of that mattered right now. She needed to go. She didn't have keys to Barry's BMW, and she wasn't about to go back inside and pull Janey away from the mêlée.

Besides, she found herself drawn to the motorcycles. Gathering the tulle and silk of her gown, she started in their direction. A walk turned into a run when she realized the lights would change, and the motorcycles would leave.

In that moment, they seemed her only solution.

The light turned green, and the engines sputtered and growled. And then, they were gone, their exhaust leaving plumes of white fog.

Except for one rider. He remained in the middle of the street, his eyes on her.

She knew him. Of course she did.

She would recognize the breadth of his shoulders, his stance, his muscular frame, anywhere, anytime.

She walked right into the street and stood in front of him.

He pulled a knife from his boot and jerked his chin toward her seven-thousand-dollar gown—a gift from Barry's mom.

"Let me do this for you." Finlay had wanted to say no to the offer, but the woman had insisted. And Finlay loved this dress. It was couture. She'd spent months creating a whole file of dresses, and then, she'd met with Knox Holliday, and together, they'd created the gown of her dreams.

But here's the thing. Barry might love me.

He might have a very good reason for not telling me.

"I wanted to wait until after the wedding."

Sure, she could see the logic in that.

Maybe. Kind of.

Actually, no. Not really.

"I didn't want to ruin this special time for you."

"I was waiting for the results of the DNA test."

But he already had those. His ex made that clear.

Nothing he said would matter because in the three months he'd known, he hadn't told her.

Finlay was sure some women could forgive what he'd done. Eventually, she could too.

But she'd never trust him the way a woman needed to trust her spouse.

And so, she nodded her permission to Jude, taking in

those intense dark eyes, the thick beard that covered a mouth she still dreamed about.

He gathered the layers of material and plunged the blade in, hacking away until the bottom half dropped to the ground. Then, he pulled off his leather jacket and held it open for her.

She slid her arms inside. It was warm from his body, and it smelled like woodsmoke and pine, like the crisp night sky in the mountains. Just like him.

And then, she climbed onto the back of his motorcycle and wrapped her arms around his waist.

He revved the engine and shot away like a bullet.

She never once looked back.

About the Author

Award-winning author Erika Kelly writes sexy and emotional small town romance. Married to the love of her life and raising four children, she lives in the southwest, drinks a lot of tea, and is always waiting for her cats to get off her keyboard.

https://www.erikakellybooks.com/

ONE GRIMM NIGHT
CHAD NICHOLAS